GILDED Mess

By Colette Rhodes

Copyright © 2021 Colette Graimes
All rights reserved

The characters and events portrayed in this book are fictitious. Any similarity to real persons, living or dead, is coincidental and not intended by the author.

No part of this book may be reproduced, or stored in a retrieval system, or transmitted in any form or by any means, electronic, mechanical, photocopying, recording, or otherwise, without express written permission of the publisher.

Cover design by: Colette Graimes

"To err is human - but it feels divine."

Mae West

RIA

CHAPTER 1

What was the over/under on my boyfriend being a serial killer who buried bodies in the woods?

I was 99% sure he wasn't, but his cabin in the forest was a lot more remote than I had anticipated, and I was starting to get the teeniest bit nervous that moving up here without actually looking at the place first hadn't been my brightest idea.

And I had a long history of not-bright ideas. Dim ideas. The dimmest.

"It's going to be so great, living together, Aurelia," Darren, my boyfriend, said with a wolfish grin as we drove up the cleared mountain pathway to his home. I clung to the truck door so hard, my knuckles turned white and my hands ached with the effort. I hadn't been off-road before, and honestly? Not a fan.

"Yeah, so great," I managed to reply, my teeth clanging together as we went over a particularly sharp bump.

"Not having second thoughts about moving into the wild, are you?" Darren teased, blue eyes flashing. "It seems like a long way up, but it's not so far to the main road on foot. Half an hour, maybe? Just turn right out of the cabin door and go straight down the slope. We have to take the scenic route with a vehicle."

I guess that made sense? My sense of direction had never been great. I knew Darren's place was secluded; it had been part of the appeal for me, and he talked about it all the time. The original hardwood floors, the old stone chimney, the peacefulness of sitting out on the covered porch in the morning without a soul around… It all sounded heavenly.

Darren and I met and dated over the past six months in Fairbanks, where he kept a tiny studio apartment to stay at during the week. He'd always talked about making the cabin his permanent base and cutting down his hours at the small law firm where he was a partner. I'd gotten a job as a server at a diner just down the street when I moved to town, where Darren frequented for lunch.

He had sauntered in, all twinkling blue eyes and coiffed blonde hair, and he'd honed in on me instantly. He was the kind of guy who knew everyone, was invited to every party, practically dripping with charisma. I'd been a pile of goo on the floor when he'd turned all that attention on little old me, in my jeans and apron, hair tied up in a messy bun.

My whole family had told me I was insane for moving to Alaska, but just a couple of days after I got here, I'd met Darren and it felt like he'd really *seen* me. I knew I'd made the right call coming here.

"I've always wanted to live somewhere isolated," I replied confidently, looking out the window at the endless expanse of trees, the leaves a mixture of green and yellow as the weather grew colder. Peace. Quiet. Privacy. Or so it seemed, I'm sure there were plenty of shifters in these woods. "And I'm excited to focus on my business."

"Jewelry. Right," Darren said unenthusiastically, but I guess making jewelry seemed a little...trivial, for a lawyer that is. Which was fine. It's not like we had to share all of each other's interests. I cared roughly zero percent about property law, or whatever it was Darren specialized in.

"Yeah, jewelry. I ordered some supplies; they're getting delivered to my old place," I said absently, thinking of Lou, my former roommate and the closest friend I'd made since moving out here.

She hadn't been as excited about me moving in with Darren as I had expected, which had been a little disappointing. The silver lining was she'd been fine with me leaving my stuff there until I'd seen the cabin and knew what I wanted to take with me. I suspected Lou was hoping I'd change my mind.

I was really going to miss our trashy movie nights. This was a little further out than I expected to be able to pop into town for a visit.

This is what you wanted, I reminded myself. A serious future with my serious boyfriend in a house we could make a home. Before I turned 30.

Tick, tick, tick. *Don't freak out now, Ria.*

"Here we go," Darren announced. "Home sweet home."

Jesus. Maybe Lou would get her wish and I would change my mind.

Pull it together. So, it was a little smaller than what I'd had in mind. That wasn't a deal breaker. Darren had insisted that he was "traditional" and didn't need me to contribute to expenses. I couldn't exactly complain about a free place to live, even if it wasn't... *precisely* how he'd described it.

It was an old log cabin — which Darren had told me — with an enormous stone chimney up one side of the house and a black shingle roof. There was a covered porch out the front with a rocking chair next to the front door that looked like the perfect place to sit and have a coffee in the morning. Maybe I could convince Darren to get a second chair so we could sit out there together.

We could spend Sunday mornings drinking hot coffee in the Alaskan chill, listening to birdsong. For a few months of the year, at least. It'd be romantic.

Darren parked the truck in front of the porch and hopped out, heading straight for the front door. I climbed down after him and struggled to scramble onto the bed of the truck to reach for the hiking pack of stuff I'd bought up to tide me over until I knew how much room I had for my things.

Not a lot, I was guessing, based on the size of the cabin.

I heaved the pack over my shoulders and struggled to pull open the worn screen door that Darren had let fall shut behind him. It creaked obnoxiously as I yanked it free, disturbing the peace and quiet. The cabin may not be what I had in mind, but the silence was everything I'd always dreamed of when I was growing up in New York.

Fresh air; trees swishing softly in the breeze, birds chirping in the background. It was everything I'd always wanted.

Perhaps it wasn't as *immediately* satisfying as I thought it would be, but maybe I just had to get used to it. My whole life, I'd dreamed of living somewhere remote and close to nature, but my family were all fox shifters and perfectly content in the city.

I'd done it, though. I was here. It was more than anyone in my family ever expected I'd do.

Darren was sitting in a rickety chair in the tiny living room when I walked in, fiddling with the satellite phone he used when he was up here. It smelled... musty. Darren had mentioned he'd been coming up here less so he could spend time with me in town, so it probably needed airing out. That was hardly a deal breaker.

God, it really was a miniscule space, though. A fireplace dominated one wall, and there was enough room for a loveseat tucked under the staircase, a wooden chair, and a small square coffee table. In the corner was a china cabinet that looked like it had been custom made for the space.

I dropped my pack at the door and decided to explore on my own, since Darren appeared to be too busy to give me a tour. I contemplated pointing out his poor manners, but it would only take me two minutes to explore the whole place anyway, I may as well do it on my own. I crossed the living room in five steps and passed through an archway that had a rifle mounted over top of it, into the kitchen area.

Okay, so it was a corner bench with a toaster oven taking up precious counter space and a mini fridge tucked underneath the bench. Darren's laptop bag took up the meager amount of counter space, the same one he'd brought with him from Fairbanks and dumped there before heading to the living room. He was probably planning on working this weekend, which was fine. It would give me time to settle in.

Maybe there was a grill outside. I could grill instead. Who needed a big fancy kitchen, anyway? Not me.

I walked past Darren again and ducked my head to climb the narrow staircase, so I didn't knock myself out on the low ceiling. Upstairs was a bedroom and bathroom, neither of which were walled off at all. I guess we'd get to know each other *really* well. There was a bathtub that would probably be big enough for me to sit in if I tucked my knees up to my chest, and a beaten-up old dresser in the corner that was unlikely to fit both mine and Darren's clothes.

The bed looked comfortable, at least. Plaid bedding, with a heavy blanket at the end for chilly nights. Functional. The wooden headboard with the elaborate engraving work was probably the most interesting feature of the house. Was that a wolf? No, a coyote? Weird.

Darren's phone rang, and I heard him let himself outside to take the call. I pulled my regular cell phone out of my pocket and confirmed what I already suspected — no signal.

This is what you wanted, Ria, I reminded myself. *A quiet life. Less noise. Fewer people. No overbearing family members reminding you constantly of what a fuck up you are.*

Lord, I was glad I did not get cellphone reception up here. My family had been blowing up my phone since I'd told them I was moving in with Darren a couple of weeks ago. If they didn't live on the opposite side of the country, they'd have been up in my face every day, I was sure of it.

Not that they'd even *met* Darren to form a judgment, but that was reason enough for my two older brothers to dislike him, apparently. They'd declared my high school boyfriend was a creep who only wanted me for my virginity before they'd met him too, it's not like boundaries were their area of expertise.

Was it any wonder I'd moved to the other side of the country on a whim?

I glanced reflexively out the window, half expecting to see the fluffy russet-colored tail of one of my brothers out there. If a fox shifter wanted to go somewhere, that's where they went, regardless of whether or not they were invited.

There was no sign of life out there, though. Just Darren's sleek black truck, looking modern and out of place in front of the aged cabin and the axe embedded in the tree stump by the porch.

Ugh, if I were a fox shifter, I could go out and explore this entire area and know exactly how to find my way back. But no, I was a mere *carrier*. My womb was the Ritz of shifter incubators.

Lucky me.

I had been living amongst humans for the past few years in Florida after I left home, and I'd been far removed from the shifter community, as far as I knew, anyway. Out here in the forest, there was no avoiding the reality that shifters were out there. I hadn't seen any, but for many different species, this was their ideal territory.

It reminded me of my failings, but at the same time it was kind of comforting. I'd grown up around shifters. My family were shifters. Maybe living among humans and not acknowledging the existence of the shifter world had been easier, but it had also felt a little hollow.

I made my way back downstairs to poke around in the mini fridge for something to make for dinner. I guessed Darren didn't come up here a lot; it wasn't as well stocked as I'd expected it to be. Would it have killed him to go to the store before we drove up?

Deep breath. Don't make a big deal about it. There was pasta and tinned tomatoes, we could have vegetarian spaghetti.

"Babe."

Oh my god, every time he said that, I thought of the pig. I thought it would grow on me, but I still hated it. I was going to have to say something. I swallowed down my immediate rejection of the endearment, turning to Darren as he stood in the archway between the kitchen and living room.

I could already tell by the apology in his voice that he was about to say something I was going to hate.

"Kev called, you know, my partner at the firm? Something has gone spectacularly wrong with this case, it can't wait. The client is flipping out." Darren held up the satellite phone like it was proof, his mouth downturned.

"It's Friday," I replied flatly, crossing my arms over my chest. "We just got here."

"I know, I know. And you've just moved in, it's the worst timing, I swear." Darren shook his head, looking physically pained at the idea of leaving me.

Darren wasn't the most naturally expressive guy. Alarm bells rang quietly in the back of my mind.

Oh well, I could get a head start on that solitude I'd been coveting, right? I'd spotted a bottle of red wine in the kitchen and there was a dirty as hell bodice ripper in my bag to keep me company.

What are men to booze and smut?

I knew when Darren suggested relocating here — so excited about us planning a proper future together — that he'd have to spend at least a couple of nights a week in town for work, but I had assumed the weekends would be for us. It was a compromise, but it meant I could focus on jewelry design during the week.

"I really need to work on making myself less essential to the day-to-day operations. I've brought it up a thousand times," Darren ranted, shaking his head in frustration. "I said to them just this week, you know, that I need to be spending less hours in the office. That Aurelia and I are moving in together and she's my priority — *my number one priority* — so I can't be working late every single night and working weekends to pick up other people's slack."

I mean, it was a nice thought, but I couldn't really envision cool-as-a-cucumber Darren professing to his staff — most of whom I'd only met once at office drinks — that I was his number one priority.

Darren let out a pained groan, pacing back and forth like he was... angry? My eyes narrowed as I tracked his movements. It felt performative. Like he was feeding me what he thought I wanted to hear. His expression was one of regret, but it didn't reach his eyes.

The alarm bells grew into a crescendo, impossible to ignore.

"Such a fucking joke to be called in like this on the weekend," Darren muttered, one theatric away from shaking his fist at the sky.

"The downside of being the boss, I suppose," I replied evenly, keeping my face carefully neutral. "Go ahead, I'll be fine."

"Babe," Darren said, turning his puppy dog eyes on me. I usually found him exceptionally attractive — for a human, at least — but he just looked slimy at the moment.

It would be just my luck that I'd moved all the way up here, spent my last paycheck on supplies to start my jewelry business, and he was a shady bastard. I'd have to call my brothers and it would turn into a whole thing about Ria and her poor life choices.

"You need to plan ahead, Ria."

"There are consequences to your actions, Ria."

"Why did you get shitfaced the night before finals, Ria? What did you think was going to happen?"

A headache was forming behind my eyes just thinking about it.

"It'll be too dark for me to bring the truck back up tonight, but I'll be here first thing tomorrow and we'll spend the entire weekend together. We were going to talk about baby making, remember?" Darren waggled his eyebrows, and I shot him a strained smile in response.

Maybe — just *maybe* — I'd let my biological clock have too big of a say on my decision to move up here. It ticked louder at the thought.

When Darren had taken me out for dinner at my favorite Italian restaurant last week and suggested moving in together, we'd talked about this. Future stuff. Baby stuff. He'd even mentioned building an extension onto this place for the nursery, and we'd both agreed on plaid and deer themed decor. Those weren't the kind of conversations you had with just anybody.

He'd been serious. *We'd* been serious, or so I thought. I wouldn't have moved up here for anything less. Disappearing suddenly on a Friday night for "work" made me wonder if I wasn't the only woman who thought Darren was serious about me.

I tended to leap before I looked, but by the time I got around to looking, I liked to think I was honest with myself about what I found.

"Sounds great," I murmured, holding myself still as he strode up and pecked my cheek. He always smelled nice — like an ocean breeze — and it had been a major part of his appeal.

Well, that, and my late-20s crisis.

"Let me get your bag," I offered, plastering my most angelic smile on my face. Clearly Darren didn't know me as well as I assumed he did, because nothing good ever came from this smile.

This was my 'I accidentally set a small fire in the laundry' smile. My 'I mixed up the brake and accelerator pedals, and I need to borrow some money' smile.

"You're a sweetheart," Darren said cheerfully, buttoning up the coat he'd only just unbuttoned when we'd arrived. I moved around the corner to grab his laptop bag off the counter, handing it to him with my smile still fixed in place.

"Stay in the cabin. You'll probably want to get a fire going too," Darren called over his shoulder as he let himself out of the front door without a backward glance.

I watched silently as the truck rumbed obnoxiously to life and he reversed fast enough to make the wheels spin. Long after the sound of the vehicle had vanished, I stayed in front of the window, staring unseeing at the trees just beyond the clearing.

Only once I was sure he was gone did I pull his regular phone out of my pocket. The one I'd discreetly swiped from his bag before he left. I'd seen him unlock it plenty of times in the months we'd been together and memorized the code ages ago, though I'd never used it before.

But if it looked like a cheater and talked like a cheater…

Fuck it. I unlocked the phone, pulling up his messages straight away. The very first sender was an unsaved contact, and I opened the thread on a hunch, finding exactly what I expected to find.

Unknown Number:

How long will you be, babbbyyyyyy? I miss you.

Me:

I'm just dropping her off, then I'll come straight back down.

GILDED MESS

Unknown Number:

She'll get pissy and then you won't be in the mood.

Unknown Number:

Why do you need her anyway? I would move in with you, baby.

Me:

It's complicated. Also none of your concern.

The phone fell from my shaking hands, landing with a clatter on the floor that seemed to echo throughout the entire cabin. I didn't want to touch it. I wanted a shower, to wash the sliminess off me.

Best case scenario: it was a friend. Or a client. They hadn't explicitly mentioned sex, right? And whoever was messaging had sounded way more into it than he had. Though Darren wasn't the most expressive person in messages, I could attest to that.

Don't be a moron, Ria.

Even if the relationship wasn't sexual — which was a generous take, since all signs were pointing towards him being a cheating fucking cheater — what I'd seen was enough red flags for me to call it and cut my losses.

Darren had been planning on ditching me here and going to see his side piece all along. He'd claimed he'd got a work call. He'd looked me square in the eyes and lied to my face.

"Fuck that noise," I muttered under my breath, pressing my cool palms against my flaming hot cheeks. God, the rage was potent, but the humiliation fucking *burned*.

Yes, I'd 100% jumped into this relationship, wanting to settle down as I stared down the barrel of my 30th birthday. No, I didn't love Darren. It had been something I'd hoped would grow. I'd never pretended that my feelings were more than what they were, but I hadn't explicitly explained them either.

Regardless, I deserved better treatment than *this*.

Now what?

I could stay the night and confront him in the morning. Endure the awkward scenic drive back down the mountain into town where I'd beg Lou for my old room back. *Ugh, no.* Then I'd have to go ask my boss at the diner for my job back, and that was more mortification than I could take. What if Darren came in? It was where we'd met, after all.

No, maybe this was the push I needed to give up on my rural living experiment and run back home to my family in New York, tail between my legs. *Ria's fucked up again. Go easy on her, though. It's hard for her, not being able to shift. She's fragile.*

I slid my hands up my heated face to massage my temple. Surely, other 29-year-olds had their shit together. This couldn't be normal.

The idea of staying here, in *his* bed, even without him was unbearable. He'd said it was only half an hour on foot through the forest, and I was pretty sure I had a couple hours of daylight left.

I mean, I was no hiking expert or whatever, but how hard could going downhill be? I hadn't even unpacked. I could just throw on my waterproof pack and go. Get this whole failed experiment over and done with.

But who would I be if I didn't sow a little chaos before I left? There was a reason my family was always bailing me out. Wasn't about to let my reputation down now.

If I was a valuable item, where would I be?

The bedroom seemed like my best bet. I jogged up the stairs, standing at the top and surveying the open space with my lips pursed, assessing.

Why did I think I was ever going to live here? *The bathroom had no walls!* There was not a single person on Earth I was comfortable enough to perform certain bodily functions in front of.

Underwear drawer.

I crossed the room in a couple of steps, pulling the top drawer open and shoving Darren's tighty whities aside, looking for... well, anything really. Something I could destroy.

Ria the Wrecker, as my oldest brother liked to call me, was out in full force.

The distinctive feel of leather under my fingers brought my search to an end. Apprehensively, I tugged at whatever I'd found at the back of the drawer, hoping I wasn't pulling out some kind of kink item Darren had used with his sidepiece. I loved a ball gag and paddle as much as anyone, but I had no interest in one with someone else's fluids on it.

Not that Darren had given any indication of having those interests, but he was a lying liar who lied, so who knows?

Turned out, I had nothing to worry about, fluids-wise. It was just a small leather pouch. I opened it curiously, eyes lighting up as I realized I'd found the fucking jackpot.

Weed.

Get. In. My. Lungs.

It had been a while, but if I ever needed to get high, it was right in this very moment.

There was a little baggie of weed, a packet of papers, and a fancy brushed metal lighter tucked in the bag, calling my name. Well, that would certainly make my unexpected evening stroll back to Fairbanks more entertaining.

I had no qualms about swiping his stash, but it wasn't really the trail of destruction I was hoping to leave behind me.

Fortunately, on a second swipe at the very back of the drawer, I struck gold. There was the sharp corner of a cardboard box next to cool metal. I tugged both items free of their underwear prison, my lips curling into a grin.

The sleek black handgun felt surprisingly heavy in my hand, a full box of ammo in the other. Not only was it something he'd miss, it seemed like a sensible thing to have on me while I embarked on my first wilderness trek. Not that I planned on using it, but it seemed like a good idea to be prepared.

It seemed like an even *better* idea to be high.

While I couldn't go back in time and undo my terrible decisions, I *could* get high and forget about them for a while like a responsible adult.

I nodded to myself. Yes, that was a good plan.

I made my way back down the stairs, stopping by the door, checking the gun was unloaded and the safety was on, and shoving it and the ammo into the top of my pack. I'd been to a shooting range a few times with my brothers, but I still felt weird carrying a firearm on me.

Besides, drugs and weapons were probably not the best combination.

GILDED MESS

"Fucking hell, Ria. You have lost your mind," I muttered, squashing my stolen goods down on top of my pack and pulling the lid down, securing the clips in place. I was still wearing the tan waterproof winter jacket over the black leggings and sweater I had left town in, with my currently spotless dark brown hiking boots and thick gray socks. I'd pulled off my dark gray beanie when I arrived, but I tugged that back on now, fighting to contain my mass of blonde curls.

I leisurely rolled a thick joint with practiced fingers, tucking it into the folded brim of my beanie, and leaving the leather pouch on the little coffee table for Darren to find when he got back.

Item one on the agenda: Get back to civilization and call my family to bail me out. Again.

Item two: Go to the bookstore and find a romance novel about a vindictive bitch who gets revenge on her cheating ex, before swanning off into the sunset, riding a new guy's monster dick while he professes how hopelessly in love with her he is.

I hesitated just as I was about to exit the cabin, feeling the weight of the world caving in on me, crushing my ribcage. I forced myself to take a deep breath before that feeling could overwhelm me. There would be plenty of time for me to lose my shit, but it wasn't this moment. Right now, I had to concentrate on getting the fuck out of here. God, all of this anguish over a guy who'd only ever given me one orgasm at a time on his best day.

Mistakes were made.

Angry at Darren, myself, and the world in general, I made a split decision to really go full Ria the Wrecker and grabbed the poker from next to the fire.

The cabin was nice, no need to take my anger out on the cabin.

GILDED MESS

The fucking phone was taunting me, though, lying on the floor where I'd dropped it. With a shriek worthy of an Amazonian warrior princess — or maybe a banshee — I drove the poker into the stupid sleek device, watching the screen shatter with satisfaction.

Better, I told myself as I shrugged on my hiking pack.

I touched the lighter in my pocket on my way out of the cabin, just barely resisting the urge to burn the whole goddamn thing down.

That would be unproductive, Ria, my brain supplied helpfully. *We don't burn down houses.*

Instead, I lit the joint, took a deep, soothing toke, and strolled into the forest, leaving my hour or so of domestic non-bliss behind me.

RIA

CHAPTER 2

So, in addition to lying about the places he was putting his penis, Darren may also have been lying about this short walk back into town, because nothing about this walk was short.

Or, *potentially*, I was lost.

But Darren was a lying fucking liar face, so I was going to blame him.

My sore feet? Darren's fault. The mud on my leggings? Darren's fault. Achy shoulders from carrying this pack? Darren's fault.

Climate change? Darren's fault. World hunger? Darren's fault.

Fuck Darren and all the Darren-y things he did to make the world a worse place.

His weed was the *shit* though. It made the walk bearable. Forget making jewelry, I was going to start a weed farm. Weed garden. Weed plantation?

Whatever it was, I wouldn't be able to do it in New York where my family lived, and where I was vaguely planning on returning. Not because I particularly *wanted* to — I'd never felt entirely at home there — it just seemed like the best option, considering the public humiliation factor of staying here and the no-money roadblock of moving elsewhere.

All of that was a moot point if I got murdered in the woods trying to find my way out. Or just died of starvation. Fucking hell, I was *famished*.

Even if I could scrounge up the cash to move to Anchorage or something, once I told my family that things with Darren were over, they'd probably freak out and insist on coming out here anyway.

Two months before my 30th birthday and I would be moving back in with my parents. Maybe I could have my brothers' old bedroom, since it was bigger than mine. That would make me feel like less of a failure, right? God, my childhood bedroom could barely fit a twin bed, and I was too old for a twin bed.

Ugh, when I was a teenager, 30 had seemed *so* far away. I was convinced I'd be married with a couple of kids by now, maybe own a ranch house in the suburbs in upstate New York, close enough to visit my family on the weekends, but not so close that I had to see them every day.

In my teenage dreams, me and my hardworking husband — who was good with his hands, *obviously* — bought a fixer upper and did it up together, picking out paint colors and tile patterns on Saturday after a lazy brunch at our local cafe.

And a few years after that, we'd have kids and do kid-stuff on weekends. Soccer runs and shit. We'd have a sensible SUV with car seats in the back, and baby wipes in the console for sticky fingers after post-game ice cream.

Basically, I didn't plan on wandering through the forest high as a kite — possibly lost? — vaguely heartbroken at this point in my life. 16-year-old Ria would shake her head in disappointment at her future self, that is for goddamn sure.

Where was the fucking road?

My leggings were filthy from repeatedly losing my footing and half sliding down the slope on my ass, and my dark brown hiking boots that had looked so cool in the store were making my feet blister like I'd dipped them directly in lava.

1/10. Would not recommend.

I couldn't see or hear a single sign that I was anywhere near civilization, but the dirt road we'd taken to get up here had been quiet, so that didn't mean anything. Maybe I was close.

Possibly, I was walking around in circles. Did that tree look familiar? Its bark was more... bark-y looking than other trees. I was pretty sure I'd seen it before.

Just when I was contemplating some kind of Hansel and Gretel breadcrumb system to keep track of where I'd been, I was pulled up short by a cabin that I *definitely* hadn't seen before, nestled among the trees like they'd cleared as little forestry as possible to make room for it.

The waning sunlight filtering through the trees limited my visibility a lot, but *dannnnnnnnnnnnnnnnng*. I could tell this house was nice.

Like, super nice.

Like, deserved to be on a show featuring rich people searching for an idyllic mountain escape with four bedrooms, four bathrooms, and granite countertops kind of nice. I bet it had been on one of those shows.

It was an A-frame cabin, two-story high with windows covering almost every inch of the front face. There was no light coming from the windows, and no smoke coming from the chimney. Maybe it was a vacation property?

Would the universe be kind enough to throw an empty vacation property in my way, right when I needed it? Previous experience pointed to 'no', but maybe I was finally getting a well-deserved break. Or a dose of good karma. Or it was whatever the opposite of Mars in retrograde was. Venus in futuregrade? That sounded like a thing.

God, I was tired. The high made my mind deliciously fuzzy, but also kind of heavy, and the pain in my feet was really getting to me. I hovered outside the property, wishing I had shifter senses so I could just *hear* if someone was inside.

Fuck it, regular ol' humans broke into houses all the time. I could totally do this. Without damaging anything, because whoever owned this place was an innocent bystander, not to be victimized by Ria the Wrecker.

I crept — graceful as a panther, I'm pretty sure — up to the front door, peering in through the windows as I passed them. It didn't look like anyone was home. Rich people usually had multiple properties, right? They were probably at their island house until the weather warmed up or something. It's not like I was going to *steal* anything, I just wanted to put my feet up for a while.

Okay, maybe I'd steal some food, but just a tiny bit. They wouldn't even miss it. No harm, no foul.

The front door was unlocked — which felt like it could be a good sign or massively foreboding — and I pushed it open tentatively, breathing a silent sigh of relief when the hinges didn't creak.

The front entry was more like a mudroom, with a wall of hooks along one side for jackets and a low shelf for shoes, though it was pretty bare. There were a couple of thin jackets hanging up, which supported my running theory that this was a summer vacation property.

Not wanting to trek mud through their nice house, I unlaced my boots and tucked them into the corner of the shelf, wincing as they scraped over fresh blisters. These boots were not worth it for the aesthetic. Next time, I was buying ugly ones that felt like pillows under my poor tootsies. I kept my jacket on, because without the fire burning it was barely any warmer than it had been outside. Without the boots, my sock-clad feet padded silently across the glossy wooden floors into the open living area.

Holy shit, this was nice. I loved *everything* about it. The massive stone fireplace. The exposed roughhewn log walls. The sturdy wooden furniture haphazardly covered in cozy blankets and soft cushions in warm shades.

I wanted to sink into the shiny floorboards and make myself at one with this house, so I never had to leave.

An enormous couch and two mismatched armchairs were arranged around a sturdy square coffee table in front of the fireplace, flanked by bookshelves on either side. The whole place could have been out of the 1950s for all the technology in the room. There was a vintage record player in the living area, and the stove in the kitchen was a proper cast iron masterpiece.

Among all the large functional furniture was the most adorable, embellished wooden rocking chair I'd ever seen. It was strangely out of place with the rest of the adult-sized furniture, but there weren't any toys or kid's paintings or anything else around that indicated a child lived here. And there were no photos of anyone, so maybe it was just a vacation rental in the *very* remote forest.

That checked out.

I couldn't pull my eyes away from the little chair. Was it actually little, or was everything else in the cabin huge? It seemed to be a house designed for giants. I wasn't particularly short, but the kitchen counter along the opposing wall looked like it would come up to my rib cage.

Maybe the chair was normal adult-sized, and my eyes were playing tricks on me?

Only one way to find out.

I mean, there probably was more than one way, but it was such a pretty chair and I wanted to sit on it.

I carefully lowered my butt into the polished wooden chair, testing to see if it could take my weight. It creaked a little, but held, and I pushed back to get myself comfy. There was something very therapeutic about a good rocking chair.

I pushed back on my heels lightly, and the entire chair fell apart beneath me in a loud clatter of wooden parts hitting the wooden floor.

"Ouch!"

That was totally going to bruise. For an hour at least, until my enhanced healing kicked in to help me out. The one single advantage to having carrier genes, except for having shifter babies, I guess.

So much for my plan to get in and out of here like a ghost, I thought as I clambered to my feet, rubbing my tender ass cheek. Shit. I definitely hadn't meant to break it. I mean, most of the bits looked like they were still whole rather than splintered, so maybe it wasn't a total disaster?

GILDED MESS

I left the mess behind me, intending to clean it up later. I definitely would. I just needed a teeny bit of food first before my stomach consumed itself. The kitchen counter wasn't quite rib-height, but it was close. It was L-shaped, set against the opposite wall of the cabin from the living area, with a pantry along the back and a sturdy rectangular dining table in the middle. It looked like it had been hand-carved, like everything else in the place.

I ran my hand over the smooth concrete counter that starkly contrasted the wooden counters underneath. It was a beautiful home, but almost by accident. Everything was rustic and functional, but it emanated that homey warmth that money couldn't buy.

It was a fancy vacation home; I'd give it that.

I snagged an apple from the fruit bowl on the dining table and went through the pantry. Mostly non-perishable, cook from scratch stuff which didn't satisfy my cravings whatsoever. I spotted a box of crackers and grabbed a handful before resuming my investigation.

Was that weird? To have a bowl of fresh fruit out in a vacant property? Maybe the last guests forgot to empty it. It was probably fine.

The fridge was fully stocked too. Was that weird? My brain was trying to tell me something, but then I spotted the beers at the bottom of the fridge and my priorities immediately shifted. *Yes, please.* Nothing like a cold beer after a long walk. I tucked the bottle under my arm, my hands laden down with snacks, and made my way up the stairs to nosey around a little more.

How often did I get to visit beautiful remote cabins in Alaska? Never. And I was moving back to New York, so double never.

Venus was in futuregrade and telling me to live my best life, and that bitch knew what was up.

The doors upstairs were open, and I let myself in to the bedroom on the right, vaguely trying to figure out if this was someone's actual bedroom or a rental property guest room. It had no photos or overly personal touches either, except for the built-in bookshelves that ran along the entire wall, seamlessly flowing around the door frame. They were packed with an eclectic mix of sci-fi, fantasy, how-to manuals, and art history books.

No romance? Disappointing.

I sat down on the edge of the bed, sinking into the alarmingly soft mattress, and finished my crackers. Ohmigod, salt was the bomb. Maybe they had chips too? I'd have to go back downstairs and look.

For now, I decided to explore the opposite bedroom. It was filled with elaborate, hand-carved furniture like the rocking chair I'd already broken with my ass. Still no photos. Just a bed, bedside tables with old-fashioned lamps, a dresser and a mirror. Maybe this really was a rental property? This looked like the kind of bedroom designed for guests.

I peeked inside the upstairs bathroom and my mouth watered a little when I saw the clawfoot tub practically calling out to me.

Ria. Come bathe in me, Ria. Your muscles are achy, and you feel all gross from walking so far. You know you want toooooo...

The bathtub made a good point. Who was I to argue with porcelain as flawless as that?

I ditched my pack and jacket in the corner and ran the water as hot as it would go, hunting around for bubble bath. Obviously, they needed to up the toiletries selection for their guests. Maybe I'd leave them an anonymous note when I left with a few vacation home tips and an apology for the broken chair. I'd write it with my left hand, so my handwriting couldn't be identified by the FBI.

Weed made me so much smarter. I considered *all* the possibilities.

Giving up my search for bubble bath, I pulled a bottle of men's body wash off the shelf instead. It was eucalyptus and mint scented, and something about it was quite... comforting. Like the menthol rub my mom would put on my chest when I was a kid. But sexy somehow. I added a bit of that to the water before stripping off my gross clothes and climbing in, letting the hot water soak into my bones.

I'd never wanted to orgasm so much from the feel of hot water on my skin. My muscles relaxed, and the blisters on my feet stung, but in a good way.

I let my eyes drift closed, tipping my head back against the back of the bath with my hair hanging over the lip so it didn't get wet. For a moment, I let myself indulge in the idea that this was my life. That I lived in this nice-ass house in the middle of nowhere, making jewelry and spending my days in solitude. I'd get lonely, but loneliness seemed like a better option than attaching myself to another asshole like Darren.

Beer. That would improve the situation. I leaned halfway out of the bath to snag the bottle from the floor and sighed in relief when the top twisted off. Venus. In. Futuregrade.

The cool liquid running down my throat helped soothe some of the burning humiliation. Embarrassment was definitely the dominant emotion at this point in the... breakup? Ugh. It was totally a breakup. And I'd have to *tell* everyone about it. My family had been concerned that I was moving too fast. My roommate, Lou, had been outwardly supportive but definitely apprehensive when I'd told her I was moving in with Darren. She hadn't particularly warmed to him any of the handful of times she'd met him.

God, was I that desperate to settle down by 30?

Maybe I was. It was an uncomfortable realization that I'd basically done everything I would have warned Lou or any of my friends against doing. I thought I was a smart woman, but apparently, I'd let the *tick, tick, tick* of my biological clock drown out my common sense.

Ugh, the weed must be wearing off. I didn't want to think about these things yet. Or maybe ever.

I lay in the bath until the water grew grossly tepid before climbing out and drying off with a clean towel from the cupboard, tidying up the bathroom behind me as I went. Maybe a power nap was what I needed to pull myself together and get back on the road. It was dark now anyway. My hiking experience was limited, but setting out as night fell seemed like an ill-advised idea. This whole expedition was probably an ill-advised idea, but I'd already begun now, so I'd have to see it through.

Besides, if there was no one in the house by now, they wouldn't be arriving in the middle of the night. There was no road nearby, and only high idiots with no sense of direction wandered around the woods in the dark.

I shoved my clothes back into my hiking pack and padded through the house wrapped in a towel, hoping I could find something more comfortable to sleep in. Tshe room opposite the bathroom with all the elegant looking, hand crafted furniture called to me, and I let myself in, looking through the oak chest of drawers. There was a selection of tops in dark colors that made me doubt my vacation home theory, just a little. These definitely looked like they belonged to one person. And they smelled heavenly. Like oranges and cloves. This room smelled like Christmas.

I pulled a faded black t-shirt out of the drawer and tugged it on, where it fell to mid-thigh and covered all the important stuff. I hunted through my pack until I found a pair of clean panties to slide on too, since I felt a little indecent prancing around a strange house with no underwear on. Even if there was no one else here.

I was a respectful intruder like that.

The bed in this room was beautiful — with a tall, carved headboard depicting the forest in elaborate detail — but it didn't really call to me. The other room hadn't either, it was more like a library with a super soft bed in it. On a whim, I hauled my pack over one shoulder and made my way back downstairs where there was one more bedroom I hadn't explored yet.

Oh, yes. This one was just right.

There were enormous slabs of rough-cut wood lined up next to each other like a giant pallet, with a huge mattress in the center, pushed back against the roughhewn log wall. In contrast to the hard materials around it, the bedding was all soft and inviting, in shades of gray and navy. It was big enough to sleep six of me, and the most inviting thing I'd ever seen. Like the other rooms, this one smelled delicious too. Woodsy. Cedar, maybe?

Oh yes, you'll do nicely.

I ditched my pack next to the bed, pulling out the handgun to keep handy in case I needed it, and crawled into the middle of the bed, sinking down into the mattress and burrowing into the blankets. It was like my own personal nest, I never wanted to leave.

Unfortunately, I would have to leave because I was very much an uninvited guest, and now my high had worn off, I was feeling vaguely guilty about that. Mostly about the broken chair. Still, they were rich. It would be fine, right?

I'd clean it up, write an apology note, and be out of their hair before sunrise.

NOAH
CHAPTER 3

My mind was always running a hundred miles a minute this time of year. We'd had the first frost already, winter was well on the way, and my to-do list seemed never ending. Plus, this year I had to plan my time around the park ranger job my brothers had insisted I take, so I had even less time on the property to prepare for the colder weather and shorter days.

Fuck it, they'd been the ones to push me out of the house, they'd just have to help out with these chores more. I'd started today by dragging them both on a fishing trip. Usually, I did these things on my own. I always had. They were the ones that wanted me to have a life outside of theirs, though, so they could add a little hard labor to their schedule.

Fishing trips were a long and necessary evil. Not the fishing itself, the bear in me loved nothing more than to fish, and most of the fishing we did in our fur. But traipsing back through the forest with our coolers was a pain in the ass.

Better than being vegetarians, though.

GILDED MESS

I glanced at my twin, Seth, out of the corner of my eye and struggled not to laugh. Out of the three of us, he was the least outdoorsy, preferring to hole up in the shed and paint. He looked hilariously out of sorts in his hiking gear, expression flitting between irritated and thoughtful as he undoubtedly contemplated new scenes to paint. His constant search for *inspiration* was probably the only reason he'd agreed to come with us.

Eli, my not-so-baby brother, whistled obnoxiously, swinging the cooler at his side *just* high enough to make me edgy that the lid would fall off. No one on this planet could raise my hackles like he could, and he was one of my two favorite people.

My chest puffed up with pride whenever I came home. It was more than four walls and a place to rest our heads at night. We'd built this place with our own hands when we were little more than *cubs*. The cabin was a big source of pride for me. It was either build a home or be homeless, but we'd still done an impressive job.

Fuck knows I didn't have much else going on these days. I didn't even particularly enjoy being a park ranger.

"What is that smell?" Seth muttered as the dark cabin came into view.

"What smell?" Eli asked absently, shoving a stray lock of hair out of his face that had escaped his stupid man bun. One of these days, I'd shave it off in his sleep.

Now that they'd mentioned it, there was a foreign scent lingering around the cabin. Not *bad* foreign. It smelled light, feminine, oddly summery. Like geraniums and grapefruit and tangerine.

Flowers and fruit. *Get a fucking grip, Noah.*

"There's someone in the house," I growled, the scent growing stronger as we approached the front door.

"Calm down, brother," Seth said lightly, giving me a pointed look. We were twins, but our personalities were total opposites.

Seth never got angry. Or never unleashed it, at least. I felt like I was never not angry.

"Calm down? There's *someone in our house*," I gritted out. "Are you demented?"

"We should probably consider *locking* the door from time to time," Eli pointed out with a shrug, looking more curious than angry, deeply inhaling the enticing scent. "That is a delicious smelling intruder."

Not good. It was a delicious smelling intruder, but Eli was likely to let that sway his judgment. They'd be best friends by the end of the night if Eli got his way.

"Let me do the talking," I ordered, glowering at him as I pushed the front door open. We'd never bothered locking it because these woods were shifter territory. No shifter was stupid enough to break into a bear's den, and if they were, a lock wouldn't keep them out, anyway.

And there wasn't much on Earth that would save them.

A pair of small muddy boots tucked neatly on the shelf was the first thing that grabbed my attention. Women's boots, surely.

"What a polite criminal," Seth remarked lightly. "Follow her lead. I don't want you trekking mud through the house."

"There's an intruder in our house and you're worried about mud?" I hissed, glaring at him.

"Yes." Seth blinked impassively at me.

"Fuck's sake," I muttered, yanking off my boots as quietly as possible. We ditched our jackets and coolers in the entryway, better prepared to fight if we needed to, though I doubted that would be the case. The faint smell of blood clung to her boots, and my gut churned uncomfortably. I wasn't used to giving a fuck about people that weren't my brothers, and I had no intention of starting now.

"Oh man, I'd been working on that chair for ages," Eli groaned as we rounded the corner, drawing my attention to the broken pile of wood on the floor that had been the rocking chair he was putting together for a customer. "Ace is going to flip."

Another rush of anger flooded me, replacing my moment of concern, and Seth grabbed my shoulder, pulling me around to face him and pinning me with his most serious 'calm down' face. "You can smell it's a human. Proceed with caution. We don't want to accidentally kill someone."

"Who said anything about an accident?" I muttered, pushing him away and prowling around the house to inspect the rest of the damage. A few crumbs on the floor, nothing too egregious, but I was past the point of feeling relaxed about anything. At this point, crumbs were on par with destruction of property.

What kind of person let themselves into someone else's home, ate their food, and broke their shit? A criminal, that's who. The kind of asshole who deserved to be behind bars. Delicious smelling or not.

Apparently, my brothers weren't on the same page as me. They looked way too relaxed about this.

I followed the trail up the stairs, expecting to find the intruder in one of the bedrooms, but they were both empty, though traces of the light scent lingered there. The bathroom was another story. The tub had clearly been used, and there was an empty bottle of *my beer* on the window sill.

"Who is this person?" Eli chuckled. "Who the fuck breaks into someone's house and takes a bath?"

"Can you stop being so cheerful about this?" I snapped.

"Can you stop being so grouchy?" Eli countered, ducking out of the way when I tried to cuff his ears. "You're just mad they took one of your beers. Admit it. It's kind of funny."

"Nothing about this is funny," I groused, pushing past my brothers and heading back downstairs when I heard the distinctive rustling of my sheets downstairs.

Oh, hell no.

"Oh dear," Seth sighed, him and Eli were hot on my heels as I quietly jogged down the stairs. The front of the cabin was dominated by the kitchen and living area, and behind the stairs was my bedroom, a bathroom, and the laundry. I pushed the door open silently, moving inside so my brothers could file in behind me.

Eli sucked in a breath, but Seth was even more curiously silent than usual.

My dick did not care that she had broken into our den. My dick was weirdly fine with it.

Probably because the little criminal looked like she'd floated down to Earth on a cloud.

Beautiful. She was beautiful.

A mass of curled blonde hair fanned out over my pillow, long dark eyelashes resting on high cheekbones with a full pouty mouth and adorably turned-up nose. The faintest streaks of tears were dried on her cheeks. Considering how innocent she looked, it was difficult to reconcile the fact that she had a) broken into our home, and b) definitely had the lingering smell of marijuana clinging to her hair.

GILDED MESS

She looked like the perfect package, but she was definitely a mess.

A mess that was sleeping in my bed. My fucking bed.

Some part of me got a kick out of that. The little intruder hadn't been shy about poking around the house — her sweet scent lingered everywhere — but she'd chosen *my* bed to rest her pretty head. Even if she was wearing Eli's oversized t-shirt.

"Can we keep her?" Eli asked eagerly.

"You want to keep the girl that smells like marijuana and tears?" I replied drolly. *And Seth's body wash,* my mind supplied unhelpfully.

"Why don't we wake her up first?" Seth muttered, his nose twitching.

"Great idea. I'll lick her face," Eli responded, more dog than bear.

"You will not," I shot back. "I will wake her." My fingers were already moving to unbutton my flannel, my bear rising eagerly under my skin. *You break into a bear's house, you best be prepared for a bear's welcome.*

"You sure about that, boss?" Eli asked, raising his eyebrows at me. "Piss is a helluva smell to get out of a mattress." I grimaced, halting my movements. I would have to burn the bed.

"Relax, big boy. I'm not going to wet my pants," the little intruder said in a husky voice, rolling onto her back and stretching out like a kitten, the movement made the blanket slip down her legs.

She wasn't even *wearing* pants. Eli's shirt rode up her tanned thighs, and an organ of mine that had no right to be responding sprung to attention.

"You'd have pissed the bed if I'd shifted," I growled, my voice more bear than man, forgetting humans weren't supposed to know about us. *Shit.*

Seth spun to face me, looking alarmed. I could see him scrambling to explain away my words, but she spoke before he could get to it.

"I'm a carrier. Shifters don't scare me," she replied lazily, tucking her hands under the pillow behind her head with her eyes still closed. Not a care in the world.

Lucky break, Eli mouthed, grinning at me as Seth sighed audibly in relief.

A carrier. So, her family could shift, but she couldn't? I didn't know much about how it worked. Seth's first shift had been two years after mine, despite us being twins, and our parents had talked about him possibly being a carrier in hushed tones. After his bear had emerged, I'd never thought about it again.

Who the fuck was this woman?

"I'm in love," Eli declared breathily, eyes trained on the hem of the increasingly indecent t-shirt.

That made the little minx crack open an eye. I'd expected to see blue, but her eyes were molten brown, flecked with gold.

Why the fuck did she have to look like that? It was throwing a real spanner in my execute-the-intruder plan.

"You are remarkably relaxed about waking up in the home you broke into surrounded by three men who could easily overpower you," Seth noted, examining her like she was a science experiment. I vaguely wondered what kind of shifters her family were, because her answering grin was wolfish.

"I have a gun under the pillow."

"That wouldn't kill us," Eli scoffed, looking even *more* turned on, if anything.

I had clearly gone very wrong somewhere with my youngest brother. Or our parents' death had irrevocably fucked him up. Or maybe he'd just been born that way.

"It would slow you down, though," she replied confidently, observing us with both eyes fully open. Maybe she was still high.

"What's your name?" Seth's intrigue was alarming me. Usually, he and I were on the same page, reining in Eli together, but I got the impression we weren't even reading the same book this time.

"Aurelia. Yours?" She ran her gaze appraisingly over the three of us. "Balls, Brains, and Brawn?"

"Why am I 'Balls'?" Eli laughed, while Seth's lips twitched at his apt 'Brains' moniker. She was a perceptive little criminal.

"You've got big ones, I can tell," Aurelia replied sagely.

"The love of my life is a genius," Eli sighed, clutching his chest dramatically. He took a step forward like he was going to jump on the bed and cuddle up to her or something, but I fisted the back of his shirt to hold him in place. "I'm Eli. These are my older brothers, Seth and Noah," he finished, gesturing at us in turn.

"What are you doing here, *Aurelia*?" Seth asked, sounding out her name like he was savoring it.

"Who cares?" Eli interjected. "Want to stay forever?"

What the hell was going on? They'd both clearly lost their minds. Maybe it was because she was a carrier. She certainly smelled more tempting than any human woman I'd ever encountered.

"This is ridiculous. You," I snapped, pinning my gaze on the woman lounging in my bed like she belonged there. "Fuck off. And you, stop talking," I added, throwing my baby brother a warning look that he confidently ignored.

"Fine," Aurelia huffed, scowling at me like I was the unreasonable one. She slid her hands out from behind the pillow, revealing the pistol and clutching it loosely at her side as she rolled off the bed, landing lightly on her feet.

"Point me in the direction of the highway and I'll be on my way," she added, sauntering over to the hiking pack she'd left against the end of the bed and hooking a strap over her elbow. She straightened, cocking her hip and glaring imperiously at me like she was fully prepared to walk out into the forest at night wearing nothing but Eli's t-shirt.

Which was... *fine*. Wasn't it? She was a criminal. Her comfort was of no consequence to me.

Eli and Seth both growled in objection and a traitorous shiver of relief ran through me that they called it, so I didn't have to. She could sleep on the porch.

"It's too late to be walking through the forest now," Seth said, no room for argument in his tone. "Stay. At least until morning."

At least? What the fuck was with the 'at least'?

"You can sleep in my bed, Goldilocks," Eli purred, shooting her that cocky smirk that usually had women falling at his feet.

Aurelia groaned, throwing her head back in exasperation. She looked about three seconds away from stamping her foot, and it was far more attractive than it had any right to be.

"Please don't tell me you're bear shifters."

"The size didn't give it away?" I snorted. Ain't no shifter bigger than a bear shifter. Fact.

Aurelia's pack slipped down her arm, landing with a light thud on the floor. She dragged it along the ground, giving me an appraising look as she stepped confidently into my personal space, hips swishing temptingly.

"Hmm," she murmured, her nose level with my sternum. "If I'm Goldilocks, does that make you the Daddy Bear?" she asked with a mischievous smile.

"I'm gonna jizz my pants," Eli muttered, making Seth groan exasperatedly.

"Not my kink, thief. Though spanking you has an awful lot of appeal," I rumbled, hoping my flannel was doing a decent job of hiding my erection.

I *really* wanted to spank her.

Aurelia's eyes flared, her teeth sinking into her plush lower lip. *Fucking hell*, we were in trouble.

"I'll sleep on the couch and be out of your fur as soon as it's light out," she announced, pulling away with visible effort. Shit, I'd barely noticed the gun in her hand and she'd definitely been close enough to do some damage.

Apparently, my dick was draining all the blood away from the organ that actually needed it.

Aurelia hauled her bag around us, heading down the hallway towards the living room. Eli recovered the quickest, trailing after her like a puppy.

Seth looked at me, amusement and wariness warring for dominance in his eyes. "We're in so much trouble, brother."

RIA

CHAPTER 4

The couch wasn't nearly as comfortable as the bed I'd been snuggled up on — too hard — but with the fire roaring and an absurd number of blankets piled on top of me, because apparently they thought humans would die at the first hint of a chill; I was pretty cozy.

The sudden appearance of the three homeowners had at least pulled me out of my pity party. I'd fallen asleep *crying* over my sorry circumstances, and that was just straight up unacceptable.

If I was going to cry, it would be when I was back in the comfort of my parents' house, blasting *All By Myself* while I ate my body weight in cookie dough ice cream.

Naturally, the answer to 'would I stay here in the house of oversized, absurdly handsome bear shifters?' was a resounding fuck no.

That is how women ended up on true crime shows, and my parents wouldn't survive the humiliation of people doing a deep dive into my life.

GILDED MESS

Aurelia Conroy was a 29-year-old spinster, who abandoned her perfectly lovely, stable family in New York to move to Alaska on a whim. Her one local friend, Lou Taylor, tells us that Aurelia — or Ria, as she was known to her friends — was exceptionally hilarious, fond of box wine, and had an encyclopedic knowledge of sex toys and romance novels.

Aurelia's internet search history shows an extensive interest in jewelry design and double penetration.

My parents would keel over dead. Then my brothers would find some way to bring me back from the dead to yell at me about our parents. And laugh at my search history. God, I should really clear that sometime.

Besides, now that my high was wearing off, I'd begun seriously questioning my sanity. No, they hadn't been home, but it was a ballsy move to help myself to their food, take a bath, steal their clothes, and lie down in one of their beds.

It all smelled so *good*, though. The clothes. The home. The men. Everything about their scent was intoxicating and soothing at the same time.

Maybe Darren had laced that weed with something else? This was not a normal reaction to strangers. Even shifters, who always smelled better to me than humans. It was a biological thing, apparently. Mom had explained that while I could be with a human, I would always feel drawn to shifters for *reproductive* purposes. Lucky me.

Though Darren was a human, and he'd smelled amazing. Too bad he was such a shitty person.

I burrowed down in the blankets Eli had found for me, waiting until the shuffling noises from the three bedrooms had stopped. Once I was certain the house was still, I silently pushed the blankets off me and dressed hastily, slipping my pack over my shoulders and grabbing my boots from by the door, carrying them between my fingers as I snuck out.

I may not have super sensitive shifter senses, but I had been raised by foxes, and I knew how to goddamn sneak.

A portable lantern sat conveniently next to the front door, and I grabbed that too, needing all the help I could get to navigate the dark forest.

The frigid night air hit me like a ton of bricks after being holed up in a blanket nest on the couch with the embers of the fire Eli had lit to keep me warm burning in the background. Fuck, he was hot. Like, really hot. I'd never been into long hair on guys before, but Eli *rocked* a man bun. He had a layer of stubble that wasn't thick enough to hide his sharp jawline and highlighted those full lips that I bet were capable of magical things. I had a radar for that sort of thing.

Eli was pinging hard on my Good Pussy Eater Radar.

Not that I thought the other two would be slouches in the bedroom. Seth, with his short hair and neat beard, would be an attentive lover, I was sure of it. His dark eyes hadn't missed a thing in the few brief moments we'd spent together. And Noah, with his rugged beard and shaggy dark hair... Noah would give me a flaming hot ass and fuck me until I couldn't walk the next day.

That weed was definitely laced with something, I'd never been so horny in my entire life.

Once I got far enough from the cabin that I didn't think they could hear me anymore, I took a moment to adjust my outfit, zipping up my jacket properly, tugging on my beanie and pulling on my boots and pack. It helped a little with the cold, but I still missed the cozy cabin and questioned my sanity a little. Or a lot. The road couldn't be far from here, though. Once I was back in civilization, I'd be fine. I'd call my family, my mom would cry, my brothers would be obnoxious a-holes, and I'd be on a plane in no time.

I flinched as I fumbled with the lantern, finally managing to switch it on. *Fuck*, that was bright. I'd be a walking, muttering beacon out there. But it had to be better than walking around in the dark, right?

Right.

Which direction was north?

I'd figured so long as I was going downhill, I'd probably be alright. Right? *Stupid Ria*. Should have paid more attention on the way up here. My boots slipped over the forest floor, even as my eyes adjusted to the surrounding darkness. I wasn't used to walking long distances, especially not on uneven terrain. I'd grown up stomping along concrete pavement in heeled boots, and while I still liked the idea of living out in the middle of nowhere, my execution needed work.

Though, that would be all for naught now, since I was throwing in the towel and moving back home, and I'd have to confess to my family that OH MY GOD YES YOU WERE RIGHT ABOUT THAT FUCKWIT DARREN. Fuck my life.

A drop of rain hit my nose, and I groaned up at the sky. Where'd my awesome luck go? It had all been going so well.

My *Venus in futuregrade* theory sounded pretty stupid right about now.

The blisters that had been almost healed after my relaxing bath and nap at the bears' house were rubbing raw inside my boots again, and my muscles ached with exhaustion. I paused next to a stump with a slight overhang that might have protected me a little from the rain. Besides, I just wanted to sit down for just a moment. Just to rest my tired feet and give my wounds a chance to heal. I still had the gun, after all. I doubted there was anything scarier in these woods than the big-ass bear shifters whose house I'd broken into, and I got out of that just fine.

I slumped down against the stump, settling between the enormous gnarled roots that had broken above the ground into the perfect Aurelia-sized spot that felt like it was made just for me. I pulled my hood over my head, hoping it would protect me from the worst of the rain, and turned off the lantern, plunging me into eerie darkness.

Just a five-minute break, then I'd be on my way. Just... five... minutes...

✱ ✱ ✱

Honestly, I probably should have died.

Even with my enhanced healing, falling asleep in the freezing cold forest in the middle of the night *in the rain* was basically a death sentence.

Fortunately for me and the many things I still had planned for my future, I woke up engulfed in an enormous bear hug. Literally. A humongous sleeping brown bear had pulled me against its chest, big ass bear arms wrapped around my waist, my face buried against its neck. Or *his* neck rather, because the gargantuan beast cuddling me smelled a lot like Noah's sheets, though with a slightly more feral, animalistic edge.

I pushed away from his chest gently, not wanting to startle the bear into attacking me, but also wanting to get the fuck away from this awkwardness. The sun was rising, beaming offensively brightly through the gaps in the trees, and shining a beacon on all the poor choices that had led me to this moment.

Well fuck you too, sun.

The bear made a rumbling noise of discontent in its chest as I shoved again, wiggling out of his grip. He must have let me go because there was no way on this good green earth I could get myself out of his hold if he didn't want me to.

God, he'd even taken my pack off without me waking up. I probably hadn't noticed while I'd been borderline hypothermic.

Or *actually* hypothermic.

His eyes blinked open, staring judgmentally at me as I shuffled backwards, hefting my ass over the root of the tree until I was comfortably ensconced in my little nest again. I didn't speak bear, but I was pretty sure what Noah was conveying with his smug bear eyes was *'you're welcome for the life saving cuddles, you fucking moron.'*

"Thanks for keeping me alive. Could you just point me in the direction of the road? I'll be on my way. Also, you have to leave because I'm not peeing in front of you in bear or man form," I added primly.

I swear to god, this 1500-pound bear rolled his stupid bear eyes at me.

I was entirely unsurprised when he didn't helpfully point me in the direction of the road and rolled onto his back, scratching himself on a root and ignoring me. Well, fine then. Be difficult.

"I'm going behind this tree to pee. Don't listen," I instructed, dragging my pack along with me in case Noah took off with it just to torture me. I was grateful he'd kept me alive, but couldn't help feeling a little disappointed that of the three of them, he'd been the one to find me.

His brothers were so much nicer.

It took me *forever* to convince my bladder to go, even though I was pretty well hidden behind the bush I'd chosen. I could still hear Noah shuffling around in all his bear glory, and my bladder was not about having an audience.

Besides, I'd had to basically strip from the waist down to go, and my ass was freezing. Men didn't appreciate how good they had it when it came to peeing on the go.

Eventually I was able to go, and redressed in the clothes I'd slept in that were now feeling pretty crusty and gross. Crusty and gross basically summed up everything about how I was feeling. If anything, the small amount of sleep had made me feel *more* tired.

Sleep when you get back to town. Come on, Ria.

I took a swig from the water bottle I'd packed before I'd left for Darren's yesterday and cursed myself for not stealing more food from the bears. Noah watched me as I pulled my pack back on and surveyed my surroundings, trying to determine which direction to go in.

"Is the road that way?" I asked, pointing through the trees. "Nod your giant furry head, yes or no."

Noah blinked at me impassively, sitting on his huge ass, content as could be.

"I know you understand me, Noah," I growled. "I grew up around shifters. Is it this way?" I tried again, pointing further… East? West? Left?

Nothing. Zero movement. Not even an eye twitch.

"Ugh, fine. I'll just figure it out myself. Nice to meet you. Thanks for not letting me die," I added dismissively.

Noah snorted, proving he absolutely understood what I was saying. The furry asshole.

Fuck it, I'd just pick a direction and commit.

I held my head up like I knew exactly what I was doing and started walking. South, or potentially east. Maybe west? Why couldn't I have just been born with handy dandy shifter genes like my brothers? I'd have shifted into a fox last night at Darren's and pranced my merry way back to Fairbanks, nice and cozy in my fur, sniffing my way as I went.

Fuck it, I'd watched plenty of reality shows where people lived in the wild, naked, and survived. At least I had clothes. I'd find my way out of here, eventually.

✳ ✳ ✳

I would not find my way out of here eventually.

I would die in this forest and they'd have to send a search party out to find me, but it'd take weeks because everyone who gave a shit about me thought I was living happily with Darren and that I just had no cell service.

By the time anyone found me, I'd be covered in my own piss, half eaten by earthworms. Actually, at least the rain would wash away the piss smell because it hadn't let up all day.

I hadn't been this tired since I'd gone to a three-day music festival for my 21st birthday and survived off beer, energy drinks, and power naps the entire time. I'd gone home, curled up in my childhood bed and slept for a week to recover while my mother intermittently force fed me vegetables and tutted about my poor liver. Until now, I didn't think it was possible to *be* more tired than that, but this was a whole new level of pain.

Somewhere behind me was a lumbering unhelpful bear, but I was doing my best to ignore him. If he wasn't going to give me directions, I wasn't going to talk to him.

I bet Eli would have helped me.

"AURELIA!"

I froze in place, my foot hovering above the stick I'd been about to stand on. Darren's voice was distant, but the dread it inspired was very much present and visceral.

Shit. I guess he realized I was gone.

He was looking for me?

Why was he looking for me?

It seemed unlikely that he was following me because he actually wanted me. Darren didn't strike me as the type to go through that much effort. Then again, he'd put effort into a whole secret relationship, so maybe I should give him more credit.

Fuck, I shouldn't have robbed him. That was probably where I went wrong.

Fuckity fuck fuck. Why had I taken that gun?

My useless companion sidled up to me, popping up on his hind legs, sniffing the air as he peered through the trees.

"Get down," I hissed, silently dropping to the forest floor and wedging myself back against a fallen tree, giant drops of rain dripping from the leaves above onto my face, crashing obnoxiously loudly onto the waterproof material of my jacket.

It was a terrible hiding spot, and I was fucked on every level if Darren came in this direction. Unless I shot him, which was a thought I only entertained for two seconds. Three, tops. Yes, he'd cheated on me, but shooting him seemed a little excessive.

"AURELIA!"

Bear Noah, who was still very much upright and looking around instead of lying down like I told him to, growled ominously in warning as Darren's voice got closer. The sound of an angry bear *should* have frightened me — logically, I knew angry wasn't the state you wanted a nearby bear to be in — but the rumble wrapped around me like a warm blanket.

Noah was a dick, but I felt strangely confident that he wouldn't turn his anger on me. I felt a lot less confident about Darren's anger.

"AURELIA! Stupid *bitch*, where are you?" Darren spat.

The hairs on the back of my neck stood up, a prickle of fear running down my spine. I'd *never* heard him this angry, but how well did I really know this guy? I'd missed some massive warning signs that had been glaring right in my face. He clearly wasn't the safe bet I'd always assumed he was.

God, it was a horrible feeling not being able to trust your own judgment.

A twig snapped nearby, the noise as loud as a gunshot in the silence. *Shit. Why was I lying on the ground like an idiot?*

Ugh, I was more mud than human at this point. On the plus side, the squelching made it a lot easier to pinpoint Darren's nearness. But that also meant if I tried to move, he'd definitely be able to hear me…

The footsteps drew closer as I debated what to do, but as soon as Darren got within a few feet, Noah moved in front of me and *bellowed*. I let out a squeak of surprise as I cowered in place, letting my unlikely ally do my dirty work for me.

The footsteps ceased immediately, I could almost envision Darren's foot hovering in the air, fear freezing him in place.

Damn it, I was in debt to Noah again.

Noah roared a second furious growl that seemed to say *fuck off* just as clearly as if he'd spoken the words in human form. That seemed to solidify Darren's decision, and I listened to his panicked, clumsy footsteps slipping through the mud grow increasingly distant, hardly daring to breathe until the sound of his escape had long faded.

For a long moment, neither one of us moved. Noah seemed to listen carefully to ensure Darren had actually left, and I was curled up tightly in a ball, trying to get my heartbeat under control and not pee my pants.

Okay.

Okay.

In hindsight, maybe traipsing out in the forest on my own hadn't been the best idea, even if it was only meant to be a half hour stroll to the highway. Apparently, wild animals weren't the only thing I should be worried about in these woods.

Ex-boyfriends were also a possible hazard to my health. He did know he was my ex, right? I assumed the smashed up phone with the messages from his side chick, plus the theft and, *you know*, leaving him would all be pretty clear signs.

Too subtle. Should have carved 'cheater' into the front door with the fire poker.

The vitriol in Darren's voice as he'd snarled *"stupid bitch"* had left me with chills. I didn't know for sure Darren would have hurt me if he'd found me alone, but I didn't know for sure that he *wouldn't*.

Though I guess I could have shot him. Just in the leg or something.

Maybe in the dick. He was actually pretty well hung, it was a decent sized target.

Seemingly satisfied that Darren had gone, Noah dropped back onto his forepaws and turned around to face me. I was trying to keep it together, to hide the vulnerability that I knew was written all over my face, but I didn't have the fortitude just yet to put my bitch face on and pretend what had just happened hadn't seriously shaken me.

Noah took two tentative steps forward, and I inhaled deeply, settling my churning stomach and calming my nerves with his comforting cedar scent.

GILDED MESS

I don't know what I expected him to do. Leave, probably. Instead, he curled up next to me, nudging and pawing until I slumped against him, closing my eyes to weather the adrenaline crash.

Why Noah wouldn't just give me directions back to the road, I had no idea, but he had saved my life for sure once, possibly twice. He was grumpy, obstinate, and difficult, and I owed him a debt I couldn't repay.

So, I snuggled against him and let his steady breathing lull me to sleep.

ELI

CHAPTER 5

Aurelia was back.

Possibly not willingly, based on the fact that she was cradled in Noah's bear arms, fast asleep, and not walking in the house under her own steam, but she was still back. I'd take what I could get.

I'd been genuinely devastated when I heard the front door open at midnight, though I felt a little better when Noah had promptly followed her. If he hadn't, Seth or I would have. It wasn't safe out there for her alone in daylight, let alone in the middle of the night. Noah was the best candidate, though. He knew the land best and was trained in how to take care of humans if anything went wrong.

Seth moved to grab her pack that Noah had dangling from one arm, while I stared dumbstruck at the woman in his arms. Aurelia's chest rose and fell steadily, a mass of thick blonde curls covering her face. Not that I needed the reminder, I'd memorized her features yesterday.

She'd said she was a carrier, but hadn't told us what kind of shifters her family were. My guess was something feline. Her defined cheekbones, small upturned nose, and almond eyes reminded me of a haughty cat.

But like… sexy. A sexy cat.

A few minutes in her company and I was smitten. Granted, we didn't see a lot of women out here in general, but I'd had passing flings in Fairbanks from time to time, and no woman I'd met came close to Aurelia. She was beautiful, sassy, and brave as hell.

I mean, she'd found out that Noah was a bear shifter, walked right up to him, and made a *daddy* joke.

How was any man supposed to resist that kind of temptation?

Maybe she was looking for a shifter mate? Or three?

Noah laid Aurelia down gently on the couch she'd so rudely vacated the night before and stepped back to shift. Even though she'd bolted, my attraction to her had only grown stronger. Obviously, wandering out into unknown woods in the middle of the night was moronic, *but* it was ballsy as hell so I could appreciate her moxie.

Seth was at Aurelia's side in an instant, pulling a heavy blanket over her slight form, then moving to relight the fire. The cold would affect her a lot more than it affected us. Shit, what if she was already too cold? She'd been out there all night.

"She's fine," Seth murmured, reading my mind like he often did. "Cuddling up to an enormous, furry bear tends to keep you warm," he added, raising an amused eyebrow at a surly looking Noah who was walking back from his room pulling up a fresh pair of sweats.

Surlier-than-usual-looking Noah.

"Wake her up," he commanded, sitting in the armchair adjacent to the sofa, gaze pinned on her peaceful face.

"What? Why?"

Noah pinned me with his scary, I-am-the-boss-do-what-I-say face and I relented with a sigh, sitting on the floor by Aurelia's head and resting my face on my forearms. I was close enough to count every single one of her thick, dark eyelashes. I should do that. She had great eyelashes.

"Today would be nice," Noah snarked, tapping his foot impatiently on the wooden floor.

"She's so pretty when she sleeps," I breathed, admiring the light freckles on the bridge of her nose.

"That is fucking creepy," Aurelia said flatly, opening her eyes and glowering at me. She didn't flinch, though. Didn't back away or let out so much as a hint of a squeal.

Because she's going to be my mate someday. Obviously. Women like Aurelia didn't come along every day, I had to lock that down. Mate her. Wife her.

After I convinced her to fall in love with me and my brothers.

"Was it too much to hope that you'd given me a lift into town?" Aurelia sighed, looking past me at my grumpy older brother.

Okay, maybe getting those two to fall in love would be a stretch. The only thing Noah loved was this house, freshly caught salmon, and *maybe* me and Seth. On a good day.

I didn't miss the way Aurelia's eyes snagged on his bare chest before she forced her glare up to his face, though. And he hadn't left her out there to die, so maybe there was hope after all.

Noah snorted. "What do you think this is? I'm not a taxi."

"Ooh, you could be," I cut in, straightening up. "We could call it a *cub* service. Like *cab* service. Get it?"

Seth groaned loudly, but Aurelia's lips twitched a little and I didn't care if my brothers thought I was lame.

"As I was saying," Noah muttered. "Not a taxi service. And I want to know why the coyote was looking for you."

"Darren isn't a coyote," Aurelia responded with absolute certainty, shaking her head.

"Darren Vaughn? He's definitely a coyote. Sorry, babe."

"I hated when he called me that, don't you start," Aurelia muttered, and I recoiled internally at being anything like Darren fucking Vaughn.

"Darren's old pack contacted us when he moved into the area. They contacted all the local shifters actually," Seth explained as Aurelia pushed the blankets down and sat up on the couch. God, she looked like she belonged here. Couldn't anyone else see it?

I glanced back over my shoulder at Seth. He totally saw it.

"Why?"

The question hung awkwardly in the air, and I knew without a doubt that Noah would be the one to answer it, because he was an asshole and weirdly bitter over the whole breaking-and-entering thing.

"Because of women like you."

"I would tread carefully if I were you, Daddy Bear," Aurelia said in a low voice, looking past me to narrow her eyes dangerously at Noah. I moved from the floor to the end of the couch with a sigh, pulling Aurelia's feet onto my lap to unlace her hiking boots. She gave me a startled look before resuming glowering at Noah, but she didn't pull her feet away.

I could never be in the doghouse with Noah around to piss Aurelia off. He made Seth and I look great.

"Darren Vaughn lost a challenge within his pack for a female coyote and apparently didn't take the loss well," Seth interjected in the diplomatic voice he usually reserved for Noah and I.

Not well was an understatement. He'd totally lost it, tried to execute the victor in his sleep and snatch the woman for himself.

Seth continued uncomfortably. "He was exiled. His pack followed him to make sure he left their territory and when he came here, they wanted local shifters to be... aware of him. In case there were unmated females or carriers around that he may find..."

"Valuable," Noah finished coolly, looking away with his jaw clenched tight. For all his shit talking, no one was more protective than Noah. There would have been no question in his mind about bringing Aurelia back here once he realized Darren was looking for her.

She was quiet for a moment, a hint of vulnerability in her expression that she was working hard to hide. Shit, I couldn't imagine how it would feel to have someone lie about something that huge. There was no fucking way Darren didn't realize she was a carrier. Humans didn't smell like that.

"It's not that I don't believe you, but it doesn't really make sense," Aurelia replied eventually, scrunching her face up and glancing up to the ceiling for a beat. "What was his plan? To pretend to be human forever?"

"You're a carrier, not a shifter," Noah stated succinctly. "He wouldn't have to mate you to impregnate you."

Aurelia threw him a filthy look, but it didn't have any real heat, and she didn't argue, the wheels in her head obviously turning. Carriers weren't coveted as mates as much as shifters were. They were pretty much human, and could have children with either humans or shifters.

I'd never objected to the idea of having a carrier mate — there were more than enough animals to go around in this house — but I knew some shifters saw them as second best, and Darren probably thought of them as an easy option. Carriers didn't need mating bites to conceive.

"Well, this is all far more fucked up than I realized," Aurelia sighed, tipping her head back against the couch. I tossed her hiking boots onto the floor and pulled off her thick woolen socks that had done little to protect her dainty feet. They were riddled with blisters in various states of healing. I'd never felt the urge to look after someone before, but I wanted to run Aurelia a bath and feed her from my hand and treat her like a princess.

I felt like she'd be into it.

"What's your relationship with the coyote?" Noah demanded. "If we're harboring you here, we deserve to know that much at least."

Aurelia's head snapped up, and she glared at Noah like she could murder him with her eyeballs. She'd seen him in bear form now, she had every reason to be afraid of him, yet she didn't look like she gave a single fuck about the fact that he was 1500 pounds and could rip her apart with his claws or teeth in three seconds flat.

"*Harboring me*? What is your deal, Noah? *You* brought me back here. I walked around all day trying to find the fucking road with your big lumbering bear ass following me, offering zero help. Don't act like you didn't know the right direction to go in," Aurelia snapped, and I turned to look at my brother with a slow grin.

"Noah is a park ranger, he knows every inch of this land," I replied confidently, selling him out straight away. "Now, why wouldn't he show you the way back to the road?"

"I don't help criminals," Noah growled. "Maybe I was waiting to see how long it took for nature to run its course and kill her out in the wilderness."

"Mm, that's usually what people do when they cuddle someone to stop them from dying of hypothermia," Aurelia replied sarcastically. "Bet your eyes are brown because you're so full of shit, Noah."

I howled with laughter and I'm pretty sure Seth snorted in amusement, which almost never happened. Seth wasn't quite as growly and furious as Noah, but he was usually pretty stoic.

"Did you eat?" Seth asked, glancing between Noah and Aurelia.

"She didn't," Noah rumbled, still glowering at Aurelia.

"I can speak for myself," she snapped.

"Then answer my question. What's your relationship with the coyote?"

"*Pushy goddamn bear asshole*," Aurelia muttered. "I was dating Darren for the past six months. I'd just moved into his place up here and realized he was still seeing someone in town roughly half an hour later. So I left. End of story."

"He was cheating on you?" I asked in disbelief. "Why would anyone cheat on you? You're perfect."

"You're very intense," Aurelia remarked, turning her critical gaze on me as Seth coughed loudly, giving me a pointed look that clearly said *cool it*. Got it, coming on too strong.

"Does that bother you?" I dug my thumbs into the arch of her foot and she groaned in relief. As discreetly as I could, I moved her foot further away from my dick. If she was going to make sex noises, he was going to respond to her call.

"Not when you're doing that magic thing to my sore feet, it doesn't," Aurelia replied breathily.

"Eli, focus," Noah growled before turning his focus back to Aurelia. "You are a thief, and I don't trust you."

"Then why did you bring me here? Why'd you scare him off?" she retorted, closing her eyes and resting her head on the back of the couch like he wasn't even worth her time.

Seth and I both looked at Noah to explain. Not why he'd chased Darren off — he was halfway in love with Aurelia too, *obviously* — but why Darren had been following her at all.

"What would you have done if he'd found you?" Noah rumbled, looking like he was about ready to hit something. "You're lucky it's been raining, or he'd be able to track every step you'd taken since you left his house."

"I'm well aware we wouldn't have been having celebratory snuggles right now if he'd caught up to me," Aurelia snapped. My grip on her foot tightened slightly at just the thought of them snuggling.

Nope. I didn't like that at all.

"We're not getting anywhere with this," Seth sighed, rubbing his temples. "Aurelia needs food and rest. Whatever unconventional methods that led to us meeting—"

"Breaking and entering?" Noah suggested.

"Calm your tits, Daddy Bear. The door was unlocked," Aurelia huffed.

"—we know Darren is capable of violence," Seth forged on, ignoring their bickering. "We're not going to turn a blind eye to the fact that you could be in danger. So stay tonight, and we'll figure out what to do in the morning."

With that pronouncement, Seth made his way to the kitchen and started crashing around in the pantry, undoubtedly making us all dinner like he usually did.

"Want a bath?" I asked Aurelia hopefully, feeling strangely eager to please and coddle her.

"That sounds amazing. I am 90% mud and sweat at this point. I can't believe you touched my feet."

Noah muttered something under his breath that sounded like he was agreeing with her, but whatever. I'd take Aurelia dirty or clean, whatever way I could get her.

"Come on, I'll run it for you," I replied enthusiastically, jumping up and scooping her off the couch into my arms, cradling her like an infant as I jogged up the stairs.

"Eli, you fucking lunatic!" she shrieked, arms wrapping tight around my neck. If I was a human, I might actually have choked.

"I've got you, Goldie. Fear not."

"I am fearing lots, actually."

"I'm a bear, Goldie. You're so tiny it's like carrying a squirrel up the stairs." I placed her down gently on the edge of the bath and got it running, annoyed that we didn't have any fancy bath stuff for her. How were we supposed to convince her to stay forever and love us if we couldn't properly pamper her?

"That is certainly the first time I've ever been compared to a squirrel," Aurelia remarked drily, inspecting the dirt under her nails with dismay.

"Squirrels are cute, it's a compliment. So, uh, do you do a lot of hiking?" I asked casually.

"I appreciate how politely you phrased that," Aurelia said, snorting a laugh. "No, I am not a regular hiker. I have no idea what I'm doing and obviously underestimated how intense it was. And how hard directions were without street signs."

"Not a country girl?" I guessed, leaning against the sink as the tub filled, the small bathroom growing steamy.

"I grew up in New York," Aurelia admitted, and my heart sank a little. Living out here in the wilderness was as far from New York life as possible. "But I never felt like I belonged there. I always wanted to live somewhere quieter, surrounded by nature."

There was hope. We weren't out of the game yet.

"I wasn't as prepared for rural living as I thought, I guess."

"I can teach you! I'm an expert at this whole living in the wild thing," I replied confidently. *Problem solved.* "I grew up out here, though we go into town semi regularly."

Instead of replying with instant enthusiasm like I hoped she would, Aurelia gave me a long assessing look that felt like it stripped me bare. I had no idea what she would find. No one had ever bothered to look at me that closely.

"Are you lonely, Eli?"

The water splashed noisily into the still filling bath; the sound echoed in the small space. It was loud enough to hide this conversation from the sensitive ears of my brothers downstairs, though it was hard to remember they were even home in that moment.

"Why would you think that?"

"Why *wouldn't* I? I mean, I'm pretty awesome and you obviously want to get in my pants, but you are seriously intense considering we just met." Aurelia crossed her arms over her chest, cocking her head to the side expectantly as she waited for my answer.

"I'm not lonely," I replied with more confidence than I felt.

I *wasn't* lonely. I had my brothers. I'd *always* had my brothers, and I always would have them. I went into town once a month to sell my creations. Occasionally I enjoyed a willing woman's company while I was there. Why would I be lonely?

"I'm *not* lonely," I repeated more forcefully. "But there's something different about you. Something exciting and different." *Something special.* "I want to get to know you. And, yes, I would quite like to get in your pants if you're open to it."

Aurelia rolled her golden brown eyes impatiently. "I bet you're a Leo. You have such *Leo* energy. You're not getting into my pants today, so if you could skedaddle, the bath is ready." She leaned over the tub to switch off the taps, giving me a spectacular view of her perky ass through her leggings.

"What if you fall asleep in the tub? It really seems like it would be safer for me to stay," I teased, sort of joking, mostly hoping she'd let me hang out with her. "I'll close my eyes and everything."

"Oh, you'll close your eyes. That solves the weirdness factor."

"Does it?" I asked hopefully.

"No, obviously not. Get out," Aurelia sighed, though I caught her smile before she turned her back on me.

"Alright, I'll leave some clothes outside the door for you. Just know that I'll definitely be thinking about you being naked in here."

I let myself out, grinning at Aurelia's mutterings about "pervy bears" as I went.

RIA

CHAPTER 6

The bathwater was just hot enough to feel like it was burning the negativity directly out of my body. And god, did I need to get rid of some negativity.

Maybe I should do a sage cleansing.

Or go to therapy.

Or all of the above.

With the benefit of hindsight and being stalked through the woods by a clearly angry man, I may have rushed the whole moving-in-together thing with Darren.

If I'd introduced him to my family first, there would have been no doubt that he was a shifter. They'd have smelled it on him, known in *seconds*, that he wasn't human.

Ugh, Vincent and Joe were going to give me *so* much shit about this. I was going to give *myself* so much shit about this. This would be one of those lying awake at night, wondering why I was such an idiot moments that would haunt me for the rest of my days.

Did Darren really only want me for my uterus? Because that was a serious blow to my ego, if so. The stupid thing was, if he'd been upfront with me... Maybe I would have been fine with it? Once upon a time I'd had dreams of falling in love and being wooed, but I was increasingly feeling like I'd settle for quiet contentment.

Wasn't that what I'd been doing by moving in with Darren, anyway? It wasn't like I was in love with him. We'd never said those words, and I'd been fine with it.

Darren *had* brought up kids pretty frequently, pointing out that I wasn't getting any younger — *thanks for that* — but our plans had never been concrete. We'd always used condoms because he'd never gotten around to going to the doctor for a test — *thank you universe that I'd held firm on that,* since he was banging someone else the whole time anyway — but if he only wanted me for my uterus, what if he'd been sabotaging them? Just the thought of him potentially tampering with my birth control sent a shiver of apprehension down my spine.

Well, he was a shifter, so that meant he couldn't carry human diseases, so I guess that was a silver lining to his lies.

Plus, I had the implant so there wouldn't be any oopsie babies on the horizon for me, but had Darren and I even discussed that? Possibly not, since we'd been using condoms anyway, and we didn't have a lot of deep conversations about anything. *Hello, Giant Red Flag. Pleased to make your acquaintance.*

I sunk further down into the water, letting the heat of the bath ward off the chill of fear that maybe I'd just had a narrow escape from a terrible future. Maybe I should call Eli back. It had been a lot easier to ignore all these uncomfortable realities when he'd been in here flirting with me like I was the most desirable woman on Earth.

It was just the kind of flattery my ego needed after the past few days.

GILDED MESS

With the taps off, the bathroom was oppressively silent, and I stared at the simple white tile walls and focused on the sound of the three guys moving around downstairs rather than letting myself be alone with my thoughts.

I still didn't really know why I was here. Noah had gone to the effort of lugging me back to the house, but he seemed so hostile about it, I don't know why he even bothered. My best guess was that he had a secret hero complex underneath all that growly belligerence.

Maybe he just knew his brothers would want to help me. They seemed a lot more... *personable* than Noah was. I had no doubt that one of them would help me get back to Fairbanks tomorrow.

Whatever it was, I was grateful. Hiking required a lot more preparation than I'd previously assumed, and dying in the woods hadn't been one of my life goals for the year.

I stayed in the bath until the tepid water made me feel gross, humming the soundtrack to *Les Misérables* under my breath to distract myself. I had problems, but I wasn't a prostitute in 1815 France, struggling to keep my child alive.

Things could be worse.

Eventually, the sounds of movement downstairs slowed and the smell of something delicious wafted upstairs. I climbed out of the bath, grabbing a towel from the cupboard like I lived here and dried myself off. I cracked the door the barest amount, wrapped in the towel to preserve my modesty, and snagged the clothes Eli had left for me outside the door. A giant sweatshirt and loose shorts that would probably come halfway down my shins.

Oh well, it wasn't like I was trying to impress them — not much, anyway. Though I was firmly of the opinion that the best way to get over Darren would be to get under someone else. Ideally someone who made me scream until my voice was hoarse and my legs were jelly. AKA Eli or Seth.

Not Noah, he was still a dick, even if he'd saved my life somewhere between one and two times.

I quickly dressed and pulled my thick hair into a side braid before letting myself downstairs. The three of them were sitting around the dining table, speaking in hushed tones that ceased the moment I appeared. Okay, so they were talking about me. Not altogether surprising, I supposed.

"I hope you like steak, Goldie," Eli said cheerfully, leaning over the corner of the table to pull out the empty chair for me. "And green beans and mashed potatoes. Seth is an awesome cook."

"It certainly smells like it," I replied, giving Seth an appreciative nod and sliding into the chair. My stomach rumbled obnoxiously loudly, and I didn't even have it in me to be embarrassed because *oh my god* food.

We each passed dishes around the table, filling our plates in silence and as hungry as I was, I attempted to be polite and not take too much. Especially because each of them looked like they could eat an entire cow for breakfast and still have room for seconds. With an irritated grunt, Noah spooned an extra helping of potatoes onto my plate without making eye contact.

He was an odd duck, that one.

Fucking handsome, though. Which was probably yet another sign that my picker was broken. Maybe it was time to accept defeat and let my mom pick me a nice shifter mate from one of her friends' many offspring, like she'd been offering to do for years.

I shivered slightly at the thought. I'd grown up with all of those guys and they were fine. Totally fine. Respectful, successful, treated their mamas well. Nothing to complain about. Maybe that was good enough.

"You don't need to be scared, Goldilocks," Eli crooned, misinterpreting my shudder. "Ain't no coyote getting past the three of us."

"She's not staying here," Noah grumbled.

"Of course, she is—" Eli began.

"No, she's not," I cut in. "I need to get on the phone to my brothers and go back home."

Eli pouted like I'd just taken his favorite toy away, though I don't know what he'd been expecting. It was one thing to break into their empty house and have a snack and a nap, but I wasn't going to just *stay* here with them. That would be weird. And inappropriate.

It was only acceptable to stay here when they *weren't* here.

"Are your brothers shifters?" Noah asked, awfully curious for someone who hated my presence as much as he proclaimed he did.

"Foxes," Eli answered confidently, grinning broadly at the confused look on my face. "Your tattoo."

Right. He'd have seen the tiny line tattoo of a fox staring up at the moon that I'd got in honor of my family when he was rubbing my sore feet like a psychopath.

"Fox. That tracks," Noah scoffed. "Why didn't they point out that your boyfriend is a shifter?"

"First of all," I began, holding up a finger and mentally preparing to chew him out. "Darren is my *ex*-boyfriend—"

"Just confirming, you're 100% single now, then?" Eli interjected hopefully.

"Secondly, they never met him."

"So you moved in with a guy your family never met, to the middle of nowhere, no less?" Noah asked in a doubtful voice that made me want to punch him in his big stupid bear face.

"I'm perfectly aware of all the bad choices I made that led me to this moment, I don't need to rehash them with you," I snapped, rubbing my temples to sooth the headache that was rapidly forming behind my eyes. I was tired, hungry, and thoroughly irritated.

"You could have been killed—"

"Noah," Seth interjected, giving his raging brother a sharp look. "Not helpful."

"Goldie," Eli pleaded, leaning across the table towards me. "I'm going into town tomorrow for work, I can escort you the whole way there. Stay here tonight. You look exhausted."

I felt exhausted. The food seemed to make me even more tired. With every bite, I just wanted to lay down and take a nap more and more.

"You can take my room," Seth offered. "I'll share with Eli. No one will bother you, I promise."

My throat was a teensy bit tight at Seth's words. I had broken into their house after all, it's not like they had to help me.

"Thank you," I replied eventually, giving Seth a tight smile since he seemed like the safest one to direct my attention at. Noah made a quiet rumbling noise in his chest that I couldn't decipher, but didn't complain.

"In case you're wondering, Seth's room is the one with all the books. You ate crackers on his bed," Eli announced into the quiet, shooting me a shiteating grin.

GILDED MESS

* * *

The trek to the private road where the guys kept their truck for trips into town was *two fucking hours,* so Darren could go straight to hell with his 30-minute nonsense. Though I had gotten lost according to Noah, but whatever. It was still Darren's fault.

Eli walked at my side the entire way, helping me when the terrain got tricky. I imagined he usually made the trek on four paws, so I appreciated him walking alongside me. Fortunately, I'd slept like a baby in Seth's bed — which was admittedly not as comfortable as Noah's, but a vast improvement over sleeping on the damp forest floor. After a shower and more food I felt human again, ready to take on the world.

Come at me, Universe. I was making life my *bitch* today. As soon as I got hold of my brothers and whined at them to come and collect me and move my shit back to our parents' house.

After that, I was making life my bitch for sure.

"Here, let me help you into the truck," Eli offered gallantly, boosting me up before I had a chance to tell him that was entirely unnecessary.

"Thanks," I muttered, blushing a little more than I liked. I pulled my phone out of my pocket, relieved to find I had both battery and reception when I turned it on.

Less relieved to see the number of missed calls and messages from Darren, growing increasingly hostile in tone.

Darren:

Aurelia, where are you?

Darren:

Aurelia, answer your phone. This is a misunderstanding.

Darren:

Where the fuck are you? I want my stuff back.

Darren:

If you died walking around the woods on your own, it's your own fucking fault. Bitch.

He was taking it well then.

"Are you okay?" Eli asked, glancing over at me. "You're breathing pretty heavily."

"Fine," I replied in a strained voice, forcing myself to breathe normally. I already knew Darren was an asshole. This was just a little extra confirmation.

My thumbs hovered over the screen as I debated whether I should reply. I had no desire to engage with him, but I also wanted to be crystal clear about where we stood.

Me:

Liar, liar, I should have set your house on fire.

We are over. Do not contact me again.

I quickly blocked his number before he could respond and opened up my social accounts to block and delete him on all of those too. Hopefully, it wouldn't alert everyone to my change in relationship status, because I was not ready for pity messages from well-meaning relatives just yet.

"Do you mind if I call my brother?" I asked, holding my phone up.

"Go ahead. I'd say I won't eavesdrop, but shifter hearing..." Eli replied with an unapologetic shrug.

I called both my brothers in succession, but there was no reply. Useless, the both of them. I briefly contemplated calling my parents, but I hated to worry them. They'd had me a lot later in life, a surprise third baby ten years after my brother, Joe, was born.

I knew they loved me, but I tried to give them as little grief as I could. Some guilt hangover from delaying their empty nest years by a decade, I suppose.

Me:

Call me? It's important.

"Could we stop off to see my client?" Eli asked hopefully as I tapped my fingernails impatiently against my phone case. "I swear I'll be quick."

"Sure," I agreed easily. He'd walked through the forest, then driven me into town. It really seemed like the least I could do.

I watched out the window as Eli navigated the streets with ease, seemingly confident making his way around town despite living out in the middle of nowhere. The streets of Fairbanks were familiar to me after living here for a year, and I liked the city well enough, but it had never felt particularly homey.

The cold was a vast improvement over the few years I'd spent living in Florida, though. I thought I'd enjoy wearing bikinis and light cover-ups all day, but when you were sweating your ass off and had already removed the maximum amount of socially acceptable layers, the appeal wore off some.

We pulled into the parking lot of a fancy furniture store I'd never been in before. I always felt like everyone would know if I walked into a store where I couldn't afford anything. Like they'd smell the poor on me somehow.

"Do you want to come with me?" Eli asked, unclipping his seatbelt. "You don't have to."

"You'd leave me alone in your truck after I broke into your house?" I teased, although I was genuinely surprised.

Eli grinned broadly at me. "Sure. It'd make life interesting if you stole it. Noah's furry ass would chase you through the entire state."

I snorted as the image of a lumbering bear chasing a truck down the highway, roaring its furious head off popped into my mind. "Tempting, but I think I'll come with you. I've always wanted to go to this store, anyway."

"Wait a sec," Eli commanded, letting himself out and moving swiftly around to my side of the truck to open my door for me while I removed my seatbelt.

"Worried I'll fall?" I asked, amused.

"A little," Eli admitted, lifting me out of the seat and placing me on the ground like I weighed nothing. For all his intense flirting, he removed his hands instantly when I stepped back. "I've got a different kind of *falling* in mind for you."

"Oh my god, do not say 'falling in love' right now. Don't do it," I warned him, giving him my sternest school teacher look, which was genuinely hard because his smile was infectious.

"Fine," he sighed dramatically. "Let's head in. I make custom pieces for Ace that he sells through his store," Eli explained. "Been doing it for a few years now. Sometimes I make to order, sometimes I just do what I want and hope he buys it."

"I'm sure he does," I murmured, remembering how beautiful the rocking chair had been before my ass had crushed it.

"I'm good at what I do," Eli replied with a smug grin, letting his eyes drift down my body for a moment, definitely talking about more than just woodworking.

I don't know how he made me feel so sexy, bundled up in my heavy clothes. It was truly a gift.

An elderly balding man greeted Eli enthusiastically when we entered the store, and I gave them some privacy, examining a gorgeous round wooden coffee table and trying to decide if Eli had crafted it or not.

"It's going to be late?" I heard the guy ask in disappointment as I drifted back towards them. "I already had a buyer lined up. They love your work, Eli."

"Sorry, Ace. It won't be super late. Circumstances out of my control and whatnot. I'll knock 10% off the price, how's that?"

Eli's tone was as affable as usual, but guilt twisted uncomfortably in my gut. I opened my mouth to admit that I was the one who broke the chair and to apologize for it, but Eli's hand found mine as I moved close by. He gave my fingers a squeeze and shot me a discreet wink, shaking his head slightly.

Ace agreed reluctantly, and I zoned out as the two of them started discussing a new project, vaguely wondering why I hadn't pulled my hand away yet.

The buzz of my cellphone in my jacket pocket grabbed my attention, and I quickly excused myself, moving next to the entrance of the store to answer it with some privacy.

"Ria? What's going on?" Vincent, my oldest brother asked, no nonsense as always.

Maybe the gruff personality was an oldest brother trait.

"Why didn't you answer?" I asked, a little petulantly. My brothers *always* answered their phones. Maybe I needed a little reassurance that they hadn't given up on me since I'd moved in with Darren against their advice.

"Busy. What's going on, Ria?"

I rolled my eyes, huffing impatiently at his non-answer. "If you say I told you so, I'll hang up and never speak to you again."

"Ria," he groaned. I knew he'd be massaging his eyeballs with his thumb and middle finger like he always did when I got myself into trouble and needed my brothers to bail me out. It was a tic he'd picked up from our dad.

"It's fine. I'm fine. I was wondering if I could borrow some money for a plane ticket, though…"

"You're moving home?" Vincent asked, considerably more pep in his voice.

"Yeah," I replied weakly. "Maybe moving out here wasn't the best decision." Though even as I said the words, they didn't feel entirely true. I was marginally less of a hot mess than I had been when I moved out here. Getting some space from my family and standing on my own two feet had forced me to grow up a little.

"Tell me what happened first. Do Joe and I need to fly out there and kick his ass?"

No.

Yes.

"Ria..." Vincent rumbled, latching onto my hesitation.

"He's a shifter. Coyote. He never told me. That's weird, right? Also, he was cheating on me, so there's that," I rushed out, the words colliding together.

"Say all that again." It was Joe, my other brother, and his voice was downright feral. Stupid Vincent, putting me on speakerphone with zero warning.

"You heard me. Coyote shifter. Didn't tell me. Was cheating on me."

There was an extended moment of silence on the line and I closed my eyes, tipping my head back and reminding myself to think happy thoughts. I wasn't getting any younger. I should probably start worrying about my blood pressure. And wrinkles.

"He wanted to get you pregnant," Joe declared.

"Yes, that's the leading theory."

"So, I'm going to kill him," Joe rumbled. A soothing feminine voice in the background seemed to distract them. Who the hell was that? She sounded like she was murmuring words of encouragement to Joe, yet it was Vincent who responded.

"Who is that?" I enquired stiffly. I was going to be *pissed* if my brothers had me divulging this humiliation in front of an audience.

There was a pregnant pause on the other end of the phone. It wouldn't be the first time my brothers had underestimated my human hearing. I swore sometimes they thought all humans were borderline deaf.

"I'm Anette," the woman eventually answered in a thick accent I struggled to place. Apparently she had bigger balls than my still silent brothers.

"How much of that did you hear, Anette?"

"All of it," she admitted guiltily.

"Never mind about that," Vincent cut in hastily. "I'll send you money for a ticket, but I'd rather have a few words with this *Darren* in person, and help you get your shit home. We can't be there for a few days, though. We're out of the country."

What the fuck? My brothers had never left the country in their lives.

"You could call Mom and—"

"No," I interjected. Maybe I could just throw all my stuff out and hop on a plane back home? It's what I'd done to get here in the first place. The logistics of moving shit across the country was hard. "I'll figure something out."

"Ria," Vincent sighed. "They don't mind helping. And I don't feel good about letting this slide. The coyote needs to be punished." Joe grunted his agreement. Before I could object, the phone was plucked from between my fingers by an unrepentant Eli.

"I absolutely agree. *Ria* will stay with me and my brothers until you can get here. If she lets me live that long—" He spun away, lifting his elbow so the phone was out of my reach.

"—my name is Eli Bernard. My brothers, Noah and Seth, are bear shifters, we live by Chena River. Noah is a ranger, you can verify his identity — Noah Bernard. We're friends of Ria, we'd never let any harm come to her."

Both my brothers started replying at once, but Eli hung up the phone, handing it back to me with a grin.

"I don't appreciate people making decisions for me," I said in an icy tone, narrowing my eyes at him and ignoring the incessant buzzing of my phone.

Eli shrugged, his grin not faltering for a second. Cocky fucking bear. "I can't force you to stay with us, but if you don't, I'll just end up stalking you for a week to make sure you're safe. And then the rocking chair will be *super* late. Poor Ace..." he sighed.

"Why would I care about that? I'm the one who broke it," I replied flippantly.

"And you feel bad about it, I can tell. You're not nearly as mean as you pretend you are, Goldie," Eli challenged, eyes full of affection he had no right to be feeling.

"I'm exactly as mean as I appear, Eli Bernard. And *that* is why I am taking you up on your offer."

"What? How is staying at our house 'mean'?"

"Because Noah is going to shit a brick. You'll see."

RIA

CHAPTER 7

Eli was still laughing as he led me out of the furniture store, a glimmer of anticipation in his eye. "It's good for Noah to be pushed out of his comfort zone. He's very set in his ways."

"What a shocking revelation," I replied drily. Noah had the soul of a crotchety old man stuck inside the body of a sexy, 30-something year old lumberjack. "How old are you three, anyway?"

"I'm 32, Noah and Seth are 37," Eli said cautiously, giving me a sidelong look like he was trying to figure out my age, or at least what was going on in my head. *Good luck, buddy. I don't even know half the time.*

"And you're all single? I'm not asking for me," I clarified quickly when Eli's eyes lit up hopefully. "I was just being nosy."

"Sure, you weren't asking for you," Eli drawled smugly. "We are all single. We always felt that we would take a mate together," he added casually as he opened the passenger door of the truck for me.

I choked a little on my own saliva, trying to play it off as a cough while I clambered awkwardly into the cab. Eli gently grabbed my waist, giving me a boost, and I almost jumped out of my skin.

Take. A. Mate. Together.

My first thought was *lucky lady*, because goddamn. Having those three on tap? She'd be ruined in the best kind of way, walking around bow legged all the time, happy as a clam full of orgasms.

Upon further reflection, I decided it wouldn't be worth it to put up with Noah's stomping all the time, even if he'd proven handy to have around in an emergency. *Good luck, hypothetical woman. You can have him.*

I cleared my throat awkwardly as Eli got into the driver's seat, hoping I could smoothly steer the conversation into safer waters. "Could we stop by my old place? My roommate, Lou, is storing my stuff there and I need some clothes if I'm going to be staying with you."

"Sure thing, just tell me where to go." Eli shot me a mischievous grin as he started up the truck, and I knew he wouldn't let me off the hook that easily. "So, no follow-up questions on the mate thing? Not curious about *why* we want to share a mate? Or how it's done? Or the *logistics*?"

"It's truly impressive that you made *logistics* sound like a four-letter word. And no, I am not curious. Zero curiosity," I replied primly, giving Eli a pointed look.

So much curiosity.

Not so much on the logistics — I'd seen porn before, I knew how all the tabs went in the slots. I was curious about how multiple people took one mate, though.

The way my mom explained it back during the most mortifying conversation of my life, after mating bites were exchanged, there was zero sexual attraction to anyone else. Maybe they all had to bite at the same time?

I hadn't thought much about it since I emerged as a carrier. If I took a shifter mate, I wouldn't be *giving* any bites, just receiving. And most shifters weren't interested in me, anyway.

Except Darren, my subconscious supplied unhelpfully. The guy who'd been booted out of his pack for being a psychopath.

I rattled off my old address while Eli chuckled quietly to himself, pulling the truck away from the curb. He was always laughing. It was one of the things I liked most about him.

It only took a few minutes for us to get to Lou's place. I'd miss the lack of traffic when I was back in New York, that was for sure.

"Wait," I said, reaching across the cab and grabbing Eli's exposed forearm. I was all bundled up in my winter coat and he just wore a navy henley with the sleeves rolled up, yet his skin was warm to the touch. Damn shifters and their superior genes. The heat of him was strangely comforting, and I had the strongest urge to slide my hand down his wrist and link our fingers.

I snatched my hand back before I did something I'd regret.

"Yes?" Eli drawled, looking at me with that amused glimmer in his eyes that both infuriated and excited me.

"Lou is a human. Well, I'm pretty sure she is," I added with a frown, remembering how wrong I'd been about that with Darren. "No shifter talk in front of her, okay?"

"Of course," Eli agreed readily.

"And rein in your intense flirtatiousness. Lou is more reserved than I am, you'll freak her out." *And I'll probably be weirdly jealous if you turn on the charm with someone else right in front of me.*

Eli frowned at me. "I'm not going to flirt with her, Goldie."

"We'll see," I muttered, pushing open the door and jumping out of the truck before Eli could come around and help me. Lou was 5-foot-nothing and all bombshell, with thick red hair, green eyes, and flawless skin.

"Let me help you down next time," Eli groused, slamming his door a little harder than necessary and rounding the truck to join me. "You could have hurt yourself."

I shot him an amused glance as he scanned his eyes over me like he was searching for injuries. "Just how fragile do you think I am? Keep your voice down when we get in there, Lou works from home. Some kind of computer thing."

Lou owned the three-bedroom place. She'd converted the downstairs into a workspace that I'd never ventured into, and the main level housed all the bedrooms and living areas. It was a slightly dilapidated place that she had grand plans to do up, but it was comfortable enough. The outside of the house was the same pastel pink as a dollhouse I'd had as a kid, and I hoped she would never paint over it.

Lou hadn't asked for my key back yet, since she knew I'd be collecting my stuff for the next few weeks. She hadn't been particularly worried about finding a replacement roommate either. I wasn't sure what kind of job she had, but it obviously paid better than my server gig had.

Silver lining to my current shit show life: No more customer service job. I could cut down my peopling by at least 80%.

I let myself in and Eli followed, glued to my back like I might need his protection in my old house. It was kind of sweet, I guess.

"Lou Lou," I called softly from the top of the stairs that led down to her basement office, not wanting to holler in case she was on a work call. I knew she had those sometimes.

"Er, Goldie?" Eli said, clearing his throat awkwardly after a long pause. "Can't you hear that?"

"Hear what?" I asked, straining my useless human ears. The basement was soundproofed because Lou said she liked to listen to music down there. I hadn't ever been in her office, though. It seemed like an invasion of her privacy.

"The... moaning."

"What?" I shrieked, before clapping my hand over my mouth. "What kind of moaning?"

"The sex kind," Eli replied matter-of-factly, before giving me an appraising look. "Have you not been getting the kind of sex you deserve, Goldie? I could make you moan."

"Focus, Eli," I snapped. "Oh my god, I can't believe she's having sex in her office. What a badass."

"I don't think there's anyone else down there," Eli replied, brow furrowed. "I can hear talking, but it sounds like it's coming through a phone or something."

Phone sex?

Oh my god. *Oh my god.* I'd opened a package of Lou's once, thinking it was mine. It had been some super high-quality webcam, and she'd been so weird and embarrassed about it, which I'd thought was strange at the time because why wouldn't she want a nice camera if she worked from home?

"Oh my god, she's totally a cam girl!" I whisper shouted.

"A what?" Eli asked, looking genuinely confused.

"You are so behind the times. Cam girls. Cam.... people. They perform on camera," I explained poorly, not entirely knowing what they did, but definitely intending to find out.

"Sex stuff?" Eli asked, eyes widening adorably.

"I mean, I guess so?" Lou had done well enough to buy her own place, and she always had her hair and nails done. "I wonder if it pays well. I could be a cam girl."

"The fuck you could," Eli growled, seeming to grow a foot in size.

"Why not? I'm cute. In the right lingerie, my boobs don't look a day over 21."

"You're a lot more than cute, and your boobs are spectacular," Eli muttered. "Everyone would want to see you naked."

"Are you trying to dissuade me? If so, you're doing a terrible job. If I can find a way to make money, I don't have to stay in New York and live with my parents forever." I pulled Eli away from the basement and into the hallway where the bedrooms were.

Mine was exactly the way I left it, and I groaned at the stacks of half-filled boxes and clothes strewn everywhere. Lou was far nicer to me than I deserved. I was an objectively terrible roommate.

"Excuse the mess," I sighed, making way to the pile of clothes on the bed.

"It smells like you," Eli replied happily, as though my scent had broken him out of his temper tantrum. "And why would you move back to New York if you don't want to?"

"Because I'm broke and I hate my old job here and have too much pride to ask for it back anyway," I explained, grabbing some warm basics to last me the next few days and shoving them into a backpack to take with me. "And moving out here on my own has been a failed experiment in adulthood, I should probably just cut my losses now."

"*Darren* was the failed experiment," Eli corrected, shoving a pile of clothes out of the way and sitting down on my bed, making himself far too comfortable in my space. "Do you like Fairbanks?"

"The city is fine. The surroundings are beautiful. Peaceful. I like living here, but that isn't everything," I sighed.

"It's a lot, though," Eli replied easily, standing up and moving over to my dresser where the framed pictures of my family were. "Are these your big brothers?"

"Hm? Yeah, Vincent and Joseph. And my parents in the silver frame," I added absently, digging through a half-filled box, looking for socks.

"Where was this taken?" Eli asked, holding up the silver frame.

"Nassau, Bahamas. When I dropped out of college the second time, I got a job on a cruise ship. My parents came on a cruise once."

God, I'd so wanted them to be proud of me for getting a proper grown job serving drinks on a ship. And hopefully to forget about the business degree I'd given up on. As much fun as being a college student in Florida had been, my brain wasn't wired for academic learning. Sitting in class had felt like a daily exercise in torture.

"Sounds fun," Eli offered, seemingly unbothered about my college dropout status. I didn't even realize I'd been bracing myself for a negative reaction — like Darren's had been — until one never came.

I supposed when you were a wild mountain man-bear, formal education didn't seem like the most important thing on Earth.

"Is that you, Ria?" Lou tentatively called up the stairs.

"It's me! I'm here with a... friend. Packing," I yelled back.

"Does everyone call you Ria?" Eli asked.

"My friends do."

"You said I was your friend," he countered smugly.

"You are insufferable. Fine, call me Ria," I groused.

"Am I interrupting anything?" Lou asked quietly, poking her head in the door. She was wearing a cute matching set of sweats, her red hair mussed and cheeks flushed. Homegirl had totally just been having paid orgasms on camera, and I was all about it.

"No, no. Just grabbing a few things and attempting to box up the rest," I replied stiffly as Lou noticed Eli, eyebrows shooting up in surprise. "This is Eli. Eli, meet Lou," I added, bracing myself for Eli to turn on the charm and flash Lou that megawatt smile.

"Nice to meet you, Lou," Eli replied politely. I let out a small breath I didn't know I'd been holding.

I don't know why I was feeling so possessive over him, we'd just met and at most, I would sleep with him a couple of times to fuck Darren out of my system before scampering back to New York. Maybe it was because my deflated ego could only take so much right now. I wanted to be the sole object of Eli's attention, for a few days at least.

"Hello," Lou replied, looking between Eli and I. "Are you a friend of Darren's?"

Eli's chest rumbled in a noise that was way more bear than human, and I threw him a warning look before returning my attention to Lou. "Ah, no. Things with Darren didn't work out."

I tapped my foot a couple of times on the floor, gently reminding it that if it wanted to open up and swallow me whole, now would be an excellent time.

"Oh Ria," Lou sighed, with way more pity than I was comfortable with. She strode into the room and threw her arms around my waist, squeezing me tight. I hugged her back, blinking furiously to keep the sudden rush of tears at bay. Lou took a step back, grabbing both my hands and squeezing them tightly. "He wasn't your Darcy?"

"He was the Wickhamest Wickham to ever Wickham," I replied gravely.

"Do you want to egg his house? I'll totally come with you. A little destruction of property is good for the soul."

Eli snorted, and I decided not to mention that I'd stolen Darren's weed, gun, and smashed his phone with a fire poker.

Then semi broke into someone else's house — *even though the door was unlocked* — and broke some furniture, stole their food, took a bath and had a nap.

Pretty much the one area I was excelling right now was destruction of property.

"Tempting, but I'm good," I said with a weak laugh. "Um, I'm going to head back to New York. My brothers will be here in a few days to help me move my stuff and potentially threaten Darren's manhood. Will that be an issue? I can move my stuff into the basement if you want to rent out this room."

Totally fishing for information.

"Not the basement," Lou replied a little too quickly. "It's fine, I'm not using this room. Don't you want to stay here until your brothers arrive? You totally can, Ria."

I mean, I *could*. That would probably be the normal thing to do in this situation, but the aggressive tone of both Darren's messages and his voice when he'd been looking for me had me a little spooked, and that was without the information about his old pack.

I glanced back at Eli, who was observing our interaction with his head tilted to the side, like we were two rare breeds of animal, interacting in the wild. I don't care what he'd told me, Eli was totally lonely.

"I'm actually going to stay with Eli," I replied, bracing myself for Lou's totally warranted disapproval. "It's kind of complicated, but don't worry, I know what I'm doing."

You said that when you moved in with Darren, Lou accused with her eyes, but she forced a smile and nodded her head.

"If you change your mind, the bed is free and you're more than welcome. Maybe you could leave me the address of where you're staying," she added pointedly.

"Great idea," Eli interjected. "My brother, Noah, is a park ranger and has a satellite phone. I'll leave you his number too, in case you want to get hold of Ria."

"Thanks," Lou said appreciatively, some tension leaching out of her at the mention of Noah being a park ranger. "I, er, need to get back to work."

"Oh totally," I replied, nodding my head a little too vigorously. *Be cool, Ria.* "We won't be long, you should get back to... Work stuff."

"Right. Work stuff," Lou agreed, side eyeing me. "Take care, okay, Ria? Call me if you need anything." She leaned in and gave me another sisterly hug that I happily returned. I'd always been pretty good at making female friends, but I hadn't been the best at keeping them. Between moving around a lot over the past decade and not putting in the effort I should, those friendships had fallen apart. *I would do better with Lou,* I promised myself. She'd been amazing, and I really would miss her when I left here.

"Come on, Ria. Let's get you packed," Eli said gently as I watched the doorway Lou had vanished through for a moment too long.

"Right. Let's do it." I exhaled and straightened my shoulders. *Onwards and upwards.*

✷ ✷ ✷

After I'd packed a backpack of stuff to tide me over for a few days, changed into fresh clothes, and boxed up the rest of my things, we drove back to the outskirts of the forest where the guys parked their truck, only to find a giant bear ominously waiting for us.

"You don't seem surprised to see him," I said wryly, as Eli parked the truck.

"Noah?" he confirmed, looking surprised. "He followed us down here, didn't you notice?"

"Obviously not," I sighed. I'd stopped bemoaning the fact that I would never shift in my early 20s, but I still had bursts of longing for all those enhanced abilities they took for granted.

"Chin up, he can't talk back when he's in his fur," Eli chuckled, climbing out of the cab. "I'll get your bag."

I undid my seatbelt and opened my door to jump out, but suddenly there was an enormous bear blocking my way, standing on his hind legs right in the doorway of the truck.

"I know you're not happy to see me again, but trapping me in the truck isn't the solution," I chided, twisting to get out and hoping he'd move.

Bear Noah huffed — an impressively judgmental sound for an animal — before hauling me against his chest with his enormous paws and guiding me to the ground while I squeaked in surprise.

"Ria is going to be staying with us for a few days until her brothers get into town," Eli announced as he moved around the truck, clapping Noah on his furry back.

Noah made a noise that could have been disinterested acknowledgement or an enraged 'fuck no'.

I think I liked this less argumentative Noah. He should stay in his fur more often.

I reached for my bag, but Eli gave me a *you can't be serious* look before shrugging one strap over his giant shoulder, guiding me towards the treeline with an enormous hand on my lower back.

"Aren't you worried someone will steal your truck?" I asked him, doing my best to ignore the lumbering bear behind us.

"This whole area is shifters," Eli explained. "All the rangers too. It took them *years* to convince Noah to join them," he chuckled as Noah huffed.

"I guess that makes sense. I grew up near a lot of fox shifter families. A few other kinds of shifters too."

"Ones that didn't mind living among crowds, I'm guessing," Eli chuckled.

"A lot of foxes are pretty happy in the city." I shrugged. Maybe that should have been my first clue that I wasn't like the rest of my family — I'd always craved the open space and quiet of rural areas.

Noah growled suddenly, and I swear I jumped a full foot into the air. "Could you not?" I asked, whirling around to face him, hand clutching over my heart. "You just took ten years off my life."

"Sorry about the scare, Goldie," Eli said quietly, his voice suddenly serious. "We just picked up the scent of a coyote shifter, and there's only one who lives around here."

"What?" I peered through the trees as though I would see him before the shifters with enhanced eyesight. "Is he here?" I whispered.

"No," Eli replied, his voice edgy. "His scent isn't fresh, but he was definitely here not long ago."

Noah growled in agreement, sniffing around wildly while I stood rooted to the spot, grateful Eli hadn't moved away from me. I mean, it could be a coincidence. Right? I could just be reading too much into things.

At the same time, I didn't think I was. Darren was looking for me.

"He cheated on me," I murmured dumbly. "Why go through all this effort?"

"Goldie, I think you might have to accept that he's not going to let you go that easily," Eli murmured, sliding his hand around mine and squeezing it reassuringly. "Not that you have anything to worry about, we won't let him get to you."

I believed him.

They'd protect me until my brothers got here to take over. Then my brothers would protect me, and my bad decisions would become everyone else's problem again, just like they always had.

RIA
CHAPTER 8

Disregarding the whole asshole ex-boyfriend and everything else I had going on, it seemed like spending a few days here would be a pretty great vacation.

Eli and Noah had accompanied me back to the cabin yesterday, then basically left me to it since they had, you know, jobs and whatever else to do. I'd basically hung out, reading the random assortment of books from Seth's bookshelf until around 4pm when I couldn't keep my eyes open anymore.

The weight of the past few days had crashed down on me in one suffocating instant, and the moment my head hit the pillow, I'd been out like a light for a solid 16 hours.

Lying in bed now, I knew the three guys had already begun their day, but I didn't have it in me to move quite yet.

While I'd been *going, going, going*, it had been easy to avoid the unpleasant feelings I'd rather not deal with. Since my moment of weakness that first night, I hadn't shed any more tears for Darren — and I didn't want to, because I knew as surely as my name was Aurelia that motherfucker wasn't shedding any tears over me — but I definitely had some ugly emotions that I needed to confront.

I blinked up at the high sloped ceiling above me, trying to sort through the jumble of feelings that were struggling for dominance in my head.

Rejection? I mean, maybe a little. A teeny bit. But I'd also been the one to pull the plug, which helped ease that emotion a little.

Embarrassment? A healthy dose of that. Embarrassment that I'd been played, but also that I'd met everyone's expectations. My parents had expressed politely worded concerns that I was moving too fast. My brothers flat out told me I was making a mistake. Lou — the only friend I had who'd actually met Darren — had been lukewarm about him at best.

And despite all of that, I still felt *disappointment* that the relationship had ended. Not because Darren was such a catch or anything, but I guess I'd thought my life was finally moving forward and now I was back to square one. I was grieving the future I'd thought I was going to have, and I had no idea what my life was going to look like now.

It couldn't possibly be more of the same. I refused to accept that.

Right, I was ticking 'pity party' off the list for today. Done. Over. *Get the fuck up and get on with your life, Ria.*

Also, after 16 hours, I really had to pee.

With a groan, I pushed out of the comfortable mass of blankets on Seth's bed and slipped out onto the landing and into the bathroom before anyone could see me. Not that they hadn't seen me looking various levels of disastrous already, but I wasn't about to add to that if I could avoid it.

I took a quick shower, glad I at least had my small bag of toiletries with me that I'd packed for Darren's. My make up skills had peaked when I was 14, so it didn't take long. I was 100% fine with foundation, eyeliner, and mascara, though my eyeliner was less emo-chic these days and my eyebrows thankfully less sperm-shaped.

I had less than zero interest in learning how to contour.

Makeup done, I dressed in a clean pair of leggings, long-sleeved top, and thick socks, intending to pull my bulky coat over my clothes, anyway.

Where was everyone? I wondered as I padded down the stairs. I assumed Noah was out... ranger-ing, but I wasn't sure if the other two were on the property or not.

As if I'd summoned him with my thoughts, Noah stormed in through the front door, looking like someone had pissed in his cereal. Obviously there was something clinically wrong with me, because all that growly energy really did it for me.

Noah's fierce gaze pinned me in place as he ran his eyes up from my sock-clad toes to my mass of blonde curls. There was nothing lascivious about his stare. It was assessing, if anything, but my body apparently didn't recognize that.

Come on, nipples. Don't sell me out now.

Damn it, I couldn't even glance down to check. He'd totally notice.

Noah grunted like I frustrated him somehow as he made his way towards me, tugging off his olive green coarse knit sweater as he went. The t-shirt he was wearing underneath rode up slightly, and I tried and failed not to look at the tempting glimpse of muscle on display. God. Damn. He was cut.

GILDED MESS

I gaped like a fish as Noah shoved his sweater roughly over my head, turned on his heel without a word, and left me standing there, swamped in fabric. Delicious smelling fabric.

Well, okay then? I'd been intending to put my jacket on anyway, but this worked. It was already warm from him wearing it, and I tried not to overthink how cozy it felt as I shoved my arms into the sleeves, rolling them up multiple times to get them past my wrists. It looked like a sweater dress and reminded me of sleeping wrapped up in Noah's bear embrace.

You need to get a fucking grip, Ria, I scolded myself, shaking my head slightly as I made my way to the front door and pulled my boots on. *You don't like him, and he doesn't like you.*

I'd had a sneak peek at the fenced-in back of the property out the window, but I took my time to explore it now. I made my way along the path that ran next to the cabin, past a large woodshed, and to a cleared area behind the house that was dominated by an enormous vegetable garden. Raised rectangular garden beds were set out in intervals lining the path right up to the treeline where I knew another building was tucked away.

I'd seen the little shed hidden among the trees from Seth's window, which overlooked the back of the house. As I let myself through the gate that kept the vegetable garden safe from animals, I realized it wasn't so much a shed as an old cottage in the forest. I could hear noises coming from inside, and I assumed that's where Seth and Eli were, though I didn't know for sure this wasn't someone's house. Maybe their parents lived here?

"Come on in, Goldie!" Eli called out cheerfully, answering my silent question.

I pushed open the heavy old wooden door, leaning on it with my shoulder to get it open. I don't know what I expected — furniture, probably — but it wasn't a workshop inside what had clearly been a living area.

I imagined it had once been a cozy home. The walls were whitewashed brick and the wooden rafters were exposed, the floors all terracotta tile. What I assumed had been the kitchen was now a workshop counter, with open shelves instead of cupboards above and below, overflowing with tools and materials.

There was stuff everywhere, but it didn't feel cluttered. Lumber was stored by length on shelves along the back wall, with scrap pieces arranged neatly in a bin on the ground. It smelled like sawdust and polish, and it was surprisingly pleasant.

"Sleep well?" Eli asked, standing behind a freestanding saw in the center of the room. "I was getting worried, but Seth told me I wasn't allowed to wake you up."

"I'm glad you didn't. I slept amazingly, thank you. What is this place?" I ran my fingers along a gorgeous hand carved cradle as I walked past, examining the space.

"It was our grandparents' cottage. We lived here ourselves when we were building the main house. Now it's my workshop and Seth's studio," Eli explained, tipping his chin at the closed door at the back of the room, presumably a bedroom once upon a time.

"Studio?"

"I'm sure he'll show you himself," Eli said with a mischievous grin. "But I don't want to share you yet."

"You know I can hear you just fine," Seth called from the other room.

"I know. That was my way of telling you to stay in there," Eli chuckled and I couldn't help but smile. His endlessly playful energy was infectious.

The door pushed open and Seth leaned against the frame, one eyebrow raised at his brother, but looking amused. "Did you even ask if our guest had eaten, brother?"

Eli's brow furrowed, and he looked adorably concerned, like I wasn't a grown ass woman who could feed myself. "Did you eat, Goldie?"

"Not yet." I shrugged. I cared more about coffee than food first thing in the morning, though it had been a long while since I'd eaten.

"Let's get you something to eat," Seth replied confidently, striding into the main workshop area and resting his palm lightly on the small of my back to guide me back out of the cottage. Eli made a noise of discontent behind us.

"Finish your rocking chair, baby brother," Seth chuckled. I threw Eli an apologetic look over my shoulder. He'd already finished the rocking chair, and I'd broken it with my big ass.

"Fine, I'll finish the chair then we're hanging out, Goldie!" Eli yelled as Seth led me back to the main house.

"You don't have to," Seth said quietly, pulling his hand away. I missed the warm weight of it instantly. "Please don't feel obligated to spend time with us because you're staying here. You don't owe us anything."

"Er, I kind of do though. Aside from the fact that you're letting me crash here for a week, there's also the whole breaking into your house thing. And Noah saving my ass. I mean, I owe you quite a lot if you think about it."

"Ain't that the fucking truth," Noah grumbled, overhearing our conversation as we entered the main house. Goddamn shifter hearing. He was sitting at the dining table with a planner book and pen in front of him, his satellite phone in the other, eyeing it like its existence personally offended him.

"Don't be a dick, Noah," Seth said lightly, moving into the kitchen and putting on the coffee pot.

"I don't think he can help it," I replied gravely, reveling in the glare Noah shot me.

"Pancakes okay?" Seth asked mildly, already pulling flour and sugar out of the pantry.

"Pancakes are great," I replied. "Let me do that, you do the coffee. I have no idea how that thing works," I added, looking at the stovetop coffee thing in confusion.

"You sure?" Seth replied in amusement. "I was going to make enough for all of us, and bears eat a lot for second breakfast."

"I'm sure. And ten points to you if that was a *Lord of the Rings* reference," I added with a laugh, moving around the kitchen to collect ingredients. It had become abundantly clear that I was no pioneer woman, but I could manage pancakes.

"It was," he replied, shooting me a small half smile. "I have a decent book collection in my room if you need something to occupy you while you're here," he added, raising an eyebrow at me.

"Oh, I've already made myself at home with your library."

"I'll bet you have," Noah snarked. "You made yourself at home before you even knew we lived here."

Was it too much to hope that they'd all just conveniently forget about that? Probably.

"About that," I said with a heavy sigh. God, I hated apologizing. "Er, I probably shouldn't have broken in. I mean, the door was unlocked..."

Seth's cocked eyebrow moved even higher as he crossed his arms over his broad chest and leaned his hip against the counter. He was unnervingly quiet, and I suspected that was by design. He was going to wait me out until I forced the uncomfortable words out.

Noah gave up the pretense of working, or whatever it was he was doing, and looked up at me with his eyes narrowed.

I could totally envision Noah laying me over his lap and spanking the attitude out of me. I could probably orgasm from that visual alone, to be honest. I'd lock that away for future reference, should I pursue my camgirl plan. Or just in case I wanted to get myself off. Either one.

"I'm sorry. I was high and thought it was a good idea," I sighed dramatically, slumping against the counter at the physical effort of apologizing, before looking up at Seth through my lashes and giving him my best puppy dog eyes. I pushed my lower lip out a little, just enough to be pouty without pouting, which I was a solid 25 years too old to pull off.

Seth snorted, shaking his head in amusement. "You're kind of a brat, you know that?" he teased.

Like... in a sexy way? Because I could totally roll with that.

Yikes, Ria. Pick a brother and go.

I really shouldn't be flirting with Seth when Eli had been all about me the past couple of days.

"Just kind of?" Noah scoffed, returning to his paperwork.

"*You're* kind of a brat," I muttered petulantly, throwing Noah a dirty look as I pulled out a bowl to mix the pancake batter in. I could have sworn he almost smiled.

"So you guys built this place?" I asked, making small talk as I prepared the pancakes.

"We did," Seth confirmed, shooting Noah a loaded look before returning his attention to the coffee. "Milk?"

"Please. That's impressive. This house is amazing. It must have taken you a while, being so remote."

"We worked on it over the course of a decade, I suppose. We lived in the cottage."

I had about a billion questions about the timeline — where were their parents? How long ago did they move in? Had they lived here since they were young? — but I bit my tongue. They were kindly sheltering me here; they didn't owe me any explanations.

"Our parents died in a forest fire," Seth continued. "This was our grandparents' place—"

"Enough," Noah growled, slamming down the satellite phone a little harder than necessary and standing up, his chair sliding backwards with a screech.

I may have wet my pants if anyone had ever spoken to me with that kind of ferocity in their voice, but Seth rolled his eyes impatiently as he handed me my coffee.

"Settle, brother."

"Silence, brother," Noah mocked, ignoring me in favor of glaring at his twin.

I was noping the fuck out of this one. There was obviously some unresolved business here that I didn't need to involve myself in. I busied myself over the stove, switching the gas on and heating the griddle, ready to pour the batter. The twins continued their silent stare-off in the background, but I was happily absorbed in my task.

It had been moments like this, quiet moments in the kitchen or in the vegetable garden I'd created in my parents' backyard, that I'd longed to live somewhere rural and quiet. I liked the idea of growing my own food and preparing it from scratch. Maybe it wasn't meant to be.

Perhaps I was destined for a life in the city where I roleplayed as a pioneer woman in my free time. I could start a social media account with a cottagecore aesthetic and post pictures of bunches of wildflowers on my thrift shop wooden dining table, or use the self-timer on my phone to take pictures of me wearing floral maxi dresses and straw hats.

"I would love to know what you're thinking about," Seth said, sidling up next to me and peeking at the griddle.

"I'm wondering if you ever shift into your bear form to scare people off if they get too close to your property. If you say 'no', I'll assume you're lying," I replied quickly, flipping the pancake I was working on, hoping it would detract from my pink cheeks. I doubted any of these mountain men had social media and they'd probably wet their pants laughing if I tried to explain 'cottagecore' to them.

"I personally haven't," Seth said, sounding amused as a chair scraped behind me, Noah apparently settling himself back at the table. I glanced at Noah out of the corner of my eye and could have sworn the tips of ears looked a little pinker.

He'd definitely gone all scary bear on a hiker before.

"The pancakes smell amazing. We've got some preserved plums and syrup in the pantry. Hold on," Seth added.

I continued pouring, flipping, and stacking while he set the table and set out the sides. If I had a cottagecore account, I would totally post pictures of this moment because I was all about it.

"I'll go get Eli," Noah grumbled, clearing his stuff off the table and stomping out the front door as I carried the platter of pancakes to the table.

"Sorry about him," Seth said with a grimace. "After our parents died, Noah really took it on himself to look after us. It's hard for him to switch that instinct off, even though Eli and I are more than capable of looking after ourselves."

"Don't do that," I said flatly, placing the platter down in the center of the table and giving Seth a loaded look.

"Do what?" he asked, baffled.

"Make me dislike him less. I'm at a comfortable level of dislike right now."

"Sorry to inconvenience you," Seth replied, lips twitching.

"Apology accepted." I sat down in the same chair I'd sat in yesterday, downing half my coffee in one gulp, amazed I'd even got through this much of the day without caffeine. It didn't taste quite the same as the way I made it, but it wasn't bad.

Noah stomped back in with a smiling Eli in tow, and the difference in their countenances almost made me giggle out loud.

"You two have been busy," Eli said with a low whistle. "I'm impressed. You're quite the *team*."

Noah gave Eli a warning look while Seth threw him that mildly curious look he seemed to have down pat. I got the feeling there was some secret brotherly communication happening that I wasn't privy to. My own brothers did it all the time, and since I'd been born ten years after Joe, I never understood what they meant either.

It had gotten easier in recent years. We could communicate with just a look that Mom was being overbearing or how Dad was working his way up to a rant.

"So you're working on the rocking chair?" I asked Eli casually, helping myself to two pancakes and drizzling a generous layer of syrup over the top of them. How bad could my life be really, when I had pancakes and syrup? Silver linings and whatnot.

"Just redoing a piece that got snapped," Eli replied, smirking mischievously at me. "I'd only roughly assembled it in the living room to take a look at it. The finished version will be more than able to bear your beautiful ass." His eyes flashed with heat and I swear I felt it all the way down to my toes.

"Jesus, Eli," Seth muttered, shaking his head.

"I was questioning your workmanship a little, I'm not going to lie," I teased, even as I shot Eli an apologetic look across the table so he knew I was, in fact, sorry.

"Not necessary, I'm great at what I do." His feet knocked against mine under the table, and I lightly kicked him back.

But I didn't pull my feet back, and neither did he.

"Modest, too," Seth added wryly, and I felt my face heat. I was playing footsies with Eli under the table and I'd barely remembered his two brothers were sitting right there on either side of us.

"No need for modesty with this level of greatness," Eli replied, totally nonchalant. "I was going to look for some branches later. Want to walk with me, *Ria*?"

Walk? How he made that sound so dirty, and how had Seth and Noah not noticed? Or maybe it was totally innocent and my mind had just permanently migrated to the gutter.

GILDED MESS

"Ria?" Seth asked, eyebrows raised.

"It's what her friends call her. AKA, me." Eli puffed his chest out dramatically and I stifled a laugh, kicking him again.

"Pretty," Seth commented lightly, sawing through his pancakes with a knife. Everything about him was so dignified and controlled, I couldn't help but wonder if he had a secret messy side.

"You can call me Ria," I offered, giving him a small smile. "You can't," I added, glancing at Noah.

He snorted. "As far as I'm concerned, your name is and always will be '*thief*'."

"Whatever helps you sleep at night, Daddy Bear. And a walk sounds lovely, thank you," I added, glancing at Eli, pretty confident my cheeks were the same color as the plums on the table.

"You don't have to thank me, just admit I'm your favorite. Hey, Daddy Bear, did you remember to thank our guest for the lovely meal?" Eli asked, never pausing to take a breath.

"Did everyone forget she broke into our house?" Noah sighed before shoving a huge forkful of pancakes into his mouth. He could talk shit as much as he liked, but he was enjoying the hell out of those pancakes. Was there any greater compliment to the chef than someone enjoying their food? I think not.

"That was *days* ago," I replied with a dismissive wave of my hand. "We've all moved on."

The conversation moved on to lighter topics and I focused on eating after my patchy diet of the past few days, but I could feel Noah's eyes burning into the side of my head the entire time and I knew with absolute certainty that Noah *hadn't* moved on.

When Noah said I'd always be the 'thief' to him, he meant it. But did that really matter?

Eli caught my eye across the table, and despite the mostly demolished stack of pancakes on the plate in front of him, he looked *hungry*.

It's just a few days, I reminded myself. *Might as well have some fun.*

RIA

CHAPTER 9

Eli and I left the cabin together, walking around the front of the house into the back garden, and out the gate that led to the forest, passing the quiet cottage in silence.

We both knew what we were doing — there was nothing coy or mysterious about it. This wasn't two horny teenagers agreeing to meet behind the bleachers with a vague but unconfirmed idea of what we were going to do. This was two horny adults off to make good on all the sexual tension between us, and I was pretty sure everyone knew that.

In the back of my mind, underneath a layer of particularly filthy thoughts about Eli, I was vaguely thinking about Seth. What he would think about me getting frisky with Eli and whether or not it would be a deal breaker. Because Seth was fucking sexy, and I wanted to see what was underneath all that brooding self-control. Even in my head, I recognized how greedy that was. I was staying here for a couple of days. It was arguably inadvisable to fuck *one* of my hosts, definitely inadvisable to fuck two of them.

My steps faltered slightly as we walked. Maybe I shouldn't fuck Eli... Maybe just a blow job. Oral sex didn't count, right? My best friend had been pretty adamant about that in senior year.

Eli looked back over his shoulder, his far-too-casual smolder morphing into a look of concern.

"Do you want to go back, Ria? If you don't feel comfortable—"

"I feel comfortable," I interrupted, immediately forgetting any of the concerns I'd just entertained in the face of turning back and *not* getting to lick Eli's abs. "Though I appreciate you checking."

"If at any point you change your mind—"

"I'll tell you," I promised. "Same goes for you."

Eli scoffed like the idea was ridiculous, his hand reaching for mine, stopping just short. I closed the distance, intertwining our fingers, marveling at just how huge his hands were.

That boded well for other parts of his anatomy, right? My lower extremities clenched in anticipation.

"Consent is for men too, you know," I chided lightly, giving his hand a gentle squeeze.

"I know," Eli replied, softening his tone. "It's just that you could probably do whatever you wanted with me and I'd beg for more."

"Bondage," I suggested instantly.

"As in you tying me up? I'd try it."

"Blood play."

"Shifters are fast healers," Eli countered.

"Watersports," I suggested with a smug grin.

"What?" Eli asked, brow furrowed in confusion.

"Pee stuff."

"Umm, if that was something you're into... *Is* that something you're into?" he asked, sounding suddenly nervous.

"Not my kink," I laughed. "I'm not judging, but if anyone ever pissed on me, things would be over very quickly, and not in the good way."

"Noted," Eli replied, breathing a sigh of relief. "Me neither."

"How much do you know about kinks living out here in the wild?" I teased.

The tips of Eli's ears went a little pink, and my eyebrows jumped up in surprise. I was probably making some bold assumptions, considering they traveled into Fairbanks pretty regularly.

"There's a club we go to sometimes," he admitted, glancing at me like he thought that might be a dealbreaker.

"Shut up," I breathed. "Like a sex club? I've always wanted to go to a sex club."

"I can recreate anything you want to try," Eli replied immediately, eyes widening in alarm. It's not like I was going to visit one *right now* just because he'd suggested it.

I'd add it to the Bucket List though. Or the Fuck-It List, which was my list of sexual escapades I wanted to have before I died. I kept it separate after my mom had expressed an interest in reading my bucket list one time.

"What kind of stuff do you do while you're there?" I asked, burning with curiosity. "Not that you have to tell me. How did you even find the place?"

"I like a little exhibitionism," Eli said with an easy shrug. I could see that. Eli dripped with confidence at all times. "We're pretty tied in to the shifter community around these parts, a few older shifters advised us to go there when we came of age..." he trailed off.

"To expend energy in a healthy way?" I guessed. My brothers had been *rowdy* as hell when they were young. Not that they'd settled down now, but they didn't have the same fuckboy energy they'd been rocking for years.

"Basically," Eli admitted. "Noah is our Alpha by default, but Seth and I are both pretty *alpha* ourselves. Sex is a way for us to exert some dominance. Consensually, of course."

"Of course," I agreed. Why did I feel jealous at the thought of them getting frisky at a sex club? It was a level of possessiveness I had no right to be feeling.

It was probably just the sex club idea. That's what I was jealous about.

"So, what's *your* kink?" he added slyly, the corner of his mouth tipping up.

Getting fucked six ways from Sunday by you and your two brothers at the same time?

I mean, I didn't know that was my specific kink until a couple of days ago, but I'm pretty sure I'd turn into a puddle of orgasms if that situation ever arose. Which it wouldn't, because Noah could barely stand to be in the same room as me and getting myself too involved with them was a bad idea anyway, but still. I had all the good clenches and flutters going on at the mere idea.

Eli cleared his throat, raising his eyebrows expectantly at me. Right, he actually expected an answer to that question.

"I'm pretty submissive in bed." Or potentially lazy, but I preferred to think of it as a kink thing. "I like someone to take the reins if I trust them enough to do so. Edging, rough sex. Light bondage, though I need to be with someone a while before I'm willing to let them tie me up. Spanking is good, but in a sexy way, not a punishment way. Safe word is red."

Not that I'd used it in a while. There had been no need with Darren, his tastes were pretty vanilla.

In hindsight, he just may have not been that into me. Our sexual encounters were always fairly brief, and I had to put in the effort to get myself off, because Darren definitely wasn't going to do it for me.

Suddenly the ground disappeared from underneath me and a muscular bear shifter had situated himself between my thighs, his chest rumbling in a steady almost growl. I wrapped my legs around Eli reflexively as he backed me up against a tree, a hungry look in his eyes.

"There's a pretty spot near here that I was planning on taking you to."

"It's pretty right here," I countered, draping my arms over Eli's broad shoulders. It was pretty too. Everything seemed saturated in color after fresh rainfall, the leaves a bolder green, the brown earth darker and richer, contrasting with the gray sky overhead.

"It was going to be romantic."

"Mm. What happened?" I asked, leaning forward to place soft kisses along his scruffy jaw, the thin fabric of my leggings and panties only dulling the feeling of him between my legs a little.

Oh my. That was a *bulge*! That was some rearrange-my-guts material right there.

"You started talking about bondage and spanking and *fuck* I can smell your arousal and if I don't taste it soon, I might die. That's what happened."

"We don't want that," I breathed, nudging his jaw with my nose so I could kiss down the thick column of his neck. "Safety first and all."

"Shit," Eli groaned, tipping his head back. It was an incredibly trusting gesture for a shifter to expose his neck like that, and the action momentarily caught me off-guard. But I wasn't about to squander the moment, so I sucked a patch of skin hard enough to leave a mark.

"Speaking of safety, I don't have any protection, so we're going to have to get creative," Eli said roughly.

It briefly crossed my mind to tell him fuck it, we didn't need condoms. I knew shifters didn't carry human diseases, and I had a birth control implant, but that seemed a little premature. We could still have fun without him putting his dick in me.

I guess.

"Boo, but okay," I replied, pouting a little against his collarbone. It was very convenient that he was just wearing a henley with a loose neckline. My stupid winter coat was getting in the way. I fumbled with the zipper, shoving it down roughly and pulling my jacket apart. "Argh, I have so many layers on," I muttered.

"And you can't take them off, because I don't want you getting hypothermia on my watch," Eli chuckled, his enormous hands sliding up the backs of my thighs until he was cupping my ass. God, he held me up so easily, like I weighed nothing. I bet he could throw me around on a bed, no problem.

New goal: Make that happen before I left.

I threaded both my hands through Eli's hair, pulling it free of the tie and messing it up a little, looking him straight in the eyes as I did.

"Look at you," Eli purred. "Holding eye contact with a predator without a drop of fear. You're something else, Goldie."

I leaned forward with a smirk, capturing his lower lip between my teeth and sucking it into my mouth. Eli's words had temporarily settled that niggling insecurity of not being a shifter that always existed in the back of my mind.

So, I couldn't shift. Regardless, I was still a fucking badass and I could hold my own with the best of them.

Eli's tongue swept over my lips and I opened readily for him, letting him take over. Kissing had never felt like this before. This was *electric*. My entire body was pressed against his, my legs wrapped tightly around his hips, his taste on my tongue, and yet it wasn't enough. I couldn't be close enough, couldn't get enough of him.

"Are you whining for me, sweet girl?" *Was I?* "Don't worry, I'll take care of you. Better be quick before my brothers come out here looking for us."

Yes. Yes. That sounded amazing.

No, wait. That was bad.

Would it really be so bad, though?

Would they watch or join in? Seth was more reserved than his brothers, but I'd seen the heat baked in his eyes when he looked at me. I think he'd join in. Maybe he'd bark orders at Eli and take charge. That was a sexy as hell visual.

Noah wouldn't join in — he was too busy having a hate-on for me. He'd sure as fuck watch, though. I'd put money on it.

"Are you going to let me slide my hand in these damp panties?" Eli asked, kissing up my jaw until he found a sensitive spot behind my ear that I didn't even know existed.

"*Yes*," I moaned, annoyed I couldn't get the friction I needed in my current position as I writhed in frustration. Eli's frame was so big that I was already testing the limitations of my flexibility the way I was. Or I was just getting old and my hips weren't what they used to be.

Fuck that. I'd take up yoga or something if it meant unhindered acrobatic sex with Eli.

"I need these leggings off," I demanded. "I won't get hypothermia, you'll keep me warm."

"With my face," Eli responded with a grin, carrying me a few feet and carefully placing me on the ground. I shoved my leggings down to my ankles ungracefully, cursing my stupid hiking boots the entire time. Eli had more patience than me, lifting me onto the wide trunk of a fallen tree and unlacing my boots one at a time, followed by my socks.

He tugged my leggings off before placing a light kiss on each ankle, pulling my thick woolen socks back onto my already cold feet.

The gesture was so unexpectedly sweet it made me a little weepy.

"I'm going to eat your pussy now," Eli announced, his declaration shoving aside any unwanted sappy feelings. I leaned back on my hands, my heels digging into the edge of the log, knees bent. Fortunately Eli had left my panties on, because I wasn't quite confident enough to go spread eagle in the harsh light of day.

I mean, maybe if I knew him a little better, you know?

Eli kneeled on the ground, looking up at me with a deliciously hungry expression before stroking over the top of my black cotton panties. Why hadn't I worn something a little sexier? Not that Eli seemed to mind. My breath caught as his ministrations grew stronger, faster. He could definitely feel the damp patch, but I couldn't find it within myself to be embarrassed about it.

Eli found my clit through my panties, circling it roughly with his thumb over the material, and my head rolled back in ecstasy. It almost felt more illicit to have him touching me over my clothes like this — like we were doing something we shouldn't. Like getting frisky in the woods at the back of his house where his brothers could walk in on us at any moment, before midday no less. The secret exhibitionist in me roared to life, and everything tightened, my body vibrated with the need to come, so, so, so fucking close.

"I don't think so, Goldie. I want to taste that orgasm," Eli chuckled, pulling his hand away.

"Then hurry the fuck up about it!" I demanded, snapping my head forward to glare at him. I mean, I quite liked delayed gratification, it always made my orgasm *that* much better. But I couldn't help being bossy about it anyway.

"Ooh, bratty, bratty. Don't let my brothers hear you talk like that," Eli teased. "You'll find yourself with a handprint on your ass. Or two."

Fuck. Me.

Maybe I didn't need him to touch me. Maybe I could come just from his words.

Fortunately, Eli didn't test that theory. He pushed my uncomfortably damp panties roughly to the side and flattened his tongue against me, circling my entrance before licking agonizingly slowly up to my oversensitive clit.

My head flopped back again, and I sunk my teeth into my lower lip, my fingernails digging into the bark so I didn't melt into a pile of goo and fall off this log.

Eli groaned like he was getting just as much satisfaction out of this as I was.

"You taste like..." Eli growled against my pussy, the end of his sentence muffled. It kind of sounded like he said "my future", but that wasn't a flavor. I wasn't about to question him when he sealed his mouth over my clit, sucking with just the right amount of pressure and fluttering his tongue like a goddamn pussy-eating champion.

I knew he'd be great at this. My radar was never wrong.

One of Eli's hands wrapped around my ankle, the other held my panties out of the way, his thumb rubbing teasingly at my entrance.

"Don't stop," I breathed as Eli's tongue did something fucking *magical*, and bless his heart, he actually listened to me, continuing exactly what he was doing until the tension that had been building and building *snapped* like an elastic band.

Pleasure flooded my body, and it took every bit of focus not to fall backwards from my precarious spot. Eli's grip on my ankle tightened, holding me reassuringly tight as my orgasm wrecked me, my nails digging hard enough into the bark to break them.

And still he didn't relent. Not until the last quaking shudders ended did Eli take his mouth off my pussy. He quickly stood, wrapping me in his arms and holding me securely as I panted against his deliciously hard chest, feeling entirely secure in his embrace.

"That's it," Eli purred. "Relax, Goldie."

Oh, I was relaxed. I gave exactly zero fucks that I was in the woods, sans pants, only a few minutes' walk away from the main house. Who needed pants, anyway?

I snuggled into Eli's chest, relishing the physical contact I hadn't realized I'd been missing. I'd been pretty short on cuddles for the past...

GILDED MESS

God, how long had it been? Darren wasn't a cuddler, and I'd almost convinced myself I wasn't a cuddler either, just to make myself feel better about it. I 100% was, though.

I liked my sex rough, and my post-sex snuggly.

"Is this a bear hug?" I mumbled drowsily.

Eli's chest vibrated with laughter, the sound and feeling warming me from the inside out, even as the cold air bit at my exposed legs. Goosebumps sprang up from the top of my socks all the way to my hips.

"I think I have to be in bear form for that? Shit, I actually will have to shift soon to warm you up if we don't get some clothes on you," Eli muttered, grabbing my leggings and extracting himself from my grip to dress me while I lounged unhelpfully on the log.

"I need a minute," I admitted drowsily, rubbing my hands over my thighs to warm them up and wishing I'd taken off my damp panties before Eli had put my leggings back on. "Then I want to return the favor."

"No way," Eli scoffed, still kneeling on the ground as he gently guided my feet into my boots, lacing them up with far more care than I ever took. "It's one thing for me to kneel in the dirt, but you definitely aren't. This was just about you, Goldie."

"Generous of you," I shot back with a smile. I felt like a queen, perched on the log, looking down at him.

"If we had a condom, I'd totally have bent you over this log and had my way with you. Don't get the wrong idea," Eli replied with a wink as he stood up, reaching forward to tuck my hair behind my ear. "Relax for a minute, I'm going to find some branches. I wasn't lying when I said I needed some," he laughed.

"It'd look pretty odd if we went back without them," I agreed, pulling my knees up to my chest and wrapping my arms around them without Eli's body heat to keep me warm.

Eli paused his cursory search of the forest floor, turning back to give me a puzzled look. "Er, no it wouldn't. You smell like a horny sex goddess and so does my face."

"Jesus, Eli. Give me some warning before you say shit like that," I chastised, feeling my cheeks catch fire.

"And miss out on that blush? I don't think so." He grinned unrepentantly.

"Here was me thinking you were a gentleman," I mumbled, pressing the cool backs of my hands to my burning cheeks. I was not shy about sex, but the idea that his face smelled like my arousal and anyone with shifter senses would be able to tell? It was kind of filthy.

"A gentleman? Rookie mistake, Goldie."

RIA

CHAPTER 10

When my legs regained sensation, I jumped lightly off the log, earning a disapproving look from Eli as I joined him looking for fallen branches on the forest floor. Once he had a decent bundle, he carried them effortlessly back through the trees towards the cottage, placing them in a pile outside the door.

I gave him a questioning glance. "Aren't you going to do something with those?"

"They're fine there for now. I'm more concerned that your lips are turning blue," Eli responded, looking genuinely concerned.

"I'm fine, honestly," I said, waving off his concern. "I'll have a cup of tea and they'll be back to normal," I assured him. Leggings had served me fine when I was inside most of the day at my diner job or in my house, but I had to admit they weren't the most practical for being out in the elements.

"Next time we leave the house, I'm making a flask of tea to carry with you," Eli announced decisively, pushing open the gate and leading me into the vegetable garden.

Before I could laugh, he clapped his enormous hand over my mouth to silence me. I seriously contemplated kneeing him in the balls until I caught the unusually serious look on his face.

"Listen," he mouthed, removing the offending appendage from my face and guiding me silently towards the side of the cabin.

His lips twitched with amusement the closer we got, but as I didn't have super sensitive bear ears, it took me a while to realize what he found so funny.

"Come on, man. She's about this tall, blonde, great ass..."

"Careful," Noah rumbled as Eli mouthed "great ass" at me, nodding in earnest agreement.

"Her scent is all over this place!" Darren yelled in frustration. "I know she's here. Fucking *aroused*," he spat.

I took a step to move around the house, ready to give that asshole a piece of my mind, but Eli's light touch on my arm halted me. His face was *all* mischief, and a little of my burning anger seemed to fizzle out at the promise of trouble in his eyes.

Just a little, though. I was still *plenty* angry.

Eli stripped off his clothes with impressive silence, and I swallowed the humiliating noise that threatened to rise up when he began tugging down his jeans and there was only bare skin underneath. God, I wanted a closer look at that V. I kind of wanted to lick it.

Would it be rude to ogle his junk right now? *Yes, Ria. Definitely rude.* Shifter etiquette dictated that you *not* perve on people when they were stripping off to shift. With some effort, I kept my eyes trained straight ahead as bones cracked and popped behind me, holding my breath until I heard the light thud of front paws hitting the ground behind me. Hopefully, the noise of Noah's lecture would drown out Eli's shift, or this was going to be a lame surprise.

Eli nuzzled the small of my back with his nose, about an inch above my ass. There was no way on earth I believed that was by accident.

Pervy bear.

Eli moved to my side, nudging me insistently and looking back over his shoulder.

Did he... Did he want me to ride him?

Was he suggesting I ride on in to confront my asshole ex on top of a 1500-pound bear like a goddamn superhero?

Obviously, yes. I was going to do that.

He laid down on the ground so I could clamber awkwardly onto his back, and I flung my arms around his thick neck as he rose onto four paws and lumbered towards the front of the house. *Shit*, this wouldn't work. I was clinging to him like a koala on a tree. There was nothing majestic about it.

I tightened my thighs around Eli's middle and pushed myself up so my palms rested flat on his back, fingers burying into his thick fur. With clumsy movements, I swung my mass of hair over one shoulder, tilting my chin up defiantly for a slightly more Warrior Bear Queen vibe.

Darren's mouth fell open as we rounded the corner and I couldn't suppress the smug smirk that took over my face, even if it ruined the icy vibe I was going for. *Check me out now, motherfucker.*

Seth bit the corner of his lip to stop a laugh from escaping, and my stomach dipped unexpectedly at how *sexy* he looked. Seth was always attractive, but not in the overtly flirty way Eli was, nor did he have the raw, borderline offensive sexiness that Noah possessed in spades.

Seth's sexiness was all half smirks, hooded eyes, and apparently a strategically placed lip bite. God, how was he doing that? I had tried lip-biting in the mirror and looked like I was auditioning for a bad porno.

Noah was not sexy lip-biting as he observed me riding into the fray on his baby brother's back. Noah looked like he was at risk of pulling a muscle from how hard he was rolling his eyes. Killjoy.

Was that... was that a sneaky dick adjustment, though? It totally was. Maybe he liked my sex goddess scent.

"Darren. Fancy seeing you here," I drawled, like I rode around on bears all the time.

"Aurelia," Darren said flatly, the barest icy edge in his tone. I wasn't fooled by his civilized facade anymore. Now I knew he was a good actor. "You seem to have gotten lost. Our cabin is further up the mountain, babe."

I raised my eyebrows slowly, letting him sweat in silence. I stole his gun and his weed, smashed his phone, and straight up told him we were finished. He and I both knew I wasn't lost.

"Aurelia," Darren said a little more forcefully, jerking his head like he expected me to follow him out of here. Eli growled in warning, and the vibration that ran up his back hit me in some unexpectedly great places.

"Darren," I mocked. "Why don't you call your other girlfriend if you're feeling lonely? Or do you not have her number now?" I asked, feigning sympathy for his busted phone. Oops.

"You cheated on her," Noah stated flatly, looking at Darren like he was a moron. It was extremely flattering. "Now why the fuck would you do something like that? She's clearly out of your league."

Was that a compliment? Had I woken up in an alternate universe timeline?

"It was a misunderstanding," Darren gritted out.

"Ex-fucking-scuse me?" I responded icily. "I saw those messages for myself—"

"You shouldn't have stolen my phone," Darren snapped. "Or my gun, or my weed for that matter."

Noah snorted obnoxiously. "Good to know you're an equal opportunity thief, Aurelia," he muttered.

"And you shouldn't have put your dick in women other than your live-in girlfriend," I retorted, ignoring Noah. "You can have the gun back, but I smoked your stash. I could apologize, but I'd be lying."

"So you're just whoring yourself out to the bears now?"

Eli growled in warning, and I jumped in surprise. I knew his anger wasn't directed at me, but I wasn't entirely comfortable having an enraged bear underneath me, to be honest.

"Eli," Noah warned gently.

"About that. When were you planning on telling me you were a shifter?" I wasn't dignifying the whoring comment with an answer.

Darren shifted his weight uncomfortably, eyes darting towards the treeline. "As far as I knew, you were a human and didn't know about shifters."

"Pretty excuse," Noah replied drolly. "But you can smell she's no ordinary human, so I call bullshit."

"Fuck you!" Darren spat, and I vaguely wondered if he was suicidal because picking a fight with Noah seemed like a terrible idea. "I challenge you for her."

Oof. I could barely see through the red haze clouding my vision. Who the fuck did he think he was?

"This isn't your archaic pack," Noah snapped. "Out here in the real world, women aren't prizes to be won. If *Aurelia* wants to be with you, she's more than capable of making that decision for herself."

Noah strode towards me, halting at Eli's side. I looked up at him in surprise, both at his proximity and his words, and Noah's mouth quirked as he gently grasped my chin, leaning in close like he was going to kiss me.

"Isn't that right, thief?"

Or was he actually going to kiss me?

Were we pretending?

I probably shouldn't be this turned on if we were pretending. Also, Noah was obnoxious as hell. I did not want to provide him with further ammo to use against me by actually *enjoying* this. But then Darren made a furious noise, and I contemplated saying fuck it, and kissing Noah anyway.

With a confident smile, I straightened, wrapping my hand around the back of Noah's neck and tugging him towards me.

"Noah?" I breathed, when our lips were a hair's breadth apart.

"Yes, little thief?" Noah's warm breath ghosted over my lips, his cedar scent drugging me when he was this close.

"Fuck off. I want Seth," I whispered.

Noah's lips curled into an amused smirk, his eyes twinkling as he looked down at me. "Be careful what you wish for, *Aurelia*. It's the quiet ones you've got to look out for."

He looked back over his shoulder and beckoned an observant Seth closer. Darren's eyes burned into the side of my face, but I didn't pay him any mind.

I'd committed to this performance now.

Shit, did I still smell like a horny sex goddess? Probably.

Noah's fingers lingered as he pulled his hand away from my jaw, his eyes dancing with amusement, probably at my blatant rejection. I'm pretty sure he secretly got off on me putting him in his place. God knows, someone had to.

Seth took his twin's place in a move so smooth it looked rehearsed. He was only an inch away from me, but unlike Noah, Seth was restrained, his hands clasped in front of him, legs spread, looking immovable and controlled. Eli shook a little underneath me in what may have been silent bear laughter. Why were they all being so weird? Maybe Seth was a virgin.

"What is it you need, sweetheart?"

Sweetheart, huh? I could work with that.

What did I need? I really hadn't thought this through. Obviously, there was no doubt there that Eli was attracted to me, and the sexual chemistry between Noah and I had been off the charts from the moment he'd found me in his bed, even if it was in an I-want-to-hate-fuck-you kind of way. Seth was far more reserved, more difficult to read.

He'd always been *nice* to me, but nice didn't mean he wanted to stick his tongue in my mouth in front of an audience.

I opened my mouth to tell him I didn't need anything, but the fucking bear underneath me chose that moment to intervene. Eli reared up a little and tipped me sideways, then Seth's chest was the only thing that stopped me from crashing to the ground. He wrapped an arm around my waist, another tangling in my hair as he dipped his head closer.

"What do you need, sweetheart?" he repeated, his grip on me just shy of painful. *Demanding.* I relaxed into it instantly, loving the feeling of being cocooned by him.

"A kiss, please."

"Since you asked so nicely..."

Seth guided my head back by my hair, and I felt the gentle tug on my scalp in places much further south. That same hand kept me in place as Seth closed the distance between us, maintaining control. God, my nipples were so hard they were probably showing through my winter coat.

I kept my eyes on Seth, my gaze dropping to his delicious mouth, tipped up ever so slightly on one side. Then he was on me, his lips on mine, his hand pulling my head impossibly closer, sexual energy passing between the two of us like a current.

My eyes fell shut, and I relaxed into the kiss, of the sensation of Seth exploring me, encouraging me, dominating me. It was far more intense than anything I could have predicted from the mild-mannered middle brother, and I loved every second of it.

Reluctantly, we broke apart, our mouths no longer touching, but hovering just millimeters apart like a magnet was pulling us together. Eli huffed underneath me, jostling me on his back and breaking the spell.

When I opened my eyes, Darren was gone.

Seth gave me a small half smile, lifting me off Eli's back and placing me onto the ground on unsteady feet.

"So, here I am, trying to dull her scent around the forest," Noah began in an unimpressed voice, arms crossed, staring at a yawning Eli. "And you take her out into the woods and make her come, alerting everyone with a decent sense of smell for miles around that she was here. Does that sound about right?"

Bear Eli snorted, wandering back around the side of the house where he'd left his clothes. Noah watched him go with his eyes narrowed.

"Aw, you've been covering my scent? I knew you cared, really," I teased, sticking close to Seth's side even though we weren't touching. He struck me as less overtly touchy feely than Eli, though I didn't have a problem with that.

"I just didn't want to attract the attention of every fucking shifter in the state. Don't read into it," Noah grumbled, his eyes flicking between Seth and I. "On that note, you might want to consider a bath."

What an asshole. But even No-Fun Noah couldn't spoil my good mood right now.

Also, perhaps he had a point. That my little forest excursion had possibly led Darren here was a little humiliating.

"For unrelated reasons, I am going to take a bath," I told Seth, doing my best to keep my voice aloof.

His lips twitched, but he didn't call me out the way Eli definitely would have. "Sounds like a great idea."

✳✳✳

After my bath, I napped a little, then picked through the extensive bookshelves in Seth's room for something to fill my time. I ended up idly flicking through an art history book, which filled me with new ideas for the kind of jewelry I wanted to make once my solder arrived at Lou's house. I hadn't entirely given up on my jewelry-making dream, but it had definitely been downgraded to a hobby rather than a career option at this point. Living with my parents forever wasn't an option, I'd have to get a real job.

Was I hiding up here? Maybe a little. I needed a little alone time to recalibrate and put some emotional walls between myself and all three of my hosts. I knew what I was like — I was a needy little puppy on the inside who lapped up scraps of attention like I was being put on a pedestal and worshipped. It was a habit that had gotten me into trouble time and time again — *Exhibit 831: Darren* — and I didn't want to fall into the same trap again.

A couple of days. I was just staying here for a couple of days, then I would be on my way. Some no-strings sex between single, consenting adults was one thing, but emotions were a hard no. Avoid. Abort mission. Do not pass Go.

As the sunlight waned out my window, I figured the least I could do was help in the kitchen while I was here. Between whatever Seth did in his studio, Eli's woodworking, and Noah's rangering, cooking was probably the last thing they were in the mood for.

I descended the stairs wearing some skinny jeans tucked into thick socks and a Ramones sweater, glad I'd packed at least one pair of pants that weren't leggings.

GILDED MESS

The three of them were already downstairs. Eli was lounging on the couch with a beer in hand, Seth was looking through the kitchen cupboard, and Noah was sitting at the dining table with some kind of report in front of him, staring at it like he could set it alight with his eyes. Not for the first time, I wondered if he actually liked his job.

Noah looked up first, and my face heated a little. He'd smelled what I'd gotten up to with his little brother this morning, then watched me make out with his twin. I was generally a pretty shameless person, but maybe it was the fact that they were brothers that was making me feel self-conscious. Who did that? I needed psychiatric help.

Noah's gaze dropped from my face to stare flatly at my jumper, his face permanently unimpressed with life.

"If you can name one Ramones song, I will eat an entire beehive in my human form."

What?

I glanced down at the black sweater with the white Ramones seal dominating the front of it. *Shit.*

"How do you even know the Ramones exist, mountain man?" I groused, feeling my cheeks heat up.

I did not know any Ramones songs, I just thought it was a cool sweater. Sue me.

"We do listen to music," Seth interjected, looking amused. He tipped his chin at the record player in the corner that I'd assumed was for aesthetic purposes only.

Like my sweater.

"So?" Noah challenged, leaning back in his chair and crossing his arms over his chest. "Bet you'd love to see me eat a beehive."

"I really would," I agreed, searching my brain for a Ramones song. Maybe something Vincent listened to? My oldest brother was the musicophile of the three of us.

"*Lola*," I said eventually, with more confidence than I probably deserved to have. It was the one song I remembered my brother blasting the loudest.

Noah looked to Seth for the answer and *ohmigod* he didn't know either, so why did I have to? I mean, he wasn't wearing their merch, but still. Hypocrite.

"*Lola*... by The Kinks?" Seth asked, visibly struggling not to laugh.

"I'm pretty sure it's a Ramones song," I replied loftily, making my way down the stairs to join him in the kitchen.

Eli, suddenly energized, leaped off the couch to go through the cupboard under the record player. *Do not call me out, do not call me out.*

I turned my back on him, busying myself getting a glass of water until the distinctive aggressive opening guitar chords of *Lola* rang out.

"Sorry, Goldie. This definitely says The Kinks," Eli called over the music, holding up the vinyl cover to further rub salt in the wound.

Noah relaxed one arm over the back of his chair, leaning back arrogantly to look at me. "Guess you're out of luck this time, thief."

I gave Eli the finger as subtly as I could, and he clutched his heart in mock injury, turning on his heel and collapsing on the couch like he'd been shot, chuckling to himself.

"You didn't know either," I muttered at Noah. "I did not come down here to have my fashion choices questioned. I came to help with dinner. What can I do?" I asked Seth, turning my back on a smug Noah and traitorous Eli.

"We have some moose meat that needs eating, I was going to make a stew," Seth replied, giving me a hesitant look.

"I don't think I've ever tried moose before," I admitted. "I can chop vegetables though?"

"Or you could come cuddle with me on the couch," Eli suggested, flopping back down.

"No, you were complicit in The Kinks fiasco," I shot back. "I'd rather chop potatoes."

Noah was notably silent, but I could feel his eyes burning into my back as I bantered with his brothers. It was unsettling, but at the same time I felt this indescribable urge to prove to him how likable I was.

When I wasn't high and committing larceny, or whatever.

Eli kept the music going, and I hummed under my breath as Seth and I worked together to cut and season the meat and vegetables. I watched him as he browned the moose meat, then we combined it all into a large pot on the stove. I'd appreciated having something to do with my hands, I felt a little out of sorts without a task to do.

"It'll take an hour or so to cook," Seth said apologetically. "I was going to do some other prep stuff in the meantime, if you'd like to hang around."

"You read my mind," I replied a little too brightly.

God, I'd always thought I was reasonably well equipped for life in the middle of nowhere. I cooked. I could bake a pretty decent loaf of bread. I'd taken a beer brewing course one weekend.

It turns out, there was a little more to living properly out in the wild than that.

I watched in fascination as Seth pulled out a bowl of almonds that had been soaking in water and added them to a blender, humming quietly as he ripped up dates and tossed them in with the almonds and blended the whole lot.

He tucked a white sack into a glass jar and transferred the thick liquidated nuts into the bag with practiced movements.

"Almond milk," Eli supplied, slipping into the chair next to me. "We try to buy as much dry stuff in bulk as we can so we don't have to go into town as much."

Maybe it was a good thing Darren had cheated on me. I was in no way equipped for life in the wilderness. Or at least not with him, anyway. He would have expected me to take care of all the domestic chores for sure.

Seth's eyes — identical in shape and color to Noah's but so much gentler — glanced up, and he offered me a soft smile as he wrung the milk out of the bag.

"There's nothing like almond milk on porridge."

"Sounds delicious," I replied with a genuine smile, biting back the avalanche of Goldilocks-themed jokes that flooded my brain.

Bears eating *porridge*. Come on.

I guess that's why the coffee Seth made tasted different — almond milk. It hadn't been *bad* though. Maybe I wasn't totally equipped for life out here, but the fact that I liked it, that I felt like it *suited* me, was a constant tease.

"Want to help me make bread?" Seth asked, looking the teensiest bit hopeful instead of his usually cool and collected self.

"Now we're talking," I replied confidently, jumping out of my chair. Bread, I could do.

SETH

CHAPTER 11

I wanted to kiss her again.

I'd made bread thousands of times, usually it was a mindless task for me, but today I could barely focus enough to get the ingredients out of the cupboard.

Aurelia — *Ria's* — lips had all of my attention. I could paint a 6-foot canvas devoted to her mouth — the poutiness of her lips, the way the corners were always tipped up mischievously... God, she was like a beautiful dream.

I wasn't as... *free with my affections*, as Eli was. I went into town reasonably often to sell my paintings, but I liked to think of myself as more selective. Or perhaps I just wasn't as appealing to the female population. I had been told more than once that I was "intense."

Ria hadn't seemed to mind, though. She relished my intensity. And Eli's playfulness, which was perfect since the three of us had always preferred the idea of taking a mate together. I couldn't imagine life apart from my brothers.

"Do you need me to show you how it's done?" Ria teased, and I realized I'd been staring at her hands for longer than was socially acceptable. Every line, curve, and edge of her body was a portrait I hadn't painted yet.

"I'm always open to learning new techniques," I replied instead.

Ria's eyebrows raised. "You'd let me take charge?"

I tilted my head to the side, studying her face to figure out if there was a double meaning to her words. I hadn't exactly held back when I'd kissed her.

"I'm not a total control freak," I replied carefully.

"Except in bed," Eli called from the couch. Ria glanced over at him, a grin overtaking her entire face. God, she was radiant when she smiled like that.

It was a testament to my extraordinary self-control that I hadn't murdered my little brother yet.

"Could you three save your fucked up foreplay for when I'm not around?" Noah grumbled, glaring at me in particular while Ria busied herself assembling ingredients from various cupboards, rolling her eyes at my grumpy twin. Noah had accepted that Eli was going to get involved with Ria — Eli was Eli, after all — but Noah undoubtedly saw my flirtation with her as something of a betrayal.

Not that I would know. Noah was a closed book when it came to talking about his feelings. As far as he was concerned, emotions were a weakness he didn't have time for, and Eli and I had always indulged his insecurities because it was convenient for us.

I regretted that call now. Not only because I was curious as hell about what Noah was thinking, but also because it was increasingly obvious that he was struggling with *something*, and that something was going to be the death of a budding relationship with Ria.

What was I missing here?

We'd always discussed taking a mate together. Our parents weren't polyamorous, it wasn't something we'd grown up with, but a nearby family of cougar shifters — the Wyatts — were polyandrous and they'd been good to us when we were trying to get ourselves set up as teenagers on our own. They'd made the idea of sharing a mate seem so easy. More than easy, *desirable*.

And maybe we were a little codependent after everything we'd been through together, but I couldn't face the idea of leaving my brothers.

I thought the three of us had been in agreement about that, but the more I thought about it, the more I realized it had been *Eli* and I pushing that line of thought. Not Noah.

Maybe he didn't want to share?

It was a chilling thought, but one I couldn't rule out after seeing the way he looked at Aurelia whenever she was flirting with either Eli or me.

God knows, he'd been asked to share enough over the years. Even before the fire, he'd been the protector out of the three of us, tasked with minding his brothers. My bear had emerged later, and my parents had infantilized me because of it.

Then after the fire, Noah had taken the lead when it came to looking after us while I'd had my head in the clouds, dealing with my trauma through my art. Someone had to be the tough one who made sure we had a roof over our heads, food in the cupboards, and kept Eli in line when he was just a little kid. It hadn't been me.

This was all premature. There was no guarantee Ria would *want* to stay with us, anyway. It was still very early days, but what would it mean for us if she wanted to and Noah wasn't on board with it? I thought if we ever found a potential mate, we'd all just *know* and it would feel right.

I stood back as Ria pottered around in the kitchen, mesmerized again as she confidently kneaded the dough, humming quietly under her breath, the sleeves of her black Ramones jumper pushed up to her elbows.

One minute she was all fierce attitude, the next she was baking, the light catching in her blonde hair, making her look almost angelic. Ria was a tangled knot of contradictions. I wanted to pick each thread, unravel them, understand what made up the complex picture that was Aurelia.

"Too bad you don't have any cornmeal, it makes the bottom of the loaf just…" Ria did a dramatic chef's kiss with flour-covered fingers I wanted to lick.

"I'm sure it'll be delicious, regardless," I replied, gently pulling the bowl away to cover it for her so she could wash her hands.

"So, Eli mentioned you had a studio," Ria said, spinning to look at me as she dried her hands on a towel. She was never particularly coy or discreet about her intentions. It was something I admired about her.

"Would you like to see it?"

"Can I?" Her eyes lit up, the golden flecks in them were almost glowing. What I would give to paint those… I wasn't sure I could capture their unique blend of tones if I tried.

"Sure. These two can keep an eye on dinner." I paused at the door to grab Ria's jacket and held it up for her to shrug her arms into.

It hadn't escaped my notice that her eyes lit up whenever one of us held a door open for her, or pulled a chair out. Basically, any time we made the barest effort at chivalry. Though I doubted *Darren* had ever done anything of the sort for her.

How had he cheated on Ria? What a fucking moron.

Testing my theory, I offered Ria my arm as we made our way out of the front door. She pursed her lips in an attempt to hide her smile as she slid her arm through mine.

The sky was already dark, and I cursed myself for not thinking to bring a flashlight as Ria's grip on me tightened. *Think, Seth.* Her eyes weren't as sharp as mine in the darkness.

I pulled her in closer to my side, easily navigating the pathway that led around the side of the cabin in the dark, through Noah's vegetable garden, back to the cottage. It was so old; it felt like it was part of the forest itself. The cottage had been in the family for generations, and we'd only made minimal changes to it over the years, even as we'd honed our construction skills.

I guided Ria up the two steps that led up to the porch and pushed open the creaking door, flicking on the lights once we were inside. I grabbed the battery-powered lantern by the door, handing it to Ria as I flicked it on.

"Thanks," she said with a grateful smile. "I'm still jealous of shifter senses, even though I tell myself I'm fine without them," Ria admitted.

"It's fine to be jealous." I shrugged. "Just so long as you don't think any less of yourself."

Ria gave me a skeptical look before striding confidently towards the closed door to my studio. Did she think less of herself? I'd never been particularly driven to reassure someone before, but I had an undeniable urge to reassure Ria. To let her know that there wasn't a single thing I would change about her.

But I didn't have the chance, because she was already letting herself into my studio with undoubtedly the same confidence that led her to break into our house. The woman treated a closed door like a suggestion.

My studio had once been the only bedroom in the cottage, one we'd shared when we first arrived here when Noah and I were 15 and Eli was 10. The only big change we'd made since converting it was to replace the small window with almost an entire wall of them that looked out into the forest, letting more natural light in.

There was a large reclaimed wood table along the windowed back wall with some of my smaller pieces on display at the back, though it was mostly functional. An easel against one wall with my current work in progress. A navy armchair in the corner furthest away from the easel where Eli sat sometimes. Paintings I had yet to transport into town were hung on every inch of wall space in the rest of the room.

Ria whistled softly, holding up the lantern and looking around the small space. It wasn't exactly private, but no one other than my brothers had even been in here. I wasn't prepared for how nervous having her in here would make me feel.

"You really like trees," Ria said eventually, squinting in the limited light.

"Trees pay the bills," I replied wryly, gesturing at the wall of landscape paintings, depicting various locations nearby. "They're popular with tourists."

"They're pretty," Ria acknowledged, giving them a passing glance before moving towards the table where some of my smaller, more personal pieces were depicted. "But I like these more."

What was happening to me? I wanted to crow like a rooster that she liked my paintings.

"They're not conventionally pretty," I said, sounding a lot more cool and collected than I felt.

Ria bent over to examine one more closely, and my gaze caught on the line of her legs in her tight jeans — about the only part of her body that wasn't covered by her winter coat.

"There's a theme here," Ria murmured, looking between the images. "But I don't think I'm artistic enough to pick up what it is. Honestly, I'm as deep as a puddle and I'm fine with that."

"I think there's more to Ria than what you let on," I replied, pulling my attention away from her legs. *When had I become such a hound?*

She hummed absently. "Eli said something similar, which means you're both going to be disappointed when you realize you're wrong. Tell me about the pictures."

I sidled up next to her, amused by her demanding attitude. Ria talked a big game, but she'd melted like ice on a sunny day when I exerted the slightest bit of dominance.

The paintings on the table were all of individual elements, painted at close range and in intricate detail. Gnarled knots in trees, wilting flowers, and broken wings. "I find beauty in the imperfections. The flaws that make up the perfect whole."

"That's a nice idea," Ria replied quietly, and I got the impression she was talking about more than the artwork.

"Browse, if you want. Take your time." I gave her some privacy, dropping into the armchair in the corner that Eli would sit in when he was ready to explode from working on his own all day. Eli needed regular interaction more than Noah or I did.

Ria moved between the paintings, holding the light up and staring at some longer than others, while I stared at Ria. Her hair was the most incredible combination of silvery white and pale gold in this light. My fingers itched being so near my paints with the urge to replicate it on canvas.

"You know," Ria began, turning to look at the landscapes on the wall. "I think I've seen these before."

"Probably. They're displayed in stores and cafes all over town — anywhere they'd take them."

"They're in *Bean There*, the diner I used to work in," Ria said, eyes lighting up in recognition as she shot me a beaming smile. "I remember thinking how beautiful they were. Why don't you display any in the house?"

"We built the main house ourselves from scratch. We started when we were teenagers and it took us ten years to complete."

Ria gave up any pretense of looking at the paintings, turning fully to stare at me. "When you were *teenagers*?"

"Our family home was destroyed by a fire. It took our parents as well. It took a few days for us to find our way here, to our grandparents' old cottage."

"Oh my god, Seth. I'm so sorry." Ria looked like she meant it too. Like our suffering genuinely pained her. That's how I knew there was more to her than she let on.

I offered her a tight smile. "It was a long time ago."

"That doesn't mean it doesn't still hurt."

"No," I conceded, tipping my chin. "Though, it's a different kind of hurt now. What about you? Any family tragedies in your formative years you'd like to share?"

"Ooh, was that deflection *and* sarcasm? My kind of man," Ria threw back with a cheeky wink.

"Is that so?" I leaned back in the armchair, surveying her with just enough scrutiny to make her squirm.

"Is what so?" she asked breathily, pupils dilating.

"Am I your kind of man?" God, I wondered if I could capture the exact shade of her blush. It was exquisite.

"You're... you're not *not* my kind of man," Ria responded, with far less bluster than usual.

"You're definitely my kind of woman," I replied, not hiding my slow perusal of her body.

Ria fidgeted on the spot, biting her lower lip as she looked at me through her lashes, adorably hesitant in the role she'd fallen into.

"What do you need, sweetheart?"

I'd never get sick of asking her that question. I'd ask her every day for the rest of her life if she'd let me.

"What can I have?"

Everything.

I glanced down at my thigh, then back up at her, letting Ria decide if she wanted to come to me. I didn't bring her out here to get into her pants, as appealing as the idea was.

I'd been walking around with an erection since I'd scented her arousal this morning when she'd emerged on Eli's back, blonde hair dishevelled and lips swollen from kisses.

Fortunately, Ria seemed to be on the same page as she sauntered over and dropped sideways in my lap, depositing the lantern on the floor, then draping an arm around my shoulders.

"Hello, sweetheart."

I wrapped one arm around Ria's back and stroked my thumb across her delicate jaw, and up to rub her bottom lip. Her eyes went hazy and her mouth parted instantly, a puff of warm breath brushed my skin.

"Hi," she said eventually.

"Can I kiss you again?"

"You can probably do anything you want to me right now," Ria admitted breathlessly. "Safe word is 'red'. Go."

I snorted in surprise. "I'm glad you're already familiar with the concept of safe words, but we're going to talk *a lot* more before we get into that territory. I like to have control, Ria. I'd like to play with you, if that's something you're interested in."

"Yes, please. All of the interest. I have it." I wasn't even sure she realized she said that out loud, and I fought to keep the indulgent smile off my face.

Despite the intensity of the moment, Ria was *fun*. An endless pool of brightness and sunshine.

"Ultimately, you are the one in control," I emphasized, wanting to ensure Ria was entirely comfortable. "Do you understand, sweetheart? I will never take anything you're not comfortable giving."

"I understand. Yellow to slow down, red to stop. This isn't my first rodeo," she added.

"I don't have any condoms, so tonight—"

Ria threw her head back with a dramatic groan. "Do none of you own condoms? What is this?" she sighed, before her head snapped back up and she gave me a wide-eyed look, like she'd been caught with her hand in the cookie jar.

"I don't mind if you're involved with Eli, too. The opposite, actually. So long as we're all honest about it," I told her, raising an eyebrow. I was *thrilled* she and Eli had connected. I'd be even more thrilled if she and Noah connected. Though if she was feeling shy about Eli and I, who knew how she'd feel about being involved with all three of us.

Slow down, I reminded myself. There was plenty of time for her to adjust to the idea.

"Right. I mean, I figured it wasn't a secret, but it's still a little embarrassing, I guess," Ria admitted, but she relaxed again in my arms.

"Why?" I resumed my gentle touches along her jaw, moving my hand down to the column of her neck underneath the collar of her jacket.

"Because you're brothers?" Ria suggested, like she wasn't sure about the answer either.

"We don't mind sharing," I murmured, wrapping my hand around the back of her neck and pulling her towards me. She came easily, melting against me as my lips brushed against her jaw, teasing her.

"When are we getting to the kissing?" Ria breathed, her eyes fluttering shut.

"Patience." I angled her head to the side to place a light kiss below her ear.

"Not my strong suit," she grumbled. I smiled against her skin, continuing my path.

Ria's hand fisted the front of my shirt, her movements becoming increasingly restless. I wanted to tease her, to tempt her, to make her forget about her shitty ex and moving back home.

"Just so you know, I haven't had a lot of action recently. I'm not usually this…"

"Responsive?" I supplied before sucking a mark at the base of her throat.

"Sure. Let's go with that."

I held her in place for a moment, leaning back to admire the mark on her pale skin. I knew it would disappear quickly — one of the few things I knew about carriers is that they had enhanced healing — but there was something satisfying about seeing my mark on her.

It wasn't an urge I'd ever experienced before.

Content that Ria was completely relaxed, I guided her face down to mine and pressed our lips together, giving her a moment to adjust.

Honestly, kissing didn't usually rank high on the list of things I wanted to do with a woman. I enjoyed it, but more as a precursor to something else. Not so with Ria. I could kiss her for hours and be entirely satisfied.

She parted her mouth in encouragement as my soft, gentle touches turned filthy and demanding. Ria whined in frustration, rubbing her thighs together impatiently.

"Why am I always wearing stupid winter clothes?" Ria muttered, pulling back slightly. "How is anyone supposed to get any action with this many layers on?"

"We can get creative," I replied, lifting her with ease and rearranging her on my lap so she was straddling me. I slid my hands to the waistband of her jeans, tugging them up and watching her reaction. She gasped, and I knew she was getting friction where she needed it.

Ria rolled her hips, leaning back slightly with her small hands braced on my shoulders. "That's it," I encouraged her, pulling the denim waistband taut. "Make yourself feel good."

"I think... I think I'm going to be embarrassed if you get me off with the seam of my jeans," she breathed, tipping her head back, her cascade of hair long enough to brush my thighs.

"I certainly hope not," I replied sternly. "You are going to come for me, just like this, and you're going to own that orgasm like the goddess you are."

"Great idea," Ria moaned, moving with greater confidence as her inhibitions disappeared. I kept one hand on her waistband, keeping the fabric pulled tight, and slid the other over the curve of her ass to squeeze her cheek. I wanted to see her bent over the table. Straddling me without a stitch of clothing on. Laid out on my bed. I wanted her every way I could get her.

"Fuck, fuck, *fuck!*" Ria whined. "I'm going to come dry humping you like a horny teenager."

"Then do it," I replied lazily. "Come."

I knew she'd take direction well. Ria went off like a rocket, biting down hard on her lower lip and arching her back as everything tightened, then relaxed again. She really had too many clothes on.

I gathered Ria's shaking frame into my arms, and she buried her face in the crook of my neck as she caught her breath. Despite the thick fabric, the smell of her arousal permeated the entire studio, and I wasn't sure how I'd ever be able to paint anything that wasn't her in this room again.

"If you two are done fucking around, dinner is ready," Noah called out aggressively from outside the cottage. Ria jumped slightly, and I pulled her in tighter, stroking my hand over her hair.

"Sorry, I forgot you wouldn't be able to hear his footsteps."

"Grumpy bear," Ria grumbled, though it lacked her usual bite. She was lust-drunk and boneless in my arms, and the idea of letting her go was abhorrent.

I shuffled her slightly so I could lean down and grab the lantern off the floor. "Here, you hold this. I'm going to hold you."

GILDED MESS

"You can't carry me all the way back," Ria protested weakly, wrapping her fingers around the handle of the lantern anyway.

"Watch me."

RIA

CHAPTER 12

After both Eli and Seth had got me off yesterday, sleeping in Seth's room by myself felt both lonely and necessary. Particularly because my willpower was pretty weak on the best of days, and I was always horny as hell in the mornings. I could never remember what I dreamed about, but I'm guessing it was a solid eight to ten hours of unadulterated filth by the state I usually woke up in.

Like right now.

Could I masturbate in Seth's bed? It was probably bad guest etiquette, right?

I laid back, sinking into the too-soft mattress, knowing all three of them had left already to begin their respective days, running my fingers over the birth control implant in my arm. Shifters didn't carry sexually transmitted diseases — I distinctly remembered my Mom panicking about these kinds of things when it emerged that I was just a carrier — and the implant would prevent pregnancy. We didn't *need* condoms.

Maybe I should bring that up today because I was not about to get off from my inseam again, and I was already desperate to come.

Don't masturbate, Ria. Where are your manners?

Would I have made the no condoms call with Darren? He'd suggested ditching them before and I'd asked him to get a test done at the doctor's, but he'd never bothered. It made sense now — shifters could hardly go get blood tests from humans — but it made me wonder for the millionth time what his intentions were.

Get me pregnant and tell me he was a shifter? Wait until after the kid was born? Take the kid and run?

God, even after yesterday's satisfying little performance in front of Darren, knowing that he'd left with his tail between his legs and probably furious, the betrayal still stung.

It was nice of the guys to let me stay here — and 99% of the time I was glad for the distraction from my real life — but sometimes I wished I was already back in my childhood bedroom. I'd be wearing my fluffiest socks, wailing *Love Is A Battlefield* into my hairbrush in front of the mirror, because if that was one thing I'd learned from my mother, it was that Pat Benatar understood my problems.

At least thinking about Darren had taken care of my morning lady wood. Boom. Dry as the Sahara down there.

I got ready for the day and made my way downstairs, back in leggings and a knit jumper I'd snagged from Seth's wardrobe that almost reached my knees and was the coziest thing I'd ever worn. It was probably a little presumptuous to help myself to his clothes, but since I'd broken into their house and got myself off on his lap yesterday, I figured we were past polite pleasantries.

As expected, no one was downstairs, and I was grateful I had the kitchen to myself as I clumsily emulated Seth's coffee-making process that I'd observed yesterday, then reheated the leftover porridge in the fridge. My clattering around eventually attracted company, Eli walking through the front door with a broad grin on his face followed by Noah, who was wearing the same stony expression he'd worn all throughout dinner last night.

"Good morning," I said over the rim of my coffee cup.

"Sleep well, Goldie?" Eli asked, leaning over the back of my chair and smacking a loud kiss against my cheek. He swiped my spoon and helped himself to a spoonful of my porridge before I could smack him away. Goddamn shifters and their fast reflexes. "Mm, *just right*."

Eli winked as Noah scoffed obnoxiously at our cheesy joke.

"Still working on the rocking chair?" I asked, sipping my coffee.

"Hm? No, all good to go. I'll move it to the truck in parts and assemble at Ace's store. I'm working on a dollhouse now," Eli replied, putting on another pot of coffee.

"Are you?" I replied, smiling as I remembered the hours I'd spent with my own dollhouse when I was a kid. "I'm sure that will make someone very happy."

"Here," Noah said, shoving his phone across the table at me. "There's bad weather coming in. You should call your brothers." I blinked at the device before looking up at him.

"He's thinking like a big brother," Eli laughed, his back to us as he poured his coffee. "Storm aside, he'd be stressing if I was staying with strangers out in the woods somewhere."

"No, because you can shift into a vicious bear and look after yourself," Noah snapped. "I'm surprised her brothers let her out of their sight."

"Hey, I can look after myself," I protested. "And my brothers have better things to do than babysit a grown-ass woman."

"Hear that, Noah?" Eli teased. "You can care about your younger siblings *and* have a life of your own."

Noah ignored him, his flat stare solely on me as he pulled out a chair and sat directly across from my spot. He held up a finger, and I sighed preemptively at where this conversation was going.

"One, you could have died when you left the coyote's house *on drugs* with no idea where you were going."

"But I didn't," I sang.

"Two," Noah continued, holding up another finger. "You could have died when you broke into our house. Trust me, it was a close call."

"But still, I didn't," I shot back stubbornly. "Thanks for not killing me, I guess."

"Three." Those fucking fingers. "You *should* have died when you ran off into the woods in the middle of the night in the rain."

"I already thanked you for that," I replied loftily, feeling my cheeks heat.

"Four—"

"Oh my fucking god, Noah!" I groaned, grabbing the phone and stabbing in Vincent's number more aggressively than necessary. "I understand the point you're beating me over the head with."

"Good," he replied, leaning back in his chair with his arms crossed. He didn't look smug, though. Just grumpy. Like my incompetence genuinely concerned him.

"Hello?" Vincent's voice was rough with sleep. He sounded rough in general, actually. Like he'd polished off a packet of cigarettes and a bottle of bourbon before bed.

"Are you okay?" I asked immediately.

"Ria?" Vincent cleared his throat, which morphed into a cough that he tried and failed to cover up. "What's up? Are you okay? Do I need to fuck up some bears?"

Noah snorted, unabashedly eavesdropping.

"Vincent," I admonished. "You sound like shit. What's going on? Where are you?"

"Don't worry about me," he rasped. "Rough night. We're in Seattle, hoping to get a flight today, but we were delayed. Answer my questions."

"I'm fine," I sighed dramatically. "The bears are fine." That sounded natural, right? He probably didn't hear the way I choked a little on that last word.

So, so fine.

"I had this whole lecture planned, but my head is pounding," Vincent admitted. "Please be safe, sis. I'm fucking stressing."

"Not so stressed that you couldn't get shitfaced last night," I pointed out drily, before shoving a spoonful of cold porridge in my mouth.

"Hey, it's a coping mechanism. There's a lot going on right now," Vincent muttered.

"There's a storm coming in tonight," Noah said in a low voice. "If they make it to Fairbanks, they won't be able to get up here until it clears."

"Did you hear that?" I asked Vincent.

"Yeah, I got it," he sighed. There was a scratching noise, like he was rubbing his beard right by the receiver. "Can I reach you on this number?"

Noah nodded in the background. "Yes, you can," I relayed.

"Well, that's something," Vincent muttered. "Please, just be…"

"Careful?" I sighed.

"Smart." *Ouch. Thanks, bro.* "I'll see you as soon as I can. Love you."

"Love you," I murmured, wondering if everyone could hear my wounded pride through my voice. I hung up the phone and slid it back across the table to a silent Noah. Eli was leaning back against the kitchen counter, sipping his coffee and watching me intently.

"One of you better talk. I feel like a bug under a microscope," I grumbled. Noah stood, the sound of his chair scraping against the floor was an obnoxious break in the silence.

"Are you done?" Noah grunted, nodding at my empty bowl.

"Yes," I replied slowly, standing and taking my dishes over to the sink to wash them. He waited a few feet away, arms crossed, an impatient look on his face. If he wanted something, he was going to have to use his big boy words and tell me, I wasn't a fucking mind reader. I finished drying my mug and bowl then turned to look at him, mimicking his posture.

"Come on."

I raised my eyebrows imperiously at him. Sure, it was nice of them to let me stay here, but I wasn't about to be summoned like a dog by anyone.

"Try again, bro," Eli chuckled.

Noah threw a dry look at his brother that almost cracked my resolve. Something about his I-am-not-amused face really got me going.

I don't know what that said about me. Daddy issues? Authority issues? Issues on my fucking issues?

"Come on. *Please.*"

"I'm not sure that's any better, but okay. Where are we going?" I asked, rolling my eyes as I walked past him to grab my beanie from next to the door and tugging it on.

"Vegetable garden. If you're staying, you're pulling your weight," Noah declared, leading me out of the house.

He glanced back over his shoulder like he thought I was going to protest, but I shrugged my shoulders as I wandered after him. I'd grown vegetables in pots at all the various places I'd lived over the years. It was one of the few methods I had for letting off steam with zero self destruction involved.

"So, what's on the agenda?" I asked, deliberately cheerful.

"Harvesting potatoes," Noah grumbled, looking straight ahead as we made our way down the gravel path that ran along the side of the house, to the maze of raised vegetable beds out the back.

God, if I actually thought about how much work they'd put into building this place and the garden at such a young age... It was a little intimidating, to be honest. Or it highlighted my lack of life achievements, at least.

I mean, those tomatoes I grew in pots at my Florida apartment had been pretty great. Probably not enough to live on out in the wilderness, but they'd tasted awesome on my signature Hangover Bruschetta.

Noah led me back to a particularly long garden bed near the back of the property that housed planted rows covered in straw.

"Will you cope getting your hands dirty, thief?" Noah drawled. "We've got to pull all this mulch off. I suppose I can find you some gloves if you need them."

"Well, aren't you a gentleman? I'll manage, thanks," I replied airily, watching Noah grab an armful of straw and emulating his actions.

We worked in silence for a while, uncovering the potato plants. Silent was how I liked Noah best. Despite the chill in the air, he was just wearing a worn black t-shirt that didn't leave a whole lot of his pectoral area to the imagination. If he was quiet, I could appreciate the view without the insults. Especially since he seemed to be marginally impressed that I was pulling my weight. Though I *just* held in a squeal when I felt a slug slithering over my hand.

He would have given me shit for that for sure.

As we cleared the straw away, an abundance of potatoes were visible right on the surface, and I had to begrudgingly admit, Noah's vegetable garden was pretty impressive. Not that he seemed particularly proud or anything.

"Do you like gardening?"

Noah glanced up at me from the potato he was inspecting in his dirt-covered hand.

"It's fine."

"What about rangering? Do you enjoy that?"

Noah huffed impatiently, like I was asking what his birth stone was, or the name of his childhood imaginary friend.

He totally had one. The grumpy ones always did.

"It's *fine*," Noah huffed eventually as I waited expectantly for his answer.

"What a fulfilling life you lead," I replied drily, sifting through the dirt and pulling potatoes free. "What *do* you like?"

"Silence," Noah muttered, but his eyes flashed with something I couldn't quite identify. Maybe he had a secret hobby he didn't want to share with me? My bet was on collecting valuable Beanie Babies. Or whittling tobacco pipes. One of those two things for sure.

I humored him for five minutes, but I couldn't help asking Noah just a few more questions. This was probably the most affable I'd ever seen him.

"So, why do you hate me so much?" I asked conversationally, pleased when Noah's confident movements faltered slightly. He was so grouchy and unapproachable, I doubted he'd been called out directly many times in his life.

"You would assume that," Noah retorted, rolling his eyes like I was the unreasonable one here.

"Let me guess — you don't think about me enough to hate me?" I suggested. Noah's brow furrowed in irritation as I gave him a sweet smile, knowing I'd just taken his stupid comeback right out of his mouth.

"You inconvenience me," Noah settled on eventually, surprising me with an honest answer instead of a meaningless barb.

"Well, I'll be out of your hair shortly," I replied, feeling a little disarmed now we weren't just insulting each other.

"Will you? My brothers might disagree with that."

For the first time, I considered whether Noah's animosity may not be a 'me' thing. I mean, I'd obviously annoyed him by busting into his house — *hello, lock your doors, asshole* — but there was more at play than I realized, and it wasn't all about me.

His brothers wanted to take a mate together, and maybe Noah was worried they were eyeing me up for the job and he wasn't interested in me that way. I'd seen his desire a couple of times, buried under a thick layer of resentment, but he might be afraid they wanted more than just sex.

I didn't think he had anything to worry about on that front.

"This is just a temporary thing," I said slowly, choosing my words carefully. "If you're worried I'm going to change my mind and demand longer, you don't need to be." Noah raised his eyebrow skeptically, and I realized I'd have to give him a little more reassurance.

"Look, Daddy Bear. My entire life has been a series of spontaneous choices and poor decisions. I'm going to be 30 in a couple of months, and I'm nowhere near where I thought I'd be in life."

"So?" Noah asked, but he sounded curious rather than sullen.

"So," I sighed, dumping another armful of potatoes into the wheelbarrow. "I'm going back to New York to be all *new year, new me*, but in September. Except I hate New York, so I'm just going to stay there for a bit until I can move somewhere else.

"Leading options right now are masturbating on camera, or getting my mom to hook me up with a nice fox shifter in the suburbs. One of her friends' sons, who has a decent job and is an all around honest man, if not a little socially awkward and selfish in the bedroom."

Noah blinked at me in bewilderment for a moment — like his brain was trying to translate my words from Ancient Greek to English — before his chest rumbled with a distinctly bear-like growl that made me lose my hold on an armful of potatoes.

"Chill out, would you?" I scolded, crouching on the ground to scoop them up. "If you make bear noises at me, I'm going to react as if there's a bear making noises at me." It was a minor miracle I hadn't peed my pants with the fright he'd given me.

"You're not doing either of those things," Noah ordered, as though he could just speak his will into reality.

"Mm, I probably will, though. Hey, if you're jealous, you should probably endorse option one. At least that way you could watch," I shot back with a saccharine smile before devoting my full attention to the immensely complex task of grabbing potatoes out of the dirt.

I was being glib about it, but I wasn't feeling great about any of the options for my future that were rattling around in my head at this point. I hadn't forgotten my jewelry design dream, but it seemed almost quaint now. *Oh sure, I'll just move in with a guy I barely know, be totally reliant on him financially while I start my own business.*

Smart move, Ria.

No reason I couldn't do that while financially depending on my parents instead, I guess. *Ugh, why was I like this?*

"Can you manage this while I get started on firewood?" Noah muttered eventually, breaking the awkward silence. I was surprised he asked, rather than issued an order. It was almost polite.

"I'm sure I can handle harvesting potatoes."

"You can," Noah replied confidently, brushing the soil off his hands. "Don't sell yourself short," he added with a pointed look.

He turned and walked away, leaving me in the garden alone with my troubled thoughts for the rest of the day, trying to decide if he was talking about more than just vegetables.

ELI

CHAPTER 13

Usually, we all got up early to start our days. Mostly out of habit, I guess. But with a storm already kicking off, we'd all elected to sleep in. Besides, we'd been so slammed yesterday with storm prep that we deserved a break. I'd seen Ria for all of half an hour over dinner because Noah had put her to work in the garden all day, and I'd made a mad dash into town to drop off the rocking chair.

I was having Ria withdrawals already.

Seth had been staying in my bed while Ria was here, which had been kind of unexpected. Noah had the biggest bed — it would be more comfortable for Seth to bunk with him — but Noah had nightmares, and Seth probably didn't want to be that far away from Ria.

I definitely didn't want to be. She'd gotten frisky with Seth in the studio, and I'd feasted on her pussy in the woods like it was my last meal, so really she should just sleep in here with us and we could all enjoy ourselves. I'd extended the invitation, but she'd looked at me like I'd lost my mind and shut the door in my face, so... Maybe tonight?

My bed wasn't really big enough to accommodate all three of us, anyway. Only Noah's bed would work for that. We'd all shared that bed when we lived in the cottage, and there was plenty of room for Ria on there too.

There was lots of room for fun activities as well, but Noah was putting a lot of effort into cock blocking himself, so that would never happen.

Well, not *never*. I just had to do some Cupid-ing to get them to stop sniping at each other for a moment and act on all that sexual tension.

"I'm going to see if Noah wants biscuits and gravy," Seth announced, lying next to me with his arms thrown over his face. We hadn't slept in the same bed since we'd finished building this place with our own separate rooms, and I didn't hate it as much as I thought I would. Those years living in the cottage were hard, but some of my favorite memories with my big brothers were made there.

"Ria would like biscuits," I replied approvingly. "We can surprise her with a nice breakfast. She probably thinks we've all left for the day already."

Seth shot me a look that clearly told me I was being a sappy romantic, but I shrugged my shoulders unapologetically. I wanted Ria to stay. The steady patter of rain on the roof that would only grow more intense as the storm rolled in was a convenient reason to delay her leaving. I wanted more than just a couple of extra days, though.

I wanted her to stay forever and fall in love with us and have a bunch of babies.

Was that too much to ask?

Maybe it was too much to ask *today*. Soon, though. I nodded silently to myself. Definitely soon.

Seth slid out of bed in his pajama pants and quietly made his way downstairs so as not to wake Ria. I doubted she'd be able to hear us over the sound of the rain up here anyway. I dozed a little, enjoying my sleep in, until I heard her door open and the bathroom door shut. A few moments later she let herself back into Seth's room, probably to get dressed, and I figured it was time to get up so we could surprise her downstairs.

I climbed out of bed and looked through my t-shirts for something to wear. Maybe I could sneak a few of my shirts into Seth's room? Ria had been helping herself to his wardrobe, much to Seth's delight, and I wanted to see her in my clothes too.

Or no clothes. No clothes would be much better.

Eventually, I dressed and grabbed one of my sweaters to see if she'd want to wear that. We'd have to get the fire going early today to keep Ria warm.

The landing was quiet and I couldn't hear any noise from downstairs yet. I crossed the short distance and paused outside the door to Seth's room, raising my fist to knock, when a breathy moan pulled me up short.

Then another. *Was she...?*

There was a muffled whine, like Ria had her face buried in a pillow, and I knew I was grinning at the closed door like an idiot. Did she have her face buried in a pillow? Was she fucking her fingers in there? Had she rolled over and used Seth's pillow to keep her quiet?

Shit, my dick was hard enough to hammer nails.

"Whatcha doing, Goldie?" I asked casually, leaning against the door. I mean, I could have left it alone, but if she wanted fingers in her pussy, mine were way longer and thicker. It would be rude of me *not* to offer. I was being gentlemanly.

"What do you think I'm doing?" Ria replied, her voice coming out a little more husky and seductive than she probably meant it to.

"I think you woke up horny and you're taking care of it on your own," I began, listening hard for her answer. *Silence.* "If you want a hand, or a tongue — your call — I'll be across the hall with my door open, fucking my hand and hoping the scent of your arousal drifts through the door."

As much as it pained me, I walked back to my room, quickly shucking my shirt and shoving my hand into my pajama pants to fist my painfully hard dick. *Oh my god, oh my god!* Ria was fucking her hand right across the hallway.

What had we done to deserve someone as funny, smart, and sexually adventurous as Ria to walk through our front door? She was my *dream woman*, and though Seth was way more chill about these things, I knew he was feeling the same way.

I flopped back on my bed, the door wide open as I stroked my dick. Would it be awkward if Seth came back now? Probably. But we'd shared a one-bedroom house all throughout our teenage years. It wouldn't be the first time I'd been busted getting myself off.

Besides, if Ria joined me, it wouldn't be awkward at all. Seth and I would be too busy making her see stars to get weirded out about it.

Thirty seconds later, the door across the hall squeaked open, and I heard Ria's light footsteps approaching before I saw her in all her rumpled, woke-up-horny glory. She was wearing Seth's shirt again — a navy t-shirt that fell to mid-thigh, and I was fucking desperate to know if she had any panties on. There was a challenging glint in Ria's eyes that made me horny as fuck. I liked that she didn't play coy about what she wanted. I'd offered to get her off, and she'd accepted with zero shame.

Maybe she was an angel? A sex angel?

"What'll it be, Goldie?" I purred, cursing myself for not having condoms as she pushed the door shut with a light *snick* behind her.

"Your dick down my throat, please."

Holy fuck, I'm pretty sure I swallowed my own tongue. "You sure?"

"Don't ask stupid questions," Ria replied, rolling her eyes as she climbed up on the end of the bed and crawled her way up to me like a sex kitten. "Lose the pants. I'm horny as hell and this is what I'm in the mood for. To begin with, anyway."

I shoved my pants off and kicked them aside faster than I'd ever moved in my life. If the lady wanted to suck my dick, then the lady could suck my dick.

Ria settled herself in between my legs, wrapping her hand around my cock and giving me a few teasing pumps, a cocky as hell smirk on her face as she pulled her thick curls to one side. She'd told me she liked to be dominated in bed, but she seemed pretty content to take the reins right now, and I wasn't about to stop her.

"I'm pretty sure I dreamed about this," she said seductively.

"Oh yeah? You woke up ready to finger yourself in my brother's bed because you dreamed of sucking me off?" I asked skeptically. *No fucking way.* She'd dreamed about something way filthier than that, I'd put money on it.

"Among other things. Fucking hell, you're big, Eli."

I grinned smugly, crossing my arms behind my head. "Hell yeah, I am."

Ria rolled her eyes, trying and failing to suppress a smile. Then, with zero hesitation, she lowered her head, swirling her tongue around the tip of my cock before taking me into her mouth. All the way into her mouth. Like she just kept going. And going. And fucking going.

Shit. No gag reflex. No fucking gag reflex at all. How was this possible? Heaven was inside Ria's mouth and all the way down her goddamn throat.

I mean, there was no way she could take all of me, but every time I'd had blow jobs in the past, they'd barely got past the tip.

"Fuckkkkk," I groaned, fisting the sheets on either side of me, trying to hold back my orgasm a little longer as Ria's throat contracted around me. I wanted this to go on forever.

I heard even footsteps pause just outside the door, too soft to be Noah's stomp. "Seth's outside the door," I gasped as Ria hollowed her cheeks, sucking my cock like a fucking sorceress. Without missing a beat, she gave a demanding point behind her at the door, then crooked her finger.

Well, okay then.

Was there anything sexier than confidence? I was going to have to think about furniture polish so I didn't embarrass myself.

"Come in," I called, my voice sounding way more strangled than usual.

Seth pushed open the door slowly, making far more noise than he usually would. I knew he was trying to be a gentleman, but the moment he saw Ria ass up on the bed, sucking my dick like it was the source of life itself, it was all over. *What a view.* I craned my neck a little, trying to figure out if she was wearing panties under Seth's t-shirt.

Ria oh-so-slowly drew back up, and I'm pretty sure I blacked out for a minute at how good it felt.

"Jesus," Seth muttered, kicking the door shut behind him.

"I'm not sure about that, but I'm definitely having a religious experience over here," I groaned as Ria released me with a *pop*.

"Are you going to join us? You both said you were fine with this whole sharing thing, right?" Ria asked, looking back over her shoulder and batting her eyelashes at Seth. As if he would say no.

"Very fine with it," I answered for both of us.

Seth kneeled at the end of the bed, still wearing his pajama pants and no shirt, then leaned over to run his hand over the back of Ria's leg.

"Oh," Ria said, sitting back on her heels suddenly. I swear my dick lurched like it was going to follow her. She shuffled on her knees towards me on the bed and grabbed my hand, guiding up to her upper inner arm. She pressed my fingers down, and I snatched my hand back in surprise when I felt something under her skin.

"Relax," Ria laughed, rolling her eyes at me before grabbing Seth's hand and repeating the gesture. He was way cooler about it than me, the asshole. "It's a birth control implant," Ria explained.

Seth clicked faster than I did. "You're saying pregnancy isn't a concern."

"And diseases aren't a concern, since you're both shifters," Ria surmised. "So if you're happy to proceed without condoms, so am I."

I all but tackled her to the bed, rolling her onto her back with a grin. My cock nestled against the heat of her pussy through the thin panties she apparently was wearing, and I could probably have come from that alone.

"I don't think so," Ria tutted. "I'm gonna need more foreplay before either of you stick your monster shifter cocks in me."

Before I could come up with a smart retort, I was shoved to the side, landing on my back next to Ria while Seth pushed her knees apart, ripped her panties clean off her body, and dove face-first into her pussy. I rolled onto my side, propping my head on my hand, watching as Ria's back arched, a moan escaping her lips.

"Feel good, Goldie?" I murmured, reaching out to toy with her sensitive nipples over the fabric of the shirt.

"Are we having a threesome right now?" she gasped. "Oh my god, we are. We're actually having a threesome. This is fucking Christmas."

"Fuck yeah we are," I replied, moving closer to capture her lips with mine.

"Remember your safe word?" Seth murmured, head still buried between her thighs.

"Safe word is red," Ria replied obediently, her lips moving against mine. Seth must have done something to reward her, because she squeaked before sinking her teeth enthusiastically into my lip.

"How do you feel about anal?" I asked optimistically.

"Big fan," Ria replied breathily. "I've always wanted to be filled up by two dicks at once, so if you two could make that dream come true, I'll be forever in your debt. It's the top item on my Fuck-It List."

"Fuck the debt thing, we're for sure doing that. Shit, my balls are hurting," I replied, my words all running together in my excitement.

"Calm down," Seth ordered, glancing up at me over the line of Ria's body. She shot me a smug grin, like she found nothing more amusing than me getting told off, but I knew it was just Seth warming up.

He was about to get bossy as hell up in here.

I kept that observation to myself, helping Ria out of the oversized t-shirt while Seth devoured her, so I had better access to her nipples. I kept my touches teasing and gentle, sensing that Seth was backing off every time Ria got close.

"Are you edging me?" Ria moaned. "Because I'll be honest, I *say* I like being edged, but I'm more of an instant gratification kind of girl."

"Mm, that's why he's doing it," I chuckled darkly, leaning over her to suck her nipple into my mouth and releasing it with a *pop*. "It's going to feel so fucking good when you come."

"It'd feel good if I came now," Ria whined.

"Patience. You have a safe word if it gets too much, remember?" Seth replied calmly before flipping Ria over easily, guiding her onto all fours and resuming his feast. Her head flopped forward, hiding her face in a tangle of messy golden curls as she let out a long moan.

"Fuckkkkkk," Ria sighed, rolling her hips back against Seth a few times before he clamped a hand down on her ass, pinning her in place.

"Let me see your face," I commanded softly, moving up the bed onto my knees so I could take in the magnificent view in front of me.

Ria looked up at me at that moment and her pupils were so blown, the brown and gold flecks of her eyes were barely visible. She licked her lips, her gaze seeking out my erection, and I wasn't about to say no to getting my cock back in her magical mouth.

I shifted forward and Ria opened her mouth eagerly, taking me as far into her throat as she could with Seth pinning her in place. She reached forward, grabbing my wrist and guiding it to her hair. I chuckled as I gathered it into a ponytail and held it firm, letting her set the pace, but guiding her movements.

Experimentally, I tugged lightly and was rewarded with a muffled moan that vibrated all the way up my cock. I wanted to learn every single thing that made Ria moan. Every sensitive spot on her body, every filthy word that made her wet, every fantasy she'd ever had. If she'd let me, I'd bring them all to life.

Seth's hand disappeared between Ria's legs and she practically screamed around my dick, writhing frantically despite her limited mobility.

"I can feel how close you are, sweetheart," Seth murmured. "Give me that orgasm."

It was either a well-timed command or Ria was a very obedient sub, because her back arched and she moaned around my cock before pulling off me, gasping for air, eyes clenched shut in ecstasy. I could watch Ria come *all day*. It was the most beautiful thing I'd ever seen.

Seth had lowered his head again, drawing her orgasm out as long as he could, never letting up. I maintained my grip on Ria's hair, stroking my cock as she rode out wave after wave of bliss. Ria would be more than ready to take us after Seth was done making her lose her mind.

Ria panted, and I took a brief break from my dick to wipe her cheek with my thumb. "So good he made your eyes water, huh?" I teased.

She squirmed away from Seth's touch and he sat back, looking proud of his handiwork as he wiped his mouth with the back of his hand.

"Oh my god, that was like a hundred orgasms in one," Ria laughed. "I think I've peaked. That was the pinnacle of my sexual experience for the rest of my life. Nothing can compete."

Seth looked smug while I growled, pulling Ria with me as I laid on my back, positioning her over me. "Don't speak so soon, Goldie. You haven't had us inside you yet."

"I'm not convinced that's physically possible," Ria muttered, bracing her hands on my chest. She lowered her hips until the heat of her pussy rubbed over my cock, making us both gasp.

"You are soaked, Goldie," I choked.

Seth moved up behind her, gathering her hair in his fist and guiding her head back until their lips met, his other hand slid over her shoulder to cup her throat. Ria relaxed into his hold, body going pliant and hips moving faster, building the friction between us.

"Ready?" Seth asked, pulling her up and meeting her eyes. Ria nodded, face hazy with lust, and I reached between us, lining myself up with her entrance. "Slow," Seth commanded, looking at me this time.

"Of course," I replied, running my hands up Ria's thighs and gripping her hips as she slowly sank down my length with a breathy sigh, eyes glazed over.

"Fuck," I gasped. "So goddamn wet and hot and tight and, holy shit…"

Think of furniture polish, think of furniture polish.

Despite my assurances that I'd fit, I hadn't actually expected her to take all of me. It had never happened before. But Ria kept going and going until our thighs touched, and she looked as high on sex as I felt.

"That feels incredible," Ria moaned. "Move me. I don't have the quads for this."

I met Seth's eyes as his mouth twitched in amusement. He wasn't naturally playful, but it was impossible not to be a bit silly around Ria.

I obliged her request, shifting my grip to the back of her thighs and holding her in place as I thrust up into her, careful at first, until she got used to my size. Seth maintained his light hold around Ria's throat, massaging it with his thumb and leaning forward to nip at her shoulders and the back of her neck.

They were only temporary marks, like the finger-shaped bruises I'd probably leave on her thighs, but I'd never felt the urge to mark a lover before, and I was confident Seth hadn't either.

I wanted to sink my teeth into her. I wanted to *claim* her.

Not today, I reminded myself. That was probably the kind of thing we should have a conversation about first.

"I'm going to come again," Ria stuttered, sounding surprised at herself.

"Hell yeah, you are," I growled. "Then we're taking this up a notch. Lube's in the top drawer," I added for Seth's benefit. We may not have condoms, but a shit ton of masturbation happened in this house. Lube, we could do.

Seth guided Ria forward until her forearms were braced on my chest, and I leaned up to capture her lips, upping my pace now I was confident she could handle it. Seth rubbed circles over her perky ass cheeks, and Ria rocked back to the sensation.

"Do it," she pleaded, glancing over her shoulder at Seth, who smirked at her.

"I'd rather keep you in suspense, sweetheart. Focus on Eli."

Ria poked her tongue out at him and I pulled her face back towards me, licking the side of her cheek.

"I'm needy. Give me your attention," I ordered. Ria snorted, but it quickly transformed into an entirely different sound as I slammed into her, giving her all of me. Maybe it was because Ria was a carrier, but she didn't seem to physically struggle with my size at all.

I felt her flutter around me and nodded at Seth, who swatted Ria's ass with a satisfying *thwack*.

"Fuck!" Ria gasped. *"Yes, yes, yes."*

He alternated sides, spanking her at an even pace until Ria's orgasm hit like a hurricane, her pussy strangling me as she fell forward onto my chest, her teeth scraping over my skin as she muffled her screams against me.

Fuck. Furniture polish. Furniture polish.

Seth moved quickly, swiping the lube from the drawer and shucking his pants. He applied it liberally to himself before kneeling behind Ria. She sighed dreamily as he began massaging her back entrance, sucking a light hickey onto my neck.

"You've done this before," I laughed.

"Anal? Yes. Threesome? No," she replied, biting me again. "I can't believe I'm starting the day with two dicks inside me. This really seems like a middle of the night, little bit drunk activity."

"Fuck that," I snorted. "I want to be awake and completely sober so I don't forget a single second of this."

Ria pushed herself up on her arms again, her eyes losing focus as Seth pushed a finger into her, then another, scissoring until she was panting with need. I wanted to tell him to hurry the fuck up because all her writhing was making it impossible to hold off my orgasm, but I knew what he was waiting for.

"Seth! Please! I need you," Ria gasped eventually, and I sighed in relief.

"Of course, sweetheart," Seth murmured, amused as he pulled his fingers free and lined up his dick. I sucked in a breath, forcing myself to stay still so she could adjust to both of us, but *holy fuck* it had already been tight.

"Oh shit, I am not going to last much longer," I muttered, my fingers squeezing the back of Ria's thighs.

"Neither...am...I," she choked as Seth pushed forward, stroking her back and murmuring softly to her, encouraging her to relax. "I feel so full. In the best way. Oh my god, how am I ever going back to regular sex again?"

You don't have to, I thought, but I didn't want to freak her out mid-threesome, so I kept the thought to myself.

Seth and I took over, alternating our movements and holding Ria between us, a limp mess of lust and need. The soft moans and keening whines as her approaching orgasm were music to my fucking ears, driving me towards my own release.

Ria slid her hand between us to toy with her clit, sending us both over the edge. My thrusts faltered as I came so hard my vision blurred. I'd never experienced anything close to it. My well was truly empty by the time Ria had finished contracting around me, and Seth fell still, bracing his hands on Ria's back as he found his release.

All three of us were sweaty, sticky, and breathing like we'd just run a marathon. Ria's hair had flown over my face, and I attempted to blow it away, too lazy and blissed out to lift my arms.

"So?" I asked, my eyes drifting shut. "Expectations met?"

"Expectations well and truly exceeded," Ria murmured, nuzzling into my chest.

"Good," Seth replied, pushing himself up with a groan so Ria wasn't taking his weight. "Give me a minute, and I'll run you a bath."

"Give me two minutes, and we can go again?" I suggested hopefully.

"We're going to need longer than that for my healing genes to kick in," Ria laughed. "Rain check?"

"Fucking rain check."

RIA

CHAPTER 14

I was a satisfied, boneless mess the entire day. Not even Noah's presence and the fact that he'd clearly heard everything we were doing upstairs could put a dampener on my mood. I mean, I didn't feel great about that fact, but I was still too high on my orgasms to really let it get to me.

It seemed like the kind of thing I'd lie in bed and beat myself up over five years from now. I'd leave it for Future Ria to deal with.

With the storm rolling in, the guys had been busy getting everything prepared. Seth and Eli moved some of their projects into the house so they could work on them here while Noah had been doing storm-prep chores outside that may or may not have been a convenient excuse to avoid all of us. I'd washed the few items of clothing I'd brought with me and then made myself useful by tidying up and baking brownies. Who didn't like brownies? That was a pretty solid 'thank you for letting me crash here even longer' present.

"Let's do family game night," Eli announced. "Or family game afternoon, rather."

"Game night?" I asked, eyebrows raised. I guess it made sense, it's not like they had a television.

"Ever played Trivial Pursuit?" Eli asked, a glimmer of challenge in his eyes.

I scoffed. "Um, yes. And I am fucking amazing at it. You sure you wanna do this, Baby Bear?"

"I'm not okay with that nickname," Eli laughed. "Does that make Seth 'Mama Bear'? Because I doubt he'd be down with that nickname either."

"I most definitely am not," Seth confirmed lightly, grabbing a well-worn Trivial Pursuit box off the bookshelf and placing it in the center of the dining table.

"And yet no one seems to care about my Daddy Bear nickname," Noah grumbled.

"It's because it suits you," I replied instantly. "We all agree."

I smiled sweetly at the filthy look Noah gave me, though it was a little less vehement than usual. He might have been warming up to me, in a grumpy, reluctant kind of way.

Maybe he'd liked hearing me come? I'd always thought my raspy voice sounded pretty sexy in bed, to be honest. Maybe instead of being a cam girl, I could record ASMR sex noises instead.

Noah's eyes narrowed on me like he could sense that I was thinking about something dirty, his stare morphing into a glare when I winked at him.

"I vote we play in teams — Ria and I versus the twins," Eli announced.

"No," Seth said immediately, shaking his head. "Ria is on my team."

"That's not fair," Eli protested. "You two are the smartest, you'll trounce Noah and I. Besides, Ria likes me more. Right, Ria?"

"Wrong," I replied flatly. "You're both... fine." That was something of an understatement, but their egos were plenty big enough, and I couldn't choose between them anyway.

"Just fine, hm?" Eli teased, eyes twinkling. "You don't want to be on Seth's team. He's not really smart, he's just good at this game because he secretly pulls out the cards and memorizes the answers," he mock whispered, dodging as Seth went to cuff him over the head.

"Jealousy isn't a good look on you, Eli," Seth replied, rolling his eyes.

"I'll take the thief," Noah announced decisively, ending their argument.

All three of us looked at him in surprise. Er, Noah was voluntarily going to be on my team? Had the sky fallen in? Were pigs flying? Maybe this was the end of days?

"I'd say this is a big step for you," Eli began, grinning at his big brother. "But you suck at this game and probably just want Ria so you can win for a change."

"I want you two to stop arguing over her," Noah grumbled.

"I knew you liked me, really." I pulled my chair around next to Noah and batted my eyelashes obnoxiously at him, while Seth pulled the game out of the box.

"Not even a little."

I'm pretty sure that meant definitely a little.

I chose the yellow wheel for Noah and I, while Eli and Seth picked the blue as we got into position on the board.

"Ladies first," Seth said, offering me the dice.

"Are you sure you want to give me any advantages? I am the kind of competitive that makes my family not want to play games with me," I warned.

"Ooh, so is Noah. Except he doesn't have the talent to back up the attitude," Eli replied gleefully. "This should be fun."

"Fuck off," Noah muttered, though I could have sworn his cheeks looked a little darker. I rolled the dice and moved our wheel onto a pink square.

"Entertainment," I announced. "Hit me. I mean us," I added hastily, glancing at Noah out of the corner of my eye.

There was a reason I was always chosen last for team sports, and that reason was that I played terribly with others.

Except in threesomes, apparently. I felt like I'd done pretty well in that arena. I was giving myself a gold medal for that performance.

"Okay, here's your question. What was Britney Spears' first song?" Seth asked, glancing up at Noah, mouth twitching in amusement.

Noah made a frustrated noise before turning in his chair to stare at the side of my face. I guessed that was his way of deferring to me for an answer? I was somewhat proud of myself that I was learning to interpret the combination of grunts, scowls, and body language that Noah communicated in.

"Hmmm. Was it *Oops! I Did It Again*?" I pondered to myself, straining my memory to the heyday of music videos and pop music. "No, no, the school girl outfit definitely came before the red catsuit. *Baby One More Time*. Final answer," I replied confidently.

"Correct," Seth said with a slow half smile that made me tingle. Ugh, he had such a hot professor vibe going on right now in his knit sweater. I flashed Noah a winning smile as he grunted at me like a barbarian.

"I *did* do good, didn't I?" I asked him as Seth and Eli took their turn. He gave me a flat stare back.

Oh yeah, he was definitely warming up to me.

I pulled their question out of the box and offered it to Noah to read, who raised his eyebrow silently in response. "Alright. I'll do the asking and the answering. I gotta say, Daddy Bear, you're not bringing a lot to the table right now. Seth, Eli, here's your question — which country produces the most coffee in the world?"

They argued quietly between themselves and I wished again for shifter hearing so I could listen in on their conversation, because it looked hilarious. Eli gestured wildly, and a vein in Seth's forehead was working overtime in response. I glanced at Noah out of the corner of my eye and noticed him watching his brothers. The usually tense set of his mouth and hardness in his eyes softened as he observed them. For all Noah's many asshole tendencies, he clearly adored his brothers. That made me dislike him a smidge less.

Actually, I'd been disliking him a lot less since we'd semi bonded over potatoes. Which was unfortunate, because Noah's hostility had been a great motivator for me to go back to New York. The more I liked him, the harder it would be to leave.

"Columbia," Eli announced. "Final answer."

"Not my final answer," Seth groused.

"I'm right," Eli shot back with totally unwarranted confidence.

"You're wrong," I laughed.

"If it's Brazil, we're taking a break from play so I can punch Eli in the face," Seth muttered. Eli grinned, not worried in the slightest.

"It is Brazil," I confirmed.

Eli leaped up from the table, crossing the room and diving over the couch with Seth hot on his heels. Noah made a strange noise I hadn't heard before — possibly laughter? — but I didn't pay him any mind while I watched Seth tackle Eli to the ground, both of them laughing as they wrestled. It was a testament to their skill that they hadn't broken any furniture while they roughhoused, because they were definitely big enough to if they landed on anything.

"I yield! I yield!" Eli laughed. "Sorry! You were right, oh wise one."

Seth snorted, standing up and reaching out to pull Eli to his feet. It was a side of Seth I hadn't seen before — more playful, more physical — and I liked it a lot.

Like, *a lot.*

Post-threesome, I'd been feeling more than a little tender, but the combination of a long, hot bath and my suped up healing genes meant I was back to normal now, and more than ready for round two.

Probably best not to put Noah through that again, I reminded myself. I could be a considerate house guest when I wanted to be.

We continued playing for half an hour as the rain poured down in sheets outside, hammering against the roof of the cabin. Inside, we were warm and cozy with the fire roaring and candlelight flickering, illuminating the darkening house even though it was only late afternoon.

There was a stuttering sound and the one light we'd had on flickered out, the reassuring hum of the refrigerator going with it.

"Generator's out," Eli groaned. "Whose turn is it?"

"Yours," Noah responded instantly. "But you don't know how to fix it."

"I'm pretty sure I do," Eli said with a nonchalant shrug.

"I'd rather not risk our already temperamental generator," Noah replied wryly. "I'll come with you. These two can start dinner, the gas is still working."

"Alright," Seth agreed. "I'll cook the fish in the fridge tonight, just in case you can't get the power back on."

Noah and Eli layered up in waterproof clothes before heading out into the storm. Noah looked his usual level of surly, but Eli was practically digging his heels into the ground as he left. I'm not sure if he naturally didn't like doing this kind of thing or if his big brothers had spoiled him by taking care of these things since he was young.

"You don't have to help cook if you don't want to," Seth said, moving into the kitchen. "I'll get you a beer and you can keep me company instead."

"How about you get me a beer *and* I'll help you cook? Compromise," I responded, feeling full of warm fuzzy feelings that had no right to be there.

"Deal," Seth replied, grabbing two bottles from the fridge and uncapping them. He passed me one and held his up, clinking it against mine before taking a long swig, eyes glued to mine the entire time, the candlelight flickering around us.

Ugh, as if this night could get any cozier and more romantic.

Danger ahead, my brain warned me.

I thought I was a pretty decent cook, but I had no idea what to do when Seth withdrew and pulled an entire fish out of the fridge for dinner. Eyeballs and all. What the fuck was I supposed to do with that?

His lips twitched in amusement as he took in my apprehensive expression. "Never filleted a fish before?"

I shook my head, wondering why I'd ever thought I could live in the wilderness. Clearly, I was vastly under-prepared for what that life would actually look like.

"I'll do the fish, you do the sides?" he proposed.

"Deal," I agreed readily. Mashed sweet potatoes and sauteed green beans, coming right up.

Oh dear, I was having another one of those this-is-domestic-bliss moments that made my chest ache. This was the real deal version of the life I'd envisioned myself having when I'd stupidly agreed to move in with Darren.

It wasn't just the lifestyle, though. It was *them*.

Noah, not so much, though I still wanted to screw the grumpy out of him. But Seth was so quietly thoughtful, and Eli was fun personified.

I thought I was just breaking into a nice house, but it was actually an incredible home, and I'd be sad to say goodbye once this storm had passed.

We worked easily together in the small space, moving around each other when we needed to, and it never felt crowded. Seth didn't fill the silence with chatter the way Eli did — not that I minded, but the quiet was nice too.

But the longer we were there, the more I noticed us gravitating towards each other. The brush of our arms as we stood side by side, or the occasional touch of our fingers as we reached for ingredients. Seth walked behind me to get to the oven, and I don't think I imagined the barest slide of his hand over the curve of my ass.

This was foreplay, I realized a little late and feeling more than a little stupid. Seth was subtle in all things, and this was no different. Each brief touch was a deliberate tease, making me chase after more contact.

With the food cooked and set aside, covered, waiting for the others to get back, the sexual tension became impossible to ignore. Seth carefully moved the board game to the coffee table so as not to lose our positions, and I swiped another beer before sitting at the dining table, needing the cold liquid to extinguish a little of the heat I was feeling.

It's not a good time, I reminded myself. *Noah and Eli could be back at any moment. They've already been gone for ages.*

Still. The electricity hadn't turned back on yet. They could be hours...

I rubbed my thighs together under the table, trying to relieve some of the ache I was feeling. *Shit*, he could probably *smell* my arousal. Goddamn shifter noses. Seth was a gentleman though, unlike his brothers. If he could scent anything, he didn't let on.

Was he tugging down his sweater a little more than usual? I was probably imagining it.

I should stand up and help him, but in my current position with my elbows resting on the table, leaning forward, my nipples that were hard enough to cut glass remained hidden behind my hair.

This was very bad. Where was Noah? I needed him to make some snarky remark about me being a criminal delinquent to squash this burning desire. Seth was walking around being unendingly sweet and obscenely attractive, and I knew from this morning that he could get freaky in the bedroom. After months of vanilla sex with Darren, my freak tank desperately needed filling.

Fuck. Fuck. Fuckity fuck fuck! I was totally going to jump his bones right here and hope for the best. I shifted around a little on the hard wooden chair, trying to get comfortable. The movement parted my thighs for the briefest moment, but I was only wearing lace panties and thin leggings. And if I could smell my arousal, Seth definitely could.

I saw the exact moment it registered. Seth had his back to me, standing in front of the sink washing a dish. His back tensed, head snapping up, his deep inhale loud enough for me to hear from my spot at the table a few feet away. I should have been embarrassed, but the fact that he knew how I was feeling, that it had affected him so viscerally, only made me hotter. My breath escaped in short pants as I tried and failed to wrangle my sexual appetite under control.

"Sweetheart," Seth drawled, still not looking at me. Oh god, I had a Pavlovian response to him calling me 'sweetheart'. I felt his voice everywhere. It traveled through my body, landing with a sharp *zing* at my clit.

"Yes, Seth?" I asked in a strained voice, attempting to sound cool and failing miserably.

I watched avidly as he turned to face me, drying his hands slowly before setting the towel down on the counter. His movements were controlled, and I knew that any intimacy between Seth and I wasn't a result of a moment of weakness, or heat of the moment passion.

It was because he *wanted* it to happen. That idea was immensely attractive.

"Sweetheart," he repeated, an almost warning edge to his voice that dared me to lie to him. "Is there something you need?"

"Do I... do you need me to tell you that I'm wet enough for you to smell my arousal from the other side of the kitchen?" I asked incredulously.

Seth smirked, a heady look of expectation in his gaze that told me he was still waiting for a proper answer. Oh, yes. There was that dominant control freak who came out to play the second I gave him the go-ahead.

Still, I didn't want to make it *too* easy for him.

"Dessert. I need dessert." I tipped my chin up stubbornly, holding his gaze even as my brain told me to submit. He was a big, alpha predator and I was defenseless prey, but I wasn't about to give him my submission unless he earned it.

"Dessert smells like a wonderful idea."

Seth prowled towards me, eyes impossibly dark with desire, but his pace was deliberately slow. Giving me time to say no. Leaving the power in my hands.

"Smells?" I repeated vaguely, twisting sideways and drawing my legs out from under the table in invitation. *Yes. Give me more.*

"Smells," he confirmed, stopping a foot in front of me.

He nodded his head once, anticipation shining from his hooded eyes. "Leggings off. Panties, too. Sit on the edge of the table."

This was probably unhygienic, but fuck it. There were candles, a roaring fire, a storm outside, and a power outage. Throw in two consenting adults who were crazy horny for each other, and it was basically a recipe for frantically fucking on the dining room table.

"I don't need foreplay," I breathed as Seth dropped to his knees and pushed my thighs apart so fast, I fell back onto my elbows.

"This is for me," he growled before flatting his tongue against my pussy and licking up to lap my clit.

"Oh fuck," I sighed, staring up at the ceiling, chest heaving as my stomach started to clench already. *Do not come,* I ordered myself. That would be embarrassingly fast.

Seth seemed determined to test my resolve though, busting out some fucking *wizardry* with his tongue that made sparks appear behind my eyes. I hoped he wouldn't edge me again, but I had a feeling if I demanded he not, he'd do it on purpose.

I mean, if I hated it, I could use my safe word, and I was absolutely confident that Seth would respect that.

I felt my release building, and sunk my teeth into my lower lip, needing to anchor myself somehow and having nothing to hold on to on the bare table. Maybe Seth was a mind reader, because he stood up at that moment, pulled up into a sitting position with his arms around my waist, and filled me with one smooth movement.

I shattered around him, clinging desperately to his shirt as he fucked me like a man possessed until one orgasm rolled into another. As soon as the high dissipated, he was on me, tongue plunging roughly into my mouth, fucking me as thoroughly as his cock was.

"Give me one more," Seth commanded against my mouth, nipping my lower lip with his teeth. "Come with me."

"Yes!" I gasped, wrapping my legs around him and digging my heels into the rough denim of the jeans he hadn't even pulled all the way down. That he was mostly dressed, and I was naked from the waist down only made our encounter sexier, more illicit.

Seth's mouth trailed down my neck and tilted it to the side, giving him better access. His teeth scraped over where my neck met my shoulder before he bit down lightly, not enough to break the skin, but enough to tip me over the edge.

I clenched around his cock, gulping down air as I dug my nails into his shoulders, clinging to him like a life raft in a storm. My name fell from his lips in a choked cry as Seth stilled, his forehead dropping to where I could feel the ghost of his teeth on my skin.

Biting was not a small thing for shifters.

A proper bite, with intent, was a mating claim. That much I remembered from my mother's sex talk.

I doubted that was what Seth had been thinking, though. We'd only just met each other. And he was going to take a mate with his brothers, anyway. I wasn't about to read into it and make things weird.

"The power's back on!" I gasped, suddenly registering the hum of the refrigerator and the increased light in the room.

"Shit," Seth muttered, pulling out messily. He glanced between my legs like he was surprised by what he found there, and I lost my battle with the giggles I was trying to suppress.

"Sorry," he said, mouth twitching. "I've, er, never not used condoms. Not before you."

"It's messy," I agreed, ignoring the weird little flutter in my chest. *Stupid.* "Hand me my underwear, would you? I'll run upstairs and clean up."

Seth did one better, kneeling down and pulling them up my legs for me, before lifting me gently off the table and tugging them up completely.

His hands lingered on my hips, and I rested mine on his chest, looking up at him. Something passed between us, a current of emotion I didn't understand, but before I could analyze it, the front door banged open.

Noah and Eli walked in the house, dripping wet with mud up to their knees. The storm raged on behind them as they stripped their filthy clothes just inside the doorway; the action kept them distracted for a moment.

I don't know what I expected to happen. Perhaps for Seth to jump away from me like I was a leper and pretend nothing had happened, which was an unfair assessment of his character. Seth had been nothing but gentlemanly. With impressive speed, he tugged his jumper over his head with one hand and yanked it over my head, my arms stuck inside the material that covered me to my thighs.

"Holy shit," Eli laughed, stopping dead in his tracks, as he moved towards us, just wearing a pair of boxers and a singlet, both of which stuck to his damp skin.

Shit, just when my libido had been settling down.

Noah snorted, striding past us without pause, like he wasn't surprised in the least. He did slam the downstairs bathroom door behind him a little harder than necessary, though.

"Well, I'm glad you guys had fun while we were out there in the rain," Eli said, grinning broadly. "The only problem is you need to clean up, and I need to clean up, and there's only one bathroom left..." he trailed off, waggling his eyebrows suggestively.

"That doesn't sound like such a problem to me," I replied, still sort of feeling like I was in the Twilight Zone. This didn't just happen in real life, right? You didn't just get to bang one hot brother in the kitchen then instantly go fuck another one in the shower, and everyone just be fine with it.

You were impaled on both their cocks this morning, Ria, I reminded myself. It was a bit late for modesty now.

"Don't take too long, dinner's ready," Seth said, pressing a kiss against my temple and stepping back as Eli snagged my hand and tugged me towards the stairs.

NOAH

CHAPTER 15

I was a coward.

A giant, useless coward.

Recognizing that fact didn't make me feel any better about it.

I had spent the night hiding in my own home, briefly stepping out to grab some food when I was sure the others had gone to bed — separately, surprisingly — before escaping the lingering scent of Aurelia and Seth that might remain in the kitchen forever now, then going back to my room.

It wasn't a secret that I was hiding apparently, since Eli had knocked on my door and laughingly told me the coast was clear before he went up to bed, but I couldn't find it in myself to prove them wrong and walk out there.

Everything smelled like her. The entire cabin. At least in my bedroom, I could keep the windows open without worrying about her freezing to death. I'd been walking around the house with the kind of boner that no amount of masturbation could cure since the little thief had a threesome with my brothers in Eli's room, *directly* above my head.

I wasn't proud of the fact that I'd gotten myself off to the sound of her moans. It would be a shame I'd have to live with long after she'd gone back to New York.

Or would it? We might be stuck with her at this rate.

Why the fuck did she have to smell so good? Like honey and wildflowers.

Pull yourself together, Noah.

I was glad I was on duty today. Usually heading out in a storm was one of my least favorite things, but the smell of clean air and damp earth was exactly the cleanse to my senses that I needed. Not that it was perfect. Even now, miles away from the house and in the pouring rain, Aurelia's scent seemed to follow me around. Maybe it had embedded in my skin and I'd be stuck with her forever.

Logically, I knew the thief smelled like temptation because she was a carrier. She was biologically designed to signal shifters that she was a viable option as a mate. A lot of shifters would overlook her because she couldn't shift herself, but physically she was no less desirable.

But even knowing that, explaining it away as just biology, there were a lot of female shifters in this area. Most of them were mated now, but even when they'd been single, they'd never smelled like that. I'd never felt drawn to them the way I did to Aurelia.

I hated it.

I hated change. I hated unpredictability. I hated risk.

Mostly, I hated anything that had the potential to cause my brothers pain. They had lived through enough pain to last them a lifetime already.

Not a single night went by where I didn't have nightmares about the fire. I had been so, *so* close to being too late to save my brothers. We weren't supposed to be home that day — our mother had sent us out into the woods for the day, which she often did when she was feeling overwhelmed — but Eli hadn't been feeling well, so I'd decided to bring him back early.

We wouldn't have been there if I hadn't dragged them back to the house.

The nightmares were fuzzy, the same broken memories flashing on repeat through my mind. The heat of the flames licking at my skin. The effort of holding my bear back so I could fit through the narrow gap to get to Eli, already unconscious from smoke inhalation. The loud, terrifying crack as the beam above us gave way and I thought I'd lost Seth forever.

The roar of his bear when he shifted for the first time, saving his life.

I rubbed my eyes, glad for the chill of the rain waking me up. The nightmares hadn't gotten any worse, but Aurelia's presence in the house hadn't helped with my sleep issues. I was fucking *exhausted* all of the time.

She was all the things I avoided. Risky. Unpredictable. And on the brink of causing my brothers a great deal of misery. She was *leaving*. Back to New York, probably to mate with a suitable fox shifter of her mother's choosing, based on what she'd told me.

I refused to entertain the other plan she'd suggested.

A fallen tree blocking the road distracted me from my obsessive thoughts about the walking, talking sin living in my house. I checked that there were no humans in the vicinity before lifting one end of the log onto my shoulders, my entire body shaking with exertion. My muscles burned, but the pain was a welcome distraction.

There was no room in my head for anything else when I was trying to breathe through the pain of burning lungs and aching muscles. Her honey and wildflower scent couldn't tease me when I could barely choke down fresh air.

I hauled the fallen tree sideways until it ran next to the road, clearing the way for vehicles, though the mud was so thick, I doubted any would come this way soon. I dropped the log with a crash, stepping back to catch my breath and brush the dirt off my hands.

If only I could find a few more of those, I could pass the day in a blur of sweat and sore muscles, then go back home exhausted enough to fall asleep instantly. I could hope.

Satisfied that this area was clear, I traipsed through the mud back into the depths of the forest, tipping my head back to let the refreshing rain fall on my face and run over my beard. It was even longer than usual. Eli often joked that my beard length was an indicator of my emotional state or some bullshit. Sue me if I was a little distracted lately and forgot to shave. It wasn't a fucking crime.

Unlike breaking and entering someone's home. That was very much a fucking crime. Why hadn't I just taken her into the police station in Fairbanks that day? They already knew me, they wouldn't have doubted my version of events for a second.

Maybe because the idea of her alone and vulnerable in a jail cell makes you want to punch something, my brain reminded me unhelpfully.

"She would have been fine," I muttered under my breath, silencing my stupid subconscious.

They weren't empty words, either. Aurelia made some incredibly stupid decisions regarding her safety that I would happily remind her about for the rest of her time with us, but she seemed like a reasonably capable person who could charm her way out of almost any situation. It was impressive, and that fact irritated me because I wanted to despise everything about her on principle.

Why did she have to be so fucking cute?

Why did they have to want to keep her?

Seth and Eli had always assumed we'd choose a mate together. We didn't *have* to, but we'd been through everything side-by-side, my brothers and I. Staying together was a choice. I couldn't imagine any of us going through something as life changing as taking a mate and starting a family separately.

If they'd ever actually asked me, I would have admitted that I wasn't as sold on the idea of taking or sharing a mate as they were. They'd assumed I was, and I'd never corrected them. Seth and I were approaching 40, and they'd never met anyone they even considered getting serious about, so why bring it up? I didn't think I'd be able to avoid the conversation much longer. They'd expect an explanation. They'd want to know *why*.

Protecting my brothers had been a full-time job for as long as I could remember. A mate would demand even more from me. Even if I wasn't protecting them *from* her, it would be another person to take care of.

Though would the thief demand too much? She could be obnoxious — though I didn't hate her obnoxiousness as much as I should — and she was disorganized, but she hadn't *asked* much of us. Each morning we'd all gone out to do our respective tasks, and she'd been seemingly happy to stay out of our way. She hadn't balked at getting her hands dirty in the garden, and had voluntarily started helping Seth in the kitchen.

Maybe she wouldn't be the worst person to live with.

Not that it mattered. It was obvious she didn't see me the same way she saw my brothers. Even if Eli and Seth wanted her to stick around, it was pointless to think about her with all three of us.

Maybe she'd like you if you weren't such an asshole.

Probably not.

Eli was funny, Seth was thoughtful. The only thing I brought to the table was protective instincts, anyway.

My phone buzzed in my back pocket and I pulled the stupid thing out, jabbing the screen clumsily as I paused to catch my breath. I'd never had a phone before I took this job, and I didn't want one now.

Chase:

How is it out your way? Need a hand with anything?

Chase Wyatt was my boss and a cougar shifter. His family lived not too far from our cabin and had helped keep us alive when we were basically kids with no idea what we were doing.

It was Chase who had nagged me into taking this job. He'd also repeatedly told me not to do shit like move enormous trees by myself, but I'd do just about anything to avoid interacting with others, even my own kind.

Me:

Fine. You?

Chase:

Feeling chatty as usual, I see. All under control here. Come for dinner tomorrow? Lacey misses you.

I almost smiled at the screen at that. Lacey was Chase's mate — she had four — and we all loved seeing her. She had been flat out and exhausted with newborn twins when we first arrived at the cottage and we'd blatantly rejected any attempts at mothering us, but she'd persisted and fallen into a fun aunt role.

Me:

Rain check. We have a houseguest.

It took about five seconds for my phone to ring, and even that was longer than I expected. I held the phone up to my ear, not even managing a 'hello' before Chase started talking.

"Don't you lie to me, Noah Bernard. Two decades you boys have lived there and you've never once had a guest," Chase teased in his permanently gruff voice.

"I'd have been happy to keep it that way," I muttered, running my hand over my wet hair with a heavy sigh.

"Oh, I know that sound," Chase laughed. It sounded like a chainsaw starting up. "That is the sound of a troubled man. Don't tell me a woman has finally gotten past your defenses, Noah."

I grunted in acknowledgment, stomping through the mud like I could force the aggression out of my body if I just put enough effort into it. Not that she'd gotten past my defenses. Not really. She was giving it a damn good go though.

"Oh dear. I can see it now — Eli is enamored, Seth is ready to paint tributes to her grace and beauty, and you're out in the rain on your own, muttering about all the ways it's going to go wrong. Am I on track?"

"I'm out in the rain doing my job. The job *you* made me take," I countered, irritated that his assessment was exactly on target.

"Now, you can't solely blame me for that. Seth and Eli wanted you to take the job too," Chase reminded me, sounding amused.

"Traitors," I muttered.

I liked my quiet life, just me and my brothers. It had taken years of Chase pleading for me to accept this job. My brothers had pushed me, thinking that it would be good for me to get out of the house. Get a hobby. Give them some freedom. Maybe they were right.

We were in a similar position again. They were going to push me more, I could feel it. Seth and Eli were attached to Aurelia, and they wanted more than just a quick fling. I was the holdout, and it would all come to a head eventually.

"Noah," Chase chided. "Change isn't always a bad thing. What's her name?"

"Aurelia." Just saying it made my chest hurt. She'd *done* something to me, and I didn't appreciate it.

"Pretty name," Chase remarked. "Why don't you bring her by the house? Have her meet the family?" he teased.

"I'm hoping it won't get that far."

"Christ, Noah. Only you would see a potential relationship as a death sentence. Go back home, try to remove the asshole lenses you see the world through for five minutes and get to know her. I'm sure she's not all bad."

I opened my mouth to list all the reasons she was *that bad*, but Chase hung up before I could get started, probably because he knew that's exactly what I was about to do. I jammed the phone back in my pocket with a huff, glancing around the area, hoping another convenient distraction would appear to put off my journey home, but it didn't look like I'd be so lucky.

The storm continued to rage around me as I looped back to return to the cabin, and although I know this terrain better than anyone, I fought for purchase in the mud and struggled to see in the heavy downpour. The days were growing shorter and colder. We needed to get Aurelia back to town and under her brothers' protection, lest we get snowed in and *really* get stuck with her. I didn't know how well humans traveled in snow, but I assumed not well. They were very breakable.

I slipped again, my pants now thick with mud all the way to my thighs. If I hadn't been working, I would have just shifted and traveled in my fur, but Chase had explicitly told me to stay in my skin when I was on duty. God, I needed to get out of these muddy clothes and have a hot shower. That was the plan. Then I would go out into the living room and make myself comfortable. No matter what happened, I wasn't going to hide from the beautiful woman who I could overpower with one hand. That much was certain.

I inhaled deeply as I walked, constantly checking for signs Darren had been near our property. With the storm, I wouldn't be able to smell him unless he was still here, and I couldn't pick up any trace of coyote in the air.

I'd rip him apart if he came back again. He was a shady motherfucker, and I didn't trust him not to leave Aurelia alone.

I already regretted not killing him the first time he showed up at the house.

I drew another deep breath and froze in place. There was something in the air that was both familiar and unfamiliar.

Impossible. My brothers and I were the only bear shifters around these parts. And yet that scent was so... familiar.

Barely allowing myself to hope, I inched closer to the source of the scent, making as much noise as I could so as not to startle them. It was never a good idea to startle a bear.

I grabbed a low-hanging branch, using it to pull my weight up over a treacherous bit of ground, the breath whooshing out of my lungs as I straightened and took in the sight in front of me.

A female bear lay on the mud-soaked ground, curled up defensively on her side next to a log. My heart stuttered in my chest as I took her in, halting me in place, but I rushed forward at her low groan of distress. Even with the multitude of other scents in the air and the rain dampening everything, I knew her scent. I would always recognize my family.

This was my mother.

My very much alive mother.

RIA

CHAPTER 16

As soon as Noah appeared in his shifted form in the distance, hauling a smaller bear next to him, both coated in mud and debris, everything changed. The three of us had been playing Scrabble as the storm raged outside, and the energy had been playful and flirty — albeit a little subdued in Noah's absence — but that disappeared in an instant.

Seth and Eli flew into action, rushing out into the downpour to help their brother. Wanting to make myself useful, but not really sure how, I threw another log on the fire and moved to grab some towels from the cupboard. I paused for a moment in front of the window, just able to make out their hazy shapes through the sheets of rain.

The three of them were supporting the weight of the bear, but Seth and Eli's attention was completely on Noah, who had shifted back and was telling them something with more emotion than I'd ever seen him express, waving an arm wildly before shoving his hand back through his sopping hair, his shoulders bunched with tension.

I shoved down my rapidly rising sense of dread and raced upstairs for more towels. Whatever it was — whoever the bear was that had them all worked up — it wasn't my business. I wasn't staying here, anyway.

Not my circus, not my monkeys.

Right?

Right.

I basically threw the towels at them as they lumbered inside, then stood awkwardly off to the side as they shifted the half-dead bear onto the couch. Seth wrapped towels around the animal, while Noah wrapped one around his waist, dropping a pile of muddy clothes, plus the phone and gun he'd been carrying in the doorway, eyeing me warily.

"Maybe she should wait in the cottage."

Ouch.

"If you need privacy, I'll give you privacy, but don't talk about me like I'm not here," I replied coolly, moving towards the front door to grab my jacket.

Noah grunted in acknowledgment, far less full of fire than he usually was. In fact, he looked almost *nervous*.

"You're not going in the cottage," Seth snapped, speaking to me but glaring at his twin. "Ria would freeze in there. Why would you even suggest that?"

"I want Ria here," Eli mumbled, looking at the groaning, half-conscious bear on the couch. Noah and Seth were tense, but Eli didn't seem to share that feeling. If anything, he looked a little sad.

His older brothers both softened when they looked at him, and I felt a swell of affection for all three of them and the bond they shared.

"Then you stick next to her, Eli," Noah announced, straightening like he was steeling himself. "I mean it. Just in case anything goes... wrong."

Eli nodded once, moving around until he was positioned slightly in front of me, a barrier between me and the bear.

They were all acting so strangely, and as much as I wanted to ask them about it, I held my tongue. Whatever was happening here was a profoundly intimate family moment. I was intruding enough as it was.

Seth jogged to Noah's room, returning with some sweatpants and a t-shirt that he tossed at his brother. Noah pulled them on quickly, not seeming to notice that the t-shirt was inside out, while I tried to study the bear on the couch without being too obvious about it. It was so much smaller than Noah's or Eli's bears. Maybe it was a female? It couldn't be a wild bear, I was sure they wouldn't be so chill to be dragged into a house, even by shifters.

Oh god.

What if they were feeling some kind of... mating connection? Maybe that's why they were acting so weird.

I was just a temporary fling for Eli and Seth. A fun distraction while I waited for my brothers to come collect me like an errant child. Even so, I didn't love the idea of them just replacing me with a permanent mate just like that.

Honestly, it stung more than Darren's cheating did, which made less than zero sense.

Noah cleared his throat, looking a combination of determined and uneasy, and I balled my hands up at my sides, digging my nails into my palms so I didn't do something stupid. Like go over there and wrap my arms around him. He just looked so... vulnerable.

"Ready?" he asked, glancing up at his brothers. Eli made a strangled noise that may have been an agreement as he moved even further in front of me, while Seth gave him a curt nod.

"Shift," Noah commanded the bear, steeling his spine. Goosebumps broke out over my skin at the authority in his voice. Noah didn't appear to exert his dominance over his brothers often, but he was definitely the most alpha of the three.

The bear on the couch shuddered under his orders, and all three guys averted their eyes as the shift began, the sound of breaking bones was the only noise in the room. A disheveled statuesque woman quickly pushed herself upright, pulling the towels tight around her body. She shook slightly, staring at the three guys as they stared back at her.

So... was this a mate thing? She was kind of old.

She blinked up at the three men towering over her, not looking nearly as terrified as anyone else in her situation ought to.

"My boys," she sighed, closing her eyes for a moment. "You're alive."

Holy awkward, was this their *mother*? Seth had told me their parents died in a house fire, but I guess their mom wasn't so dead after all?

Now that I looked a little closer, she had the same dark eyes as all three brothers did. Her hair was dark as well, but flecked with gray, and I could see a little of Eli around her jaw. She was younger than I would have expected, definitely younger than my mom.

"Mom?" Eli asked hesitantly. The vulnerability in his voice broke my heart. I reached out to stroke his back, but pulled my hand back at the last second. He'd said he wanted me here, but that didn't necessarily mean he wanted my affection right now.

"All grown up, aren't you my little Elijah?" the woman replied stiffly, her tight smile seeming forced. I suppose it would be pretty weird to see your children after so long, all grown up.

"How is this possible?" Noah choked out.

"I could ask the same question," she replied, turning her attention to her oldest son. Was it my imagination, or did her face soften a little? "I've been living in Anchorage. A friend in my quilting club has a fascination with the State Parks. She noticed a new ranger, Noah Bernard, in Fairbanks and asked if he was any relation. Well, I thought that couldn't be possible, so I looked for myself..."

If I was a charitable person — which I was not, as a general rule — I'd assume she was filling the silence with chatter, and that's how she handled awkward situations.

At the same time... was she not interested in how her kids were doing? Apparently not.

"I was supposed to be going to a quilting convention this weekend, but curiosity got the better of me, so I headed to Fairbanks and..."

If this were a reality show, I'd be looking directly at the camera right now, doing my best 'she can't be serious' face.

"I can't say I'm surprised you ended up at your grandparents' old place. I'm glad you built something a little less squalid though, I always hated that cottage," she continued obliviously, surveying the beautiful cabin her sons had built on their own as teenagers with mild interest.

I think... I think I didn't like this woman.

Finally, her assessing eyes landed on me. I was wearing leggings, thick woolen socks, and Eli's oversized sweater, and couldn't have felt more exposed.

"Who is she?"

Yikes. The Arctic chill in her voice was enough to make my teeth chatter. It didn't look like I'd be bonding with their mother any time soon.

Which is fine. You are leaving.

"Oh, this is—" Eli began, voice full of affection.

"Aurelia is staying with us until the storm clears," Noah cut in, determinedly not looking at me. "Aurelia, this is our mother, Bernadette Bernard."

Bernadette Bernard? What a mouthful.

Noah's answer had obviously displeased his brothers. Eli's lips flattened as he glared at his big brother, while Seth fidgeted silently, giving me an apologetic look that did nothing to sooth my bruised ego. Nothing Noah had said was untrue, but it wasn't the full picture either. He'd diminished the connections I had with both Seth and Eli, and it was a shitty feeling.

But I guessed I was nothing to him, so what did it matter?

Bernadette exhaled dramatically. "Good. I thought I would need to have an uncomfortable conversation with my sons about the importance of mating with their own kind."

"That really won't be necessary," Noah muttered, looking immensely uncomfortable. *Good.*

"We were about to prepare dinner," Seth announced, speaking for the first time to smooth the tension. "I'm sure you're hungry."

"Famished!" Bernadette sighed. "Though I would prefer to shower first."

"I'll show you to the bathroom," Noah offered, while I backed into the kitchen to help Seth with dinner and do something with my restless hands.

Awkward. It was so, so awkward.

I didn't have the social skills for this kind of situation. A scenario like this required specialist training.

Bernadette padded along behind Noah to the downstairs bathroom, making backhanded compliments about the cabin the entire way, and I was pretty sure a vein in my forehead was twitching.

As soon as the shower was running, Eli exhaled loudly, leaning back against the kitchen counter, running his hands through his hair, pulling strands free from its tie. "Well, this is all very unexpected," he murmured.

"Very," Seth muttered with a tightness around his eyes that I'd never seen before.

I pulled the potatoes towards me as Seth washed them, cutting them into smaller pieces so they would cook faster. The stew we'd made together earlier was ready, sitting on a low heat on the stove, filling the cabin with the smell of seasoned meat.

"But a good kind of unexpected, right? You must be excited," I hedged.

Seth grimaced slightly. "I never had a close relationship with my mother. She never particularly wanted children, and when she thought I was a carrier... well, she favored Noah pretty heavily after that. I was closer with our father. He was flawed, but he loved us. They never had a happy mating."

I blinked, slightly overwhelmed at the amount of information he'd just thrown at me. It was maybe the most words I'd ever heard Seth say in one go.

"My memory of these things isn't as good," Eli offered. "But I remember Mom and Dad fought a lot. Like *a lot*. She bitched. He drank. It wasn't good."

The idea was a little foreign to me, honestly. Shifter mates weren't like human spouses. *'Til death do us part* was entirely literal, and they wouldn't even be remotely attracted to anyone else after they'd mated. All the mated couples I'd grown up around had been sickeningly happy.

"They mated as teenagers," Seth added under his breath. "I think at our grandparents' behest and more because they were both bear shifters than anything else."

Yikes.

Noah emerged from down the hallway, looking tense. He'd been thawing on me in the past couple of days, but it looked like we were all the way back at the beginning now, judging by the cool glare he shot my way.

"Sleeping arrangements," he grunted.

"I'll take the couch," I replied instantly.

"What? No," Eli objected. "You can just share with—"

"Don't even finish that sentence, Eli Bernard," I warned. I was not hopping into bed with Eli and Seth while their mother slept across the hall. A girl had standards.

"One of us can take the couch," Seth volunteered. "You don't need to, Ria."

"You're all giant, I'll be the most comfortable there. And it'll probably only be for one night longer," I added quietly, looking at Noah. Eli's eyes bored into the side of my head, but I refused to look his way. I wasn't sure what I'd find there.

Noah glanced out the window at the dark forest, rain still coming down heavy outside. "Two, I think," he sighed, scrubbing his hand over his face.

"Right, two nights on the couch won't kill me." The awkwardness might, though.

"Last time you said you'd sleep on the couch, you ran away," Eli grumbled.

"Even I'm not quite idiotic enough to go out there in the middle of a storm, Eli," I replied softly, shooting him an indulgent smile. Some of the tension leached out of him instantly.

"I'll make the bed," Noah muttered, stomping off up the stairs. "Stop flirting. Mom won't like it."

"Fuck that," Eli muttered under his breath, making Seth snort, but foreboding crept up my spine.

Nothing was going to be the same with Mom around, that much was for fucking sure.

✵ ✵ ✵

The awkwardness hadn't dissipated by the time Bernadette emerged after her shower, wearing Noah's clothes and looking mightily irritated about it. She sat down directly opposite me at the table, her unimpressed gaze trailing over the venison stew, mashed potatoes, and sliced bread.

"It is *so* nice to be in my skin again," Bernadette sighed dramatically, helping herself to a spoonful of mashed potatoes. "That was the first time I'd shifted since the fire. I prefer not to."

Her sons gaped at her. Despite not being a shifter, I was right there with them. I'd never met a shifter who'd deliberately tried to suppress one half of their nature.

"Why?" Eli asked bluntly, earning him a warning glare from Noah.

"It's a little uncivilized, don't you think?" Bernadette responded absently, spooning stew on top of her potatoes.

I had entered the Twilight Zone. That's what this was. There was no other explanation.

For a while we ate in awkward silence. It was obvious that all three guys had a million questions between them, but maybe no one wanted to go first.

Bernadette's hawkish gaze caught on me again, and I stared blankly back at her, contentedly eating my dinner. One reason my family had been so surprised that I couldn't shift was that right from birth, I'd never had a prey response to predators, and I wasn't about to start now.

It was probably just a lack of self-preservation instincts, but whatever. I'd play it off like I was a badass.

"You know, my worst fear when I realized you were alive was that you had taken ill-advised mates," Bernadette sighed. "It's such an important decision to make, one that requires parents to be heavily involved. Not that your father would have been any help."

"You only knew for sure Noah was alive," Eli pointed out. It was weird hearing his voice without the usual laughter in it. He sounded stiff and uncomfortable, and I hated that for him.

"I knew if Noah had made it, you two had," Bernadette replied, looking oddly smug. "Noah would have never let anything happen to you. He was always so good about looking after Seth when his bear didn't emerge."

Holy favoritism, Batman.

"Seth's bear emerged the night of the fire," Noah offered hastily, shifting awkwardly in his seat. "It took both of us to get Eli out that night."

Seth was silent, but his dark eyes flashed with pain, and my heart ached for him. When I was 12, I'd gone over to the neighbor girl's house — Charlotte. Her family were fox shifters too, and we'd played together most days. We'd been trying to emulate a hairstyle from a magazine with twists and butterfly clips when Charlotte's first shift had begun.

Her parents had sent me on my way pretty promptly, but I remembered the agony she was in as if I'd seen it yesterday. For years, when I thought I was a late bloomer and would shift too eventually, I'd lived in constant fear of that pain.

I couldn't imagine how traumatizing it had been for Seth to go through that while his house burned down around him, trying to keep himself and his brothers alive, not knowing where his parents were.

Bernadette turned her attention back on me, dark eyes narrowed in displeasure. All of her sons had inherited her eyes, yet they looked nothing alike, not really. Bernadette's were colder, shrewder than any of her sons'.

"So, *Aurelia*," she began, taking great pains to draw out my name like it was the most ridiculous thing she'd ever heard. "Tell me about yourself."

What on Earth for? I was the least interesting topic of conversation at this table.

"She's just staying here for a while," Noah interjected. "There's not much to tell."

For once, I was grateful for Noah's abruptness. I didn't really want to get into the details of *why* I was staying here with this woman, and it seemed he didn't either.

"So you've said, yet the scent of her and your brothers' *activities* is all over this house," Bernadette snapped, glaring at the son who appeared to like her the most.

Oops. Probably should have cracked a window.

Eli's grin was unrepentant, while Seth raised an eyebrow at his mother, though I could have sworn the tips of his ears looked a little pinker.

"I'm just staying here until my brothers can come get me," I replied tightly. "Once the storm clears, I'll be on my way back to New York."

Eli tried in vain to disguise his growl with a cough, but no one was fooled. It was flattering, but I didn't for one second think that was about *me* in particular. Eli, more than his brothers, seemed to get lonely out here. He'd mourn the loss of my company, but I doubted it was *me*-specific.

"Your scents—"

"Are hardly anyone's business but our own, Mother. We're all adults here," Seth interrupted smoothly. She looked at him like she'd never seen him before, and I wondered briefly what Seth had been like as a teenager for her to seem so unnerved by him.

"Fine, I'll let it be," she grumbled. "Are your brothers carriers too?"

Rude. "They're fox shifters."

"Foxes," she hummed disapprovingly. This was fast shaping up to be the most awkward dinner of my life, and I'd once had to sit through a family dinner with my then-boyfriend after his mom walked in on me giving him a blowjob in the bathroom. "Are they mated?"

"No."

"Three children, all unmated?" Bernadette confirmed, as if her own children weren't in the exact same position.

The Lady Catherine de Bourgh energy was strong with this one. Also, the hypocrisy.

"Correct," I replied with a saccharine smile. *You are a guest. You are a guest. Mind your manners.*

"How disappointing for your parents," she remarked lightly. Eli met my incredulous look with one of his own, and I was reassured knowing I wasn't the only one who thought this was *crazy*. Seth was always the hardest to read with his impassive expressions, and Noah was still staring at his mom like he was seeing a ghost.

I supposed that's what she was, but not the good kind of ghost, like Patrick Swayze. Or Casper. She was the kind of ghost you called the Ghostbusters to eliminate. In my opinion, anyway.

"Parents want grandchildren in their old age," she sighed, finally turning her disapproval on her own sons. Seth's facade cracked spectacularly — he was practically gaping at his mother.

I was reminding myself on loop that this was not my business. That I shouldn't get involved. That I'd be out of here soon, anyway. However...

"I assumed parents who thought their children had died would just be happy to have live children," I said lightly, looking up from my meal to make eye contact with Bernadette.

Yeah, bitch. I said what I said.

Noah choked on his beer, breaking the sudden silence, and Eli beamed at me like I'd made all his Christmas wishes come true.

"Obviously," Bernadette replied coolly, looking back at me with I'm sure as much thinly veiled dislike as I was projecting at her.

I'd really never thought of myself as a hateful person. I mean, I hated Darren, but he was basically it. Bernadette, I could see myself hating, though. She'd been living in Anchorage, hanging out with her quilting circle, just... content? Had she even looked for her sons?

Now she'd shown up when they were fully grown, bitching about grandchildren and suitable mates, without acknowledging at all how hard their lives had been on their own.

The twins had raised themselves and Eli. They'd all built this home together from scratch, found careers and passions, maintained their brotherly bond through everything, and she was seriously complaining that they hadn't reproduced yet?

Aside from everything else, they were dudes. They could have kids when they were 90 if they wanted to. Like The Rolling Stones.

I shoveled food into my mouth as quickly as I could without looking totally unladylike, glad that my dig seemed to take Bernadette's attention off me for a while. She asked politely about what Seth and Eli did for work before gushing over Noah, who seemed to grow more uncomfortable by the minute, whilst also glowing a little under his mother's praise.

Maybe he was a little starved for affection? It sounded like he'd always been doing everything for everyone else, putting himself last. Unease coiled in my gut at the thought. Tensions between him and his brothers were already high due to my presence. His mother could really drive a wedge between them if they weren't careful.

Noah glanced briefly at me, his expression unreadable. "Your bag is in Eli's room for now, we'll put some blankets on the couch for you later."

I couldn't decide if he was dismissing me or giving me an out, but either way I wasn't about to look a gift horse in the mouth.

"Great, I'll leave you all to reconnect," I offered stiffly, already standing and backing towards the stairs, wanting to get the fuck away from this nightmarish family reunion.

"Better late than never," Bernadette scoffed, earning her two disapproving glares from her younger sons and a solid blank look from her robotic eldest.

I pretended my puny human ears hadn't heard as I escaped up the staircase, disappearing into Eli's room as quietly as I could and pulling the door behind me, disappointed it didn't have a lock. Maybe it was petty, but didn't want to be around any of them right now. I didn't want to hear the details of their reunion with the woman who'd just made me feel two inches tall. I already knew I wasn't gracious enough to act happy for them.

Petty, thy name is Aurelia.

Not that Seth and Eli seemed particularly thrilled either, but I'm sure they'd get there in time. She was their long-lost mother, after all.

I pulled the beaten-up historical romance novel out of my pack and made myself comfortable in the middle of Eli's bed, hoping the familiar love story would offer me the distraction I needed from my own messy love life.

You don't have a love life, Ria. Your ex-boyfriend is a lying liar who lies, and you're fooling around with a couple of guys while you hide out at their house, waiting for your big brothers to bail you out again.

I peeked out the window, trying to determine if the rain had eased or not. If it had, I was getting the fuck off this mountain *tomorrow*. I had my own family reunion to get to, and I was going to give my mother the hug of her life in gratitude for her *not* being like Bernadette.

RIA

CHAPTER 17

"You're squishing her."

Vaguely, I registered Eli's panicked whisper as a warm body wrapped around me, jostling me from my nap.

"I am not," Seth rumbled quietly, his chest vibrating against my back as he spoke.

"Share," Eli muttered, pressing himself against my front, his hand rested on my thigh, over the leggings and sweatshirt I must have fallen asleep in on top of Eli's covers while reading my book.

Shit. Book. Hiding in Eli's room. *Bitchy Bernadette.*

I shot upright; the movement startled both Seth and Eli into yanking their hands back, and shuffled on my butt to the end of the bed, annoyed they could probably see perfectly in the dark how awkward the movement was.

"Where are you going?" Eli asked, mystified.

"Couch, remember?"

"You don't have to—" Seth began.

"Nope. The weirdness factor is way too strong," I whispered, climbing off the end of the bed. "Besides, the bed is too small for all of us."

"Noah left blankets on the couch for you," Seth sighed, shushing Eli when he began protesting. "Please don't feel you have to leave. You sleeping here is no one's business but our own."

It was a sweet sentiment, but Judgy Mother was judgy. I wasn't about to invite any extra criticism.

"Sleep well," I whispered, pulling the door open as quietly as I could and slipping out onto the landing. The house was dark and silent except for the steady pattering of rain on the roof, still warm from the fire that had been burning all evening. Fortunately, I didn't see anyone as I padded down the stairs in my woolen socks, clinging tight to the bannister so I didn't fall and break my neck in the dark.

It was strange to feel so uncomfortable moving around the house. Right from the moment I'd walked into this house like I'd owned it, I'd felt so at home. Right now, I actually felt like the intruder I had been on that first day.

I curled up in the fetal position on the couch, the faintest glow of the embers in the fireplace illuminating the space. There was a pile of far more blankets than anyone could ever reasonably need on the arm of the sofa, and I pulled a couple over me, burrowing down until I was comfortable.

Cedar.

God, it almost felt like an insult that Noah had given me a blanket that smelled like him. A final *fuck you*. Was that how he meant it? Probably not. But I was tired and grumpy and petty. He could have told me I was the most beautiful woman he'd ever seen, and I would have assumed he meant it as a taunt.

For hours, it felt like sleep eluded me. I was too exposed in the living room to fully relax, and the rain that had sounded so soothing during the day when I'd been playing board games with Seth and Eli now tormented me. It reminded me I was stuck here, even as an idiotic part of my brain did a happy dance, not wanting to leave.

Eventually, my exhaustion dragged me under, for a couple of hours at least. By the time I woke, light was filtering through the windows, the rain had stopped, and the house was still silent. Glad they'd slept in, I got up as quietly as possible, grabbing clean clothes and my toiletry bag from the pack Noah had left next to the couch and scampering into the downstairs bathroom.

I hadn't been in here before. It was smaller than the upstairs bathroom — no tub — but felt more cozy and masculine with the dark blue tiles instead of the bright white ones upstairs.

It would probably wake Noah up, but fuck it, I needed a shower. My eyelids felt like sandpaper and my muscles were stiff from sleeping on the couch. He could deal with waking up a little early. Besides, I was still irrationally annoyed at him.

I pulled my hair up into a bun, stripped out of the gross clothes I'd slept in, and cranked the hot water. The moment it hit my skin, some of the tension leached out of my body, and my head cleared.

I was a flawed person. I leaped before I looked. Talked too much, listened too little. Depended too much on others to fix problems of my own making.

But I never overstayed my welcome. That's one lesson my mama taught me that actually stuck.

Quickly finishing my shower in case Noah stormed in here while I was stark naked to yell at me for waking him up, I pulled on my most functional pair of leggings, a warm top and socks, ready to slip my hiking boots and jacket over top, then went extra hard on the foundation to cover up my dark circles.

By the time I emerged, Eli, Noah and Bernadette were all sitting around the dining table while Seth busied himself in the kitchen, apparently responsible for feeding them all without any help.

Bernadette spared me a glance as I headed over to the couch to pack up my bedding, before returning to the conversation like I wasn't here. Fine by me.

"Black coffee, if you please, Seth," she called. I already thought she was a psycho, but if I hadn't, the black coffee would have confirmed it. Gross.

"Well, I feel much more *human* after some sleep," Bernadette announced, accepting the coffee Seth put on the table in front of her before he returned to the stove to make more. "Pity about my clothes," she added, looking down at the oversized collection of items from her sons' wardrobes in dismay. "Though I'm sure my sons will help me get some new ones."

"Let me help with the porridge," Eli muttered, pushing away from the table, leaving Noah with Bernadette.

Eli shot me a longing glance from across the room, but I gave him a subtle shake of my head. Aside from the awkwardness of him showing affection while his mom was right there, glaring at me, I needed to put some physical distance between us for my own sake.

Seth strode over to me as I finished folding up blankets, passing me a steaming cup of milky coffee with a soft, half smile. His fingers brushed against mine as he handed me the cup, lingering a little longer than necessary.

"Sit, if you like," he murmured, nodding at the window bench. "Breakfast will be a while."

I gave him a grateful nod, taking my liquid gold and curling up by the window, trying to make myself small and inconspicuous for perhaps the first time in my life.

"Well, I suppose the quiet out here is nice, if you're into that sort of thing," Bernadette began. Or maybe she'd already been talking, and I'd just tuned it out? I'd left my manners somewhere back at Darren's tiny cabin.

"How long are you staying, Mom?" Eli asked, forced casualness in his tone.

"As long as she wants, of course," Noah shot back through gritted teeth.

"Of course," Eli agreed tightly.

The rain had cleared, and the sky outside was a brilliant blue, like it was taunting me about yesterday's foul weather. The clear sky had briefly perked me up, until I noticed the disastrous state of the ground. 'Mud' was too generous a term for the river of sludge that the ground had turned into.

It was going to be a grueling walk back to town, but I'd take swimming in mud over spending the day in Bernadette's company, waiting for the ground to harden.

"You should have moved to the human world," Bernadette forged on. "It's been so lovely. No territorial shifters to worry about. No stripping off all the time. It's a far more... dignified way of life."

I chanced a look back at Noah, Seth, and Eli, who were stonily silent after their mother's declaration, presumably thinking the same thing I was thinking.

How nice that you were off living a dignified life amongst humans while your young sons struggled to get by on their own, thinking you were dead.

"There were payouts, some money from your father's family, and such. Enough to buy a beautiful home in Anchorage," she continued obliviously, waving her hand absently in the air. "Due to… circumstances, I may have to sell. Though you could come join me — there are far more employment opportunities for you in the city, and the house is big enough for all of us. You'll be far more comfortable there than you are here."

Don't get involved, Ria. Not your place.

"We're quite happy where we are," Seth said evenly, the tick in his jaw obvious even from the other side of the room, before he turned back to the stove. His back was stiff with tension, and my fingers itched to rub it.

"Well, you can't know that until you've experienced something else. I am glad you haven't been holed up in that tiny old cottage the entire time. This structure is at least an improvement over that monstrosity, though the finishings are a little… low-end. Your father's parents never had any taste. That cottage was a hovel."

If she couldn't turn into a bear and rip me the fuck apart, I'd have taken a swing at her. My meager self-preservation instincts won out, but it was a close call.

How. Dare. She?!

That cottage *meant something* to them. When they'd been all on their own in the world, that was their little safe haven. Both Seth and Eli were artists — Seth with his painting and Eli with his woodwork — and they'd both chosen that little building full of memories to work in, and she'd called it a monstrosity.

Not only that, but calling the main cabin a mere "improvement" was a fucking joke. This place was amazing, and Noah, Seth and Eli had built it with their own blood, sweat and tears when they were *kids*. Who did she think she was to piss on their hard work like that? Low-end, my ass. While she'd been living off inherited money in the suburbs, assuming her sons were dead and never bothering to come back?

"We love this house," Eli said firmly, glaring accusingly at a silent Noah, more visibly uncomfortable by the second.

"I'm going to get more firewood," Noah grunted, his chair squeaking across the ground as he stood quickly, striding towards the front door as fast as he could without jogging. *Coward.*

"You were always my little country boy," Bernadette said fondly, reaching over to pinch Eli's cheek like he was a toddler and not a grown-ass man.

I tried to hold my snort, but a bit of it escaped, anyway. A sort of strangled, derisive noise that I tried to smother with a fake cough into my coffee cup.

Bernadette spun in her chair to face me, pinning me with a look that was way too hostile considering we'd just met yesterday. Usually, it took me much longer to get people to hate me.

"The storm has cleared, no reason for you to hang around."

God, this lady really was a barrel of peaches.

"It's not safe to walk out there yet," Seth replied smoothly.

"Of course it is. It's a little mud. It's dangerous having her in the house like this, you know. You might get... ideas. More than you've already had." She sniffed haughtily while Eli shot me a flirty wink behind his mother's back.

As much as I hated to agree with her on principle, she was right. The storm had stopped. My brothers were most likely in town, ready to go. I was already feeling more attached than I had any right to be after just a few days together, but this was always meant to be temporary. Better to rip the band-aid off now.

Besides, I might punch Bernadette in the face if she kept up the snide comments directed towards both me and her own children. She didn't have any stuff, so robbing her or destroying her things was out. Maybe I could set her hair on fire?

Bad Ria! You are working on becoming a better person, remember? I really had been on my best behavior while I was staying with the guys. They had kindly taken me in and kept an eye on me while I waited for my brothers to take over babysitting duty. I'd done the most to be respectful and grateful for their generosity.

Because you like it here. I silenced that thought. *All* the flashing danger signs in that direction.

I downed the rest of my coffee and left Seth and Eli inside while Bernadette was holding court, working herself up to espouse the benefits of suburban living again, shoving my feet into my hiking boots and plodding through the squelching mud to the woodshed where I could hear Noah splitting logs at superhuman pace.

Holy back muscles.

It's not like I hadn't seen Noah shirtless before, but standing behind him, watching his muscles flex and ripple as he raised the axe over his head and brought it down with breath-stealing precision was a level of sexual energy I hadn't been prepared for this early in the morning.

The *thwack* of the axe hitting the wood made me jump, startling me out of whatever ill-advised sexual thoughts I'd been having towards my least hospitable host.

"See something you like?" Noah drawled as he glanced back at me over his shoulder, voice dripping with arrogance.

"Well, I did, but you turned around and ruined the view with your face," I snarked.

Noah snorted, strolling over to the log pile and grabbing another piece. I was woman enough to admit that it irritated me that I could never get a rise out of him. Noah was impervious to my insults, and it frustrated the hell out of me.

"So, did you just come out here to check out my ass?"

Whack.

"Why would I check out *your* ass when you have an identical twin? His doesn't have a stick wedged all the way up it. Makes for better eye candy."

"What do you want, thief?" Noah asked exasperatedly, ditching the axe and turning to look at me, hands resting low on his hips.

He didn't look jealous, but there was that glimmer of *something* behind his eyes that always appeared when he thought about me with his brothers.

"I want to go home."

"Good."

God, neither of us sounded happy. I knew where the edge of bitterness in my voice came from, but I couldn't explain his. There was a long pause where we both stared at each other, trying in vain to understand one another.

"My mother told us last night that you were a threat to us, you know. She's right," Noah said quietly, closing the distance between us.

Right, I guess that explained his bitterness. Noah hadn't trusted me to begin with, and that had only gotten worse now he'd started mainlining his mother's special brand of poison.

And he thought *I* was the threat.

"Well then, I'll be on my way and you'll never have to see me again," I replied coolly, crossing my arms over my chest protectively.

He was standing just inches away from me, his cedar scent even more potent after exertion. A rivulet of sweat ran down his defined chest and I forced my eyes upwards, tipping my head back to meet his dark eyes.

Noah gave me a long look, his expression shuttered. He could be thinking about how glad he was to get rid of me, or about how Seth and Eli would take it, or what to have for dinner tonight. He was such a closed book; I didn't even know where to begin with what was going on in his head.

"It will be a hard trek," Noah began, his jaw ticking wildly. "I'll need to carry you."

"No thanks," I responded instantly. Even if Noah was in his bear form and unable to communicate, that was a level of awkwardness I just didn't need to experience, ever. "My brothers can meet me in the woods. They'll be in town by now."

"Sure. Call them," Noah grunted, pulling his satellite phone out of his back pocket and shoving it roughly in my direction.

"Thank you." The words sounded strangled as I forced them out around the rapidly expanding lump in my throat.

I blinked away the foolish tears that were welling up, bending my head over the phone so my hair obscured my face from Noah's view, and punched in Vincent's number a little harder than necessary.

Why was this bothering me so much?

Eli, Seth and I had a fun little fling for a few days. Noah was wary of me in the beginning and wary of me now, that hadn't changed. I was leaving here with fun memories that would go a long way to replacing the soured memories of Darren. Plus, I had plenty of new material in the finger vault for future masturbatory sessions. I had no reason to feel sad about leaving.

"Ria?" Vincent's voice pulled my head into the present and killed any thoughts of masturbating stone dead.

"Yeah, it's me."

"Fucking hell, we have been losing our shit, Ria. I can't believe you've been out there in that storm. Where are you? We're coming to get you."

There was so much certainty in his voice that I lost the battle with the tears I was trying to hold back, sniffling a little and frantically scrubbing my cheeks with the heel of my hand.

"Why are you crying? Did someone hurt you?" Joe growled, he and Vincent scuffling over the line to hold the phone.

"I'm just glad to hear your voices, that's all," I reassured them.

"It's okay, sis. We'll be home soon," Joe said softly. Right, home. *New York.*

"Er, Noah, could you maybe give me some coordinates or something?" I asked, not looking at him.

Considering how gruff he'd been, his fingers were surprisingly gentle as he pried the phone out of my grip and began discussing coordinates and meeting points with my brothers.

God, the idea of a long, protracted goodbye with these guys was far more painful than walking out on Darren ever was. Maybe it was a good thing Bernadette had returned from the grave when she had. There would be no steamy farewells with her here, trying to murder me with her eyeballs.

Noah hung up, looking tense as he tucked the phone away, glancing up at the house. He tipped his head, gesturing for me to follow him as he moved behind the woodshed. Further away from sensitive ears.

I followed without hesitation. Noah had a strange hold over my emotions – his words cut deeper than anyone else I'd ever met – but I didn't feel in any physical danger with him for a moment.

He looked more uncomfortable than I did. *Guilty*, I realized. Noah was a man on the precipice of doing something he knew he shouldn't, and it wasn't my feelings at risk.

"I could ask my brothers to help me clear some fallen trees." He hesitated, shifting on the balls of his feet. "The opposite direction of where you and your brothers are headed."

I gave him a long look, giving him a moment to reconsider. Would it be easier on me to escape like a thief in the night? Yes, definitely. But it wasn't my feelings Noah had to worry about.

"You want me to disappear like a thief in the night?" I confirmed flatly.

He hesitated for a moment, and I watched the internal battle play out in his eyes. With visible effort, Noah squared his shoulders, pulling himself up a little straighter.

"You are a thief in the night. If you leave now, I won't report the stolen firearm you're carrying."

I blinked up at him, waiting for the anger or betrayal to set in. It didn't, though. I mostly felt disappointment. Disappointment that the past magical few days were ending on such a sour note.

Disappointment that I'd made a shitty call in taking that stupid gun, along with an extra helping of disappointment that Noah was throwing that decision in my face.

"It's better for everyone this way," he insisted, though I don't know which of us he was trying to convince more.

There was a long pause, an understanding passing between us. Noah was a protector. He'd faced fire and battled the elements over the years to keep his brothers safe, and he was trying to do it again — perhaps protecting me as well, in his own way — as best he knew how.

He was wrong. Not all wars were waged on battlefields, and not all wounds came from attacks. That was his lesson to learn, though.

"I hope you know what you're doing, Daddy Bear," I murmured, turning away and leaving him standing in the dirt alone.

SETH

CHAPTER 18

Ria returned, even more subdued than she'd been before she left if possible, followed shortly after by Noah, who was carrying an armful of firewood and a chip on his shoulder the size of Mount Denali.

I slammed his bowl of porridge down in front of him a little harder than necessary, shooting him my best *thanks, asshole* look. We had more than enough firewood to last the next couple of days. There was no reason to leave us alone with *Mother*, who'd been extolling the virtues of just pretending we weren't shifters and moving into her lovely four-bedroom suburban home in Anchorage, selling insurance to humans, and yet also finding a bear shifter mate because keeping the lineage pure was somehow essential, even if she despised what that lineage was.

Nothing made sense anymore.

I was glad she had survived the fire, of course I was. But the two decades in between hadn't softened Mother at all, and she'd been a hard woman to begin with.

"There's such a lovely park near my home," she was telling Noah, who was either swallowing this bullshit or at least the best at pretending. "It's a great way for me to spend time with nature when I feel like I need to shift, without giving in to the urge."

Eli glanced up at me from across the table where he was wolfing down his porridge, his eyebrows raised to his hairline. *I know what you mean.*

"I have only been in my ranger position for a couple of months, it wouldn't be a good look to quit now," Noah muttered. God, I hoped that was an excuse. If he was actually considering moving, I'd disown him. "Speaking of, I could use some help clearing fallen trees," he added, clearing his throat as he looked between Eli and I.

"Today?" Eli asked hesitantly. We both looked at Ria, whose head was bent over her porridge bowl, seemingly absorbed in her meal.

"This morning," Noah replied stiffly. "Sorry, Mom. Will you be okay here for a couple of hours?"

Mom sighed dramatically. "I suppose. I am very tired from my trek up here. It is rather ridiculous to live so far from the road, you know."

"Great," Noah said quickly. "We'll be gone a couple of hours and you can rest. After that, we're all yours."

Speak for yourself...

Ria stood and collected our bowls as soon as we were done, shooing me away when I tried to help her with the dishes.

"Go, go. Noah needs you."

I moved right behind her, a few loose curls that had escaped from her tie fluttered against her neck under my breath. Ria's breath hitched, an almost imperceptible gasp, enough to give away how affected she was by me.

It was incredibly flattering.

"Join me in the studio when I get back from this stupid errand," I murmured, my fingers running down the back of her arm, hidden from view by my body. Not that I was being overly discreet, but I knew my mother's presence had made things uncomfortable for Ria, and I hated that.

I wanted to win her over, not drive her away.

"That sounds fun," Ria replied cautiously, filling the sink. She didn't relax into me as I hoped she would, but we weren't entirely alone either. Maybe later.

"I'll see you soon," I promised, squeezing her arm once before moving towards the front door to pull on my jacket. Noah was already waiting for me, looking tense, while Eli was trying to shake off Mother.

"Is this safe for your brothers?" she called to Noah, sounding doubtful. "They were never as *confident* outdoors as you," she added.

"Weird how much changes in twenty years," Eli interjected, striding into the kitchen and smacking a firm kiss on Ria's temple, audience be damned.

"See you in a bit, Goldie."

"Take care," Ria breathed, looking back at us with a sad smile on her face.

Don't worry, sweetheart. We won't leave you alone with our mother for long.

✳ ✳ ✳

I wasn't a park ranger.

That was a very deliberate choice on my part. I had no interest in doing Noah's job. I didn't even like helping with Noah's regular household chores — fishing, hunting, chopping firewood, and so on. I quietly hated every moment of doing those tasks when Noah roped us in to help, but it wasn't fair to expect him to do them alone.

Even if no one ever helped me cook. Not that I was bitter.

Today was worse than usual, though. The ground was a nightmare to navigate after the storm, my mood was already foul from all the retorts I'd bitten back this morning when I was talking to Mother, and leaving her and Ria alone together seemed like the worst possible idea ever.

We only had a day or so left with Ria. Her brothers were probably in Fairbanks already, waiting for her, and I could feel the tick of the clock, counting down the moments we had left together.

Eli wanted to ask her to stay, he hadn't been shy about that. We'd both hoped to talk to Noah about that, but our mom's sudden reappearance had delayed that conversation. Eli glanced at me, a question in his face, but I discreetly shook my head in warning. Noah wasn't in the right frame of mind for that conversation right now, but when Eli got an idea in his head, he was like a dog with a bone. And Ria was more than just an idea. He'd pinned his future hopes on her staying with us, and he wasn't about to just let it go.

"Noah," Eli called to get his attention. Noah grunted in acknowledgment — a brief, irritated sound that would signal to any sensible person that danger was ahead.

"I — *we* — wanted to talk to you about Ria—"

"No."

"No?" Eli repeated incredulously.

"No. N-O. *Fuck* no. We're not talking about her now or ever. If I never hear her name again, it will be too soon," Noah groused, stomping ahead while Eli and I stood rooted to the spot.

I knew Noah and Ria hadn't connected, but there was a level of hostility in his voice I hadn't expected.

"What did she ever do to you?" I demanded, jogging to keep pace with my twin, slipping over the treacherous terrain. "What possible reason could you have for talking about her like that?"

"All the same reasons you should have. If you'd think with the head on your shoulders for a minute, you'd see them," Noah snapped. "She's a criminal. She stole drugs. A weapon. Broke into our house. Charmed you idiots into letting her stay with us."

"Jesus, you could not be more dramatic if you tried," Eli groaned. "Ria never suggested staying with us, *I did*. She was pissed about it too."

"And Darren's a sack of shit, so who cares if she robbed him?" I added under my breath.

Was it ideal? No. She could give the gun back though. Maybe repay him for the weed.

No, he cheated on her *and* hid the fact he was a shifter. He basically owed her one high.

"I already know what you want to talk about," Noah said tightly. "And my answer is no. Come on, this way."

Eli opened his mouth to argue, but I rested a hand on his forearm, shaking my head more forcefully this time. If we pushed now — with Noah as borderline feral as he currently was — he'd only dig his heels in more.

Ria wouldn't stay now even if we asked her to, anyway. She'd just come out of a serious relationship, she barely knew us, and she'd dragged her brothers all the way out here. We couldn't realistically expect her to give up everything, move in with us and agree to be our mate, even if Noah was on board with it.

No, I needed to pull Eli aside and tell him to pump the brakes. We could get her phone number, court her long distance. Whatever it took, I was willing to put in the work.

Patience was not one of Eli's virtues though, and he released a distinctly bear-like growl as he shook my hand off. To my great relief, he said nothing. We couldn't risk screwing this up — we had to deal with our mother too. Women like Ria didn't come around very often, and I wasn't going to let her slip through my fingers. Not even if my father, grandparents, and all my long-lost cousins came back from the grave.

Shit, we really needed to talk about this — all of this — but it would have to wait until Noah was feeling less savage. I don't even know why he'd dragged us out. We'd wandered around aimlessly, occasionally moving logs that he would easily be able to shift himself, and it had taken every ounce of my self-control not to lose my patience.

I was the most understanding person on this Earth about Noah's coping mechanisms or lack thereof, and I was closer than I ever had been to giving him a black eye and telling him to get the hell over himself.

What felt like *hours* later, Noah's pace faltered as we approached our property, and Eli came to a sudden halt. Even without the faint trace of fox shifters that lingered around the edge of our territory, I'd know Ria wasn't there without needing to go inside.

When she'd been here, the cabin had pulsed with her warm, playful energy. It seeped through the boards and made the whole house seem like it was glowing from the inside.

Ria had gone, and that light had gone with her.

I closed my eyes and waited as the *whoosh* of a flying fist cut through the air. I didn't turn around. It pained me to see my brothers fight.

Noah grunted at the impact, stumbling back a step, but it didn't sound like he made any move to block it.

"You fucking two-faced sack of shit!" Eli yelled, going after Noah again. "How could you? You knew she was important to me! To us!"

"She asked to leave," Noah countered, his voice thick. With a heavy sigh, I turned around, realizing that Eli had broken Noah's nose.

"Did she ask to sneak away without saying goodbye, or was that your idea?" I asked quietly, my voice halting Eli's movements as he went to swing again.

Noah was silent, jaw clenched, staring at me. Blood streamed from his nose, running over his beard, and I could see in his eyes that he was pleading with me to understand why he'd made this call. I didn't understand, though. I didn't understand any of the choices he'd made when it came to Ria and the way he acted around her.

"Noah," I said sharply. "Answer my question. If this was your decision, you need to own that."

"I pointed out it would be better for everyone if she left," Noah bit out, eyes shifting guiltily. "Do you really want to make a fool of yourself, begging some girl to stay, permanently stay, just because she was fun in bed?"

Usually, I intervened between Noah and Eli after the first hit. One was a freebie, after that they had to sit down and talk like adults. But that was for minor disputes, not Noah disrespecting the woman we had come to care so much about, so when Eli launched himself at our older brother, I crossed my arms and watched.

"Don't—" *Punch.*

"Fucking—" *Punch.*

"Talk—" *Punch.*

"About her—" *Punch.*

"Like that!" *Punch.*

Eli had Noah pinned to the ground and was laying into his face. Noah had his arms up defensively, blocking the blows, but he made no move to push Eli off because he knew he was wrong. He fucking knew it.

Ria was more than 'some girl who was fun in bed.' She was smart, resilient, curious, interesting. A burst of color in a world that had grown increasingly dull and gray as each year passed.

I left them to it, rolling around on the forest floor, coated in blood and mud as I dragged my feet back to the foreboding house. Not only would Ria not be there, my mother *would* be. And god knows what kind of send-off she'd given the woman who'd carved out a piece of my heart and taken it with her.

With a fortifying breath of fresh air, I pushed the front door open, removing my boots, hat, and jacket and setting them aside in the entryway. All the windows in the cabin were open, and it felt like another knife in the heart that Ria's scent was being blown away like it had never been here at all.

"Seth?" Mom called from the kitchen. It should have felt good having her here, shouldn't it? I should've felt happy that after all this time thinking we'd lost her, she was healthy and content.

It didn't feel good and I didn't feel happy. I felt weirded out, and angry that she'd never bothered to look for us, usually followed by confusion as to whether or not I was allowed to feel angry.

If Ria was here, I'd ask her about it. She had seemed plenty angry at my mother for all three of us.

"I'm here," I sighed, moving around the corner into the kitchen.

"You need to go to the grocery store," Mom muttered, looking through the cupboards. My eye twitched in irritation.

"Unlikely," I muttered. "We stock up in bulk."

"I suppose we just have different tastes then," she sighed heavily, wrinkling her nose as she examined a jar of split peas. I distinctly remember her cooking this exact kind of food when we were kids, but if I had to guess, she liked to pretend that reality didn't exist. "Where are your brothers?"

"Conferring."

I moved around her to fill up the kettle. My mind was racing, trying to figure out what to do. Should I go after Ria? She had asked to leave, I wanted to be respectful of her wishes. Plus, her brothers likely wouldn't take kindly to me forcing myself into her life if she didn't want me there.

At the same time, the idea that this was just *done* was hard to reconcile. I wanted to hear it from her lips. I needed closure.

"I hope they're not fighting about that *girl*," Mom said coolly, narrowing her eyes accusingly at me.

"Ria is a grown *woman*," I sighed, taking a deep breath to maintain some semblance of calm. First Noah, and now Mom. If everyone could stop fucking *disrespecting* her, that would be great. "And yes, they are."

"I must admit, I'm surprised she left with such little fuss. I thought she'd hang around, making a spectacle trying to convince you or Eli to take her as a mate," Mom commented lightly, moving towards the living area. "Make me a cup of tea, would you? You remember how I like it."

The callous way she'd spoken, the casual cruelty had me rooted to the spot in shock. Mom didn't even *know* Ria. She'd spent less than 24 hours in her company. I wanted to drop the conversation entirely, but Mom had been the last person to see Ria, and I wasn't too proud to admit that I was fishing for information.

"Ria isn't like that. *At all*," I added forcefully. "I hope you didn't imply anything like that when she left."

"What makes you think I talked to her at all?" Mom replied loftily, settling in on the couch and resting her feet on the coffee table.

I swallowed down the hot rush of rage that rose in my chest. My self-control was not for nothing. When I lost my temper, I made Noah look sweet.

"Anyway, it was all very anticlimactic. She packed, lugged her things to the door — such a production — then waited outside until her brothers collected her." Mom waved her hand dismissively while bile burned at the back of my throat at the picture she painted.

I hated the idea of Ria waiting outside, ankle-deep in mud, like an unwanted interloper. God, I hoped her brothers had navigated the journey back okay with such precious cargo. A frisson of panic split my chest at the thought.

I spun on my heel and jogged up the stairs, ignoring Mom's demands for tea, and headed straight for Eli's bedroom. The window was open, linen stripped from the bed. Had Ria done this, or Mom? I couldn't decide which option was worse. I slammed the window shut, keeping in the last vestiges of Ria's honey and wildflower scent, then sat on the edge of the bed, cradling my head in my hands.

The corner of a note stuck out from under the bedside lamp and I reached forward, gently tugging it out without allowing myself to get my hopes up.

Seth,

One day I'll see your work in a gallery somewhere and I'll say, "the guy who painted that got me off with my own jeans."

Jokes! Kind of.

I'll say, "the guy who painted that was one of the kindest souls I ever met, and I hope he finds true happiness someday."

Ria x

My throat felt uncomfortably tight as I reread the words so many times, they imprinted on my brain for eternity.

You would have made me happy.

Had she ever felt the same way? Or had we never given her the chance to even entertain the idea?

Maybe I should have made our intentions clearer. Surely there was a way we could have done it without scaring her off.

Why hadn't we at least asked for her phone number?

The door banged hard against the wall as Eli stomped inside, traipsing mud everywhere, his muscles shook with the effort of holding back his shift. I don't think I'd ever seen him so angry.

"There was a note for me under the lamp," I said quietly. "Check your side."

That seemed to break him out of his haze a little. Eli moved faster than I'd ever seen him, holding himself back from throwing the lamp across the room at the last moment when he spotted the torn edge of the paper. He dropped to the edge of the bed and I watched as he read and reread it, eyes scanning over the paper as fast as they could go.

"Sorry, Goldie. I can't do it," Eli muttered, shaking his head.

"Can't do what?" I asked quickly, eager to know if she'd left a phone number or any kind of contact details in Eli's note.

He looked up at me with his brow furrowed, but attempted to give me a tight smile. "Forgive Noah."

"She asked you to?" I breathed, the ache in my chest expanding. Eli nodded, pulling his gaze away from me to stare at the wall ahead of him, jaw tight.

"She said he just wants what's best for us, and asked me to forgive him."

"Fuck," I swore softly, lying back on the bed and banging my head lightly against the headboard. If anything, that knowledge made me feel even worse. She'd been unceremoniously booted out of our home and she'd still had the grace to think of us and try to mend bridges that she hadn't broken.

Ria's arrival may have escalated the disconnect Eli and I had been feeling with Noah, but she hadn't *caused* it. For years, we'd pushed him to get his own hobbies, a job, a fucking *life*. He'd devoted every waking second of his time to us since he was 15 years old, he needed a break. *We* needed a break.

I wanted him on my side — I still wanted us to take a mate together — but he had to see Eli and I as equals for that to happen. That he'd gone behind our backs and against our wishes showed very clearly that he still didn't.

Ria may want us to forgive our older brother for his overprotective flaws, but I wasn't sure I could. Not when the cost had been so high.

"How are we going to find her?" Eli asked, kicking off his filthy boots and lying back on the bed next to me with a heavy sigh. "She could be on a plane already if she left right after we did. Noah was not fucking around."

I doubted that was the case. She still had to grab her things from her old place, and I was certain her brothers would want a word with Darren, but I didn't want to put ideas in Eli's head.

"I don't think Noah was lying when he said she asked to leave," I said quietly.

"Yeah, but that was just because of Mom," Eli shot back quickly. "Not us. Well, not us *two*."

"Maybe not us two," I agreed. "But we come as a package, all three of us. Maybe…" I rubbed my forehead, unable to get out the words I'd been intending to say.

Maybe it wasn't meant to be?

How could that be true when Ria and Noah had never had a chance to connect? For reasons that were entirely his fault, they'd barely gotten to the point of civility, let alone any further than that.

"I'm not giving up," Eli promised, glaring at me like he dared me to disagree. "It's Ria. She's it. I'm not giving up."

"Nor am I," I replied, tipping my head in acknowledgment. "But I think… I think we have work to do here, first."

I'd been trying to tune out the low murmur of voices downstairs, but they were impossible to ignore. Maybe Ria was our future, but we couldn't offer her that until we dealt with the present.

RIA

CHAPTER 19

Leaving the Bernard's home was far worse than leaving Darren's house. Granted, I didn't have that sweet, sweet marijuana buzz to take the edge off, but also I felt like I was leaving something more behind this time.

Besides, this time I was doing the walk of shame with my brothers, which made it a hundred times worse. Vincent was in human form, carrying my pack and half carrying me as we slid over mud and climbed over debris. I only had my light backpack, the one I'd grabbed when Eli and I had gone back to Lou's place, and I was barely managing with that. Every step I took, I sunk several inches into the sludge, and my center of gravity vanished.

It would have definitely been easier to wait another day before making this journey. Not that Noah had given me much choice.

Joe trotted along next to us in fox form, leaping and darting and making it look oh-so easy. I didn't feel like he needed to be in his shifted form, but I was grateful for it. Joe was the less filtered of the two of them. For my own sanity, I was glad he couldn't speak right now.

Vincent cleared his throat, shooting me a sidelong look that I returned with a raised eyebrow, daring him to tell me off while I was in this mood. *Proceed with caution, big brother.*

"Come on, Ria. I can't not say anything," Vincent complained.

"You've been not saying anything for the past hour. Just keep doing that. You're doing a magnificent job."

"We flew all the way back to the States—"

"Yeah, let's talk about that," I interjected. "You two have never left the country, you wouldn't even come on a cruise when I worked on the ship." Joe made an impressively disgruntled sound at that, for a fox. "Where were you?"

Vincent had dark blonde hair and skin as fair as mine that flushed beet red when he was embarrassed. Like right now.

"Denmark."

I blinked a couple of times, thinking I must have misheard him. I was expecting him to say "Mexico." Maybe "Canada."

Denmark was far away. My brothers weren't the most cultured of guys — I was honestly surprised they'd even *heard* of Denmark.

"This wouldn't have anything to do with... Anette, would it?"

Vincent tensed and Joe straight up snarled. The sound gave me a fright and I lost my footing, falling hard on my ass in the mud.

"Shit," Vincent muttered, hauling me up with a hand around my upper arm. "Are you okay?"

"Fuck you, Joe," I grumbled, glaring at him as he circled my mud-covered legs and nuzzled my knee apologetically as I swatted him away.

"She's a touchy subject for both of us," Vincent sighed, glancing nervously at Joe like he expected him to pounce. "Best not to bring it up."

"Oh, so you want me to not talk about it?" I asked sweetly, throwing his words back at him.

"Fine," Vincent snorted, his mouth twitching. "Truce. You don't bring up, you know. And we won't bring up the bears."

I startled, tightening my hands around my light backpack. "You mean Darren."

"I don't think I do. Don't get me wrong, we'll be having words with the coyote, but you sound more upset now than you did when I talked to you on the phone while you were staying with them. Do I need to have a word with them too?"

"Definitely not," I replied, shaking my head vigorously. My brothers were pretty tough dudes, but Noah, Seth, and Eli would eat them for breakfast. "They've been very gracious hosts. They took me in and gave me somewhere to stay, plus told Darren to back off when he came to plead his case—"

Joe snarled again and Vincent's hand shot out preemptively to steady me before I went ass over tit again.

"—calm down, Joe, oh my god. We all told him to get lost, and he did. I stole something from him though, so you know, I should probably give that back." I shrugged, hoping they wouldn't ask too many questions about that.

"Ria," Vincent sighed.

"You wanted to go all Protective Big Brother on him, anyway! We'll drop it off then, kill two birds with one stone," I said defensively.

"Drop what off?" Vincent pressed, a low warning in his voice.

"*Schmun*," I muttered, kneeling in the mud since I was already filthy and pretending to adjust my hiking boots. Such interesting laces. I should spend more time down here staring at them. However long it took Vincent to calm down would suffice.

"Gun!?"

"Keep your voice down!" I hissed, quickly standing and jabbing him in the ribs with my elbow. "Who knows who's out here?"

"We do, we can scent them," Vincent hissed back, glaring at me. "Ria, you can't go around stealing people's weapons, are you out of your fucking mind? How are you not in jail yet?"

There had been plenty of close calls. The blonde hair and overall angelic face probably helped, honestly.

"It was a spur-of-the-moment decision. I thought it would be a good idea to be armed if I was strolling through the forest on my own," I replied haughtily. "I didn't think of it as *stealing*, per se."

"You never think, that's the problem," Vincent replied, throwing his hands up in exasperation. "You just do whatever you want with zero consideration for the consequences and wait for someone to bail you out of your messes. Rinse and repeat."

Fucking ouch, bro.

Was he right? Yes. Had I had those exact same thoughts about myself countless times over the years? Absolutely.

Did it hurt any less to hear it coming from someone else? No. Not even a little.

I was a fuckup who kept fucking up, and everyone was sick of my bullshit. I was sick of my own bullshit.

I swallowed around the uncomfortable tightness in my throat, dropping my eyes to the ground and blinking back the hot tears burning behind them. My brothers hadn't made me cry since I was a little kid, and I wasn't about to break that streak now.

"Ria," Vincent sighed.

"Can we just get back, please?" I asked quietly, a slight tremor in my voice giving me away. "The only time I have not been reflecting on what a screw up I am over the past week was when I was spending time with... Anyway, whatever. It doesn't matter. The point is, I'm more than aware of my flaws. You won't need to bail me out again, I can promise you that."

Joe made a pained noise, brushing along my legs, and I trailed my fingers over the russet-colored fur on his back. I meant it. I couldn't promise that I wasn't going to fuck up again — I knew myself better than that — but I definitely wasn't going to call Vincent and Joe if things went wrong. Maybe if I got better at fixing my own problems, I'd be less inclined to get into trouble in the first place.

"I didn't mean it like that, Ria," Vincent pleaded. "I don't want you to feel like you can't call us if you're in trouble. Look, let's just leave it for now. Focus on getting back to New York. Mom and Dad don't know you're coming home, right? They're going to be so excited to see you."

Sure, until they found out I had no money and nowhere to live and had to mooch off them again.

"Can't wait," I murmured.

* * *

"Ria!" Lou squealed, pulling me in for a hug as soon as I appeared on her doorstep, covered in mud from head to toe with Vincent and a now-human Joe flanking me. "I'm so glad you're not in 15 pieces scattered across the wilderness," she sighed.

"Er, likewise?" I replied with a strained laugh. "That's a very specific fear."

"You know I watch a lot of true crime documentaries," Lou said seriously, looking suddenly flustered as she took in my brothers. I was surprised at how nonchalant they were. Lou was fucking hot. If women got my motor going, I'd have for sure made a move on her, but they weren't showing any interest at all.

They were over a decade older than her, which may have been part of their hesitation. Or it was the mysterious Danish lady that we weren't supposed to talk about. I was leaning towards Option B.

"Lou, these are my brothers, Vincent and Joe. They've, er, come to help me pack."

"Aw, you're seriously moving home?" Lou asked, deflating.

"Yeah." I shook my head as if I could physically shake off the tangled web of emotions that was sticking to my skin. "I guess it's time," I added brightly, shooting her a fake smile I knew she could see right through.

"Well, I'm going to New York for a... work thing, in a couple of weeks. Maybe we could catch up?" Lou asked hopefully. A little bit of warm and fuzzy permeated the cold and miserable.

"I'd love that," I replied honestly. Not everything about my time in Alaska had been bad, and I wanted to hold on to the good memories.

"We should get a move on," Vincent prompted softly. "Our flight leaves in a few hours, and we still need to do that other thing..."

"Are you going to beat up Darren?" Lou laughed. "I saw him outside his office today, so he's definitely in town."

"Not helpful," I muttered, moving towards my old bedroom. I wasn't totally averse to my brothers scaring Darren a little — at best he'd been shady to me, at his worst, downright nefarious — but I didn't want them making a scene in the middle of town.

"Very helpful, thank you," Joe called over his shoulder as the two of them followed me to my old room. The first thing I noticed on my bed was the packages of jewelry making supplies I'd ordered before I'd left for Darren's cabin, thinking I was going to start an at-home career as a jewelry designer. It seemed like a ridiculous dream now, but I wasn't about the throw away the supplies I'd spent my last paycheck buying.

God, I'd lived in this room for a year. I'd had Darren visit me here, fucked him a few times even, but all of those memories seemed vague and fuzzy. When I was in here now, all I could think of was Eli looking around, examining my photos, sitting on the edge of my bed as I told him about my family and dropping out of college.

I barely knew him, and I was pining like we'd been in a serious relationship. I needed my head checked. Or a hobby.

Joe and Vincent brought their practically empty suitcases in from the rental car they'd picked up at the airport, and I pulled out the one I used to move here from Florida, brushing off the dust that had accumulated while it sat in the back of my closet.

"So, we pack your shit, threaten to slice your ex's balls off, then head to the airport?" Vincent suggested, accepting the box of things I handed him to load into his suitcase. "Actually, maybe we should allocate some time for you to shower. You look like a swamp monster."

"I missed you too, big brother," I replied drily. "How firm are you on the whole ex-threatening thing?" I sighed, pulling my hair up into an enormous messy bun on my head. I couldn't wait until I had a chance to wash it and put some product in again. A week using men's 3-in-1 shower gels had been hell on my curls.

Even if Seth's menthol body wash had smelled glorious.

"Pretty firm," Vincent replied easily.

"Or — hear me out here — we could just let sleeping coyotes lie?"

Honestly, Darren seemed like a whole lifetime ago. I was still semi angry about the whole situation, but it just seemed less... *emotionally significant*, after the past few days.

"Can't we just pay him a visit at his office?" Joe muttered, packing the unopened jewelry supplies into his suitcase. I was impressed it had taken this long to say anything, but maybe the whole Anette situation was messing with him more than I thought. "He fucked you over. Who cares if we humiliate him a little?"

"You'll also be humiliating *me*, and I'm not okay with that," I protested, angling myself in front of my suitcase and frantically shoving sex toys in as fast as I could go.

It's not like I had a lot — I read reviews obsessively and saved up to only buy things I knew I'd love — but I had enough that my brothers would ask awkward questions if they noticed them.

Or tease me about why I needed them, which was much more likely. As if toys were solely a stand-in for sex, instead of a great enhancer for couples to use.

Not that I'd missed my collection over the past week when I'd had two excellent penises at my disposal. *When I'd had a threesome.* I was going to dream about that for the rest of my life.

"Earth. To. Ria!" Joe said loudly, clapping his hands to catch my attention. I shoved the last bullet vibrator in my bag and turned around to give him my best death glare. He knew how I felt about being clapped at.

"We did not come all the way here to *not* tell this guy to go fuck himself," Joe grumbled. "Come up with a plan, Ria."

"Fine, fine," I relented. "He gets lunch every day at the diner where I used to work. Corner him on the way back to his office, if you must. Outside. With no witnesses."

"Deal," Joe replied with a savage grin.

Between the three of us, we had all the most important stuff packed within half an hour. I set aside a few clothes I thought Lou might like and boxed up whatever was left to donate on our way through town. It was a fast and clinical end to my time here.

Vincent and Joe sat on my old bed, staring at their phones and ignoring each other while I left to quickly shower and pull on clean, mud-free clothes. Those two had always been as thick as thieves, so the weird tension between them made me nervous. It wasn't like them to let a woman come between them.

That I'd come between Noah and his brothers was not lost on me, but I'd bowed out gracefully, hadn't I? Ria the Wrecker was a distant memory. I was mature and gracious now.

It was a less satisfying feeling than I expected. Maybe maturity would grow on me.

We loaded up the rental car while Lou watched from the doorway, and I gave her an extra squeeze when it came time to say goodbye.

"Message me when you land, okay?" she sniffed. "And I'll see you in a couple of weeks and you can show me around NYC."

"Okay," I agreed with a watery smile. "I don't live in, like, the middle of Times Square if that's what you're thinking. But I will definitely give you a tour."

Lou pulled me in again for a last hug, and I sniffled a bit into her bright pink hoodie. I hadn't cried when I left New York, or when I left Florida. The difference this time was I didn't *want* to go.

Vincent cleared his throat, and Lou and I broke apart. "Kick his ass!" Lou called as I climbed into the backseat, though I didn't know if she was talking to me or my brothers. Probably my brothers.

I gave Vincent directions to Darren's office, my voice sounding disinterested to my own ears.

Were the guys back from Noah's fake log-clearing venture this morning? Did they know I was gone? Were they mad? Hopefully, the notes I left them would help with that.

It wouldn't help Eli. He'd be furious. The thought made my heart hurt.

We parked near Darren's office and I instructed my brothers to wait in the alleyway next to the building — like proper goons — while I hovered on the sidewalk, scrolling through pictures of influencers with flat abs and no pores, vaguely considering whether I should join a gym when I got back home.

Probably, right? Maybe I could replace my almost-30, no-kids crisis with an almost-30, slowing-metabolism crisis.

Darren emerged from the diner, paper lunch bag in hand, and spotted me almost instantly. *Scented* me, rather. His nose twitched a second before his head whipped around to look at me, and the reminder that he was a shifter was the healthy dose of anger I needed to snap me out of my morose mood.

Fucking asshole.

I gave him an imperious look before turning on my heel — with a seriously impressive hair flip, I might add — and strutting into the alleyway like the Fairbanks sidewalk was my own personal catwalk.

Joe rolled his eyes dramatically, but I could see him trying not to laugh. They were both leaning against the wall, arms crossed, looking suitably intimidating.

I had to give Darren credit for his moxie. He'd confronted the bears, bold as brass, and he swaggered into the alley with that same energy, though he must have been able to scent Vincent and Joe from the street. Mediocre men usually possessed unwarranted confidence in spades, though.

"Aurelia," Darren sighed, spreading his arms like I was going to give him a hug.

"You are insane," I said flatly, crossing my arms over my chest as my brothers flanked me. "This is not a reunion. I'm going back to New York. We're here to threaten your manhood."

Darren dropped his arms to his side, tilting his head as he took me in. His body language said that he was relieved to see me, hopeful that I was here to reconcile, but his eyes were flinty. The contradiction made me feel uneasy.

"So you're the asshole who cheated on our baby sister," Vincent growled. "*Lied* to her," he added, his nose twitching.

"This has all been a misunderstanding," Darren sighed, giving me a genuinely pained look that had me second guessing myself for a moment. "It pains me to see you leave, Aurelia, especially like this — with things so uncertain between us — but I respect whatever decision you feel is right."

He looked so unnervingly contrite that my brain seemed to hiccup for a second. Had this been a misunderstanding? No... Right? He'd cheated on me. Kept his true nature from me. Shown the extent of his rage when I'd left.

This was an act. It was bullshit. It was *gaslighting*. But even recognizing those facts, I still felt the weirdest sliver of guilt, like I was the one at fault here.

"Just before you go," Darren continued, face suitably somber. "I need you to know that I'm as in love with you now as I was before, and I haven't given up on us. Whatever space you need in New York, you have it. Just know that I'll be waiting for you."

So... he loved me *zero* then? He loved me zero now, just like he loved me zero when we were together. Maybe *I'll be waiting* was meant to sound like a promise, but it sounded more like a threat.

While I was all about being an independent woman and standing on my own two feet these days... I kind of wished Seth and Eli were here. Shit, I'd even take Noah at this point.

"Why did you lie to her, then? If this is how you felt?" Joe growled, and to my horror I realized my brothers might actually be buying this act.

"I could hardly just bring up the fact that I'm a shifter to a human," Darren said defensively, glancing between my brothers. "I couldn't be *sure* she knew about our kind."

Vincent and Joe looked at each other over my head, looking very much like they thought that was a reasonable excuse, and I contemplated punching them both in the balls.

"And the cheating thing was a misunderstanding," Darren continued, the very picture of remorse. "An overenthusiastic ex-lover who didn't respect the bounds of my relationship. If you'd stuck around to talk to me about it, Aurelia, you would have known that." He sighed heavily, like he was disappointed in me, and I glanced nervously up at my brothers again.

"Ria has a tendency to burn shit to the ground and ask questions later," Joe muttered, giving me a sidelong look.

I swear my jaw hit the concrete pavement. The *betrayal*. Yes, I did have a tendency to do that, but I wasn't a liar and I wasn't stupid.

Though I was in a burn-shit-down mood now for sure. I reached into my purse and grabbed the gun I'd wrapped in an old t-shirt, taking a few steps forward and shoving it roughly at Darren, who grabbed it with surprise.

"The weed is gone, but you can have this back. Don't wait for me, we are done. I cannot emphasize enough the level of done we are, actually."

"Aurelia—"

"No, fuck you. You're a fucking liar, and I'm not falling for your bullshit. Though now I feel sorry for whoever your side chick was, because undoubtedly you were feeding her some sorry story about why you had to keep her a secret. I hope she ditches your ass too."

"Let's go!" I yelled over my shoulder at my useless brothers, shoulder barging Darren as I stormed out of the alleyway towards the rental car.

Fuck them. Fuck Darren. And fuck Noah.

Fuck all of this.

ELI

CHAPTER 20

I stomped through the woods in my human form, tempted to shift, but holding myself back. In my bear form, my emotions were more primal and easier to process. But I'd come so close to marking Ria as my mate, I was worried that if I shifted, I'd end up chasing her down.

Or trying to, anyway. I was pretty impressive in bear form, but not run-to-New-York impressive.

The last two weeks had been the longest of my life. Ria had been gone longer than I'd even known her, and somehow I felt like I was losing my fucking mind without her. Or maybe I'd already lost it, I don't know.

Why the fuck hadn't we got her phone number? Her last name? Because we thought there was more time. There was time until there wasn't. Until Noah had decided that he — god, king, ruler of the family — didn't want her around anymore.

Seth had stolen Noah's work phone and copied out her brother's phone number, just in case Noah got any ideas about deleting that too just to be spiteful, but we hadn't used it yet. If I'd had my way, we would have, but Seth was holding back. Insisting that it wasn't *time* yet. Like he was some kind of Love Yoda or some shit.

Fuck, I wanted to hear her voice again.

Nothing felt right with Ria gone. She'd carved a place in our home without even knowing it. Her scent belonged there, mixing with ours. Her laugh, her sarcastic sense of humor, the quiet way she found something in common with each of us. Even with Noah, who'd been an asshole to her since day one.

The house my brothers and I had built and lived in together for years felt foreign and hollow without her.

I had to believe Ria would have stayed if we'd asked her. She would have at least considered it, even if she wasn't ready right now. But we hadn't given her the chance because Noah was a stubborn prick and our mother had come back from the dead and wasn't even nice.

This was not how family reunions looked in movies. People were usually all excited and crying and hugging when they found long-lost relatives. Mom just wandered around the house, criticizing everything, refusing to talk about the fire, and telling us both that we needed to find nice bear shifter girls to settle down with — *individually* — and at the same time, that we needed to move to the human world and put all this shifter nonsense behind us.

It was like she preferred living as a human, but hadn't quite been able to shake off the shifter supremacy brainwashing she'd grown up with yet. Well, that was Seth's theory, anyway. He remembered our grandparents better than I did and said they'd been pretty old-school, and that was why our parents had been encouraged to mate *for life* when they were still teenagers.

My memories pre-fire were pretty vague, but I remember Dad being way more fun, especially with me and Seth, who were never Mom's favorites. He'd usually been blitzed out of his mind though, which probably helped.

I walked further and further from the house, pushing through the thicker growth of this uninhabited area of the forest. I doubted my brothers were in the house either, none of us were dealing with Mom's presence well. We were grown men, we could tell her to get fucked when she insulted us. Right?

Or maybe a less extreme option was to just sit down and chat to her about just... going home. We didn't have to live together to get to know one another again.

For some reason, she had decided to hang around even though living out in the wilderness seemed to make her objectively miserable, and we were all hiding from her. Noah had been pulling triple shifts — *good*, he was an asshole, I didn't want to see him — while Seth and I spent every second we could in the cottage, which Mom seemed to particularly despise.

You have to talk to each other.

My subconscious sounded like Ria, all husky and impatient.

I *knew* we had to talk. Whatever anger I was harboring towards Noah, we had to sort that shit out. Seth had flat out told me we couldn't pursue anything with Ria until we'd sorted both the Noah situation — and the Mom situation — but fuck. Noah was a prick, Mom kind-of sucked, and I didn't know how to reconcile that shit in my head.

She'd obviously been through some shit and I knew what it was like for trauma to change a person. I'd been pretty young when the fire happened, but Noah in particular hadn't emerged as the same 15-year-old he'd been before that night.

Whatever happened though, he'd done his best to prevent his negativity from affecting us. Well, until now. Though I didn't think Noah would have been quite such a Grade A prick and shoved Ria secretly out the door if Mom hadn't hated her on sight. Before she'd come along, he'd been warming up to Ria.

They played Trivial Pursuit on the same team. That *had* to mean something.

Shit, I thought if any of us would be susceptible to a long-lost relative with an agenda, it would be Sensitive Seth.

Or me, Eager Eli, always desperate for love and affection.

Not No-Fucks-To-Give Noah.

To add insult to injury, the day after she left, Noah had found a note from Ria in the eaves of the woodshed. We'd all assumed he hadn't got one because there was nothing left in his room and also, he was an asshole. But apparently Ria wasn't going to leave him out, even though he was never *in*.

I was desperate to know what it said, but Noah refused to tell me or Seth. I didn't think it was the reaming-out that he deserved though, based on his reaction to it. If anything, he had looked ashamed.

Good.

Ria had a way of seeing more than we meant for her to see. She'd clocked that I was lonely straight away, I bet she saw some things in Noah that he wasn't proud of.

Maybe I'd steal it. I hadn't been through my big brother's stuff in over a decade, but now seemed like a good time to pick up the habit again.

I stomped around aimlessly, no real direction in mind, just needing to put some space between me and the home I'd always loved. Some space between me and the memories of Ria that felt baked into every corner of the place.

Some space between me and the brother who'd ripped away our chance at a happy future, and the mother who was fucking gleeful about it.

Was it too much to ask that there was some trace of Ria left in these woods? It felt too much like she'd never existed at all.

As I walked, the distant sound of feminine sobbing reached my ears. I froze, my foot hovering in midair. Oh man, distressed humans were not my area of expertise. For all of Noah's many flaws, he was the one who helped people who got lost in the woods. Shit, I couldn't just leave, though. What if she was in trouble?

Warily, I followed the noise, hoping I was making the right decision. The closer I got, the more my hackles raised. This was Darren's territory, I could smell the coyote's lingering scent everywhere. It wasn't fresh, though. He wasn't here. A crying woman at Darren's cabin couldn't be a good sign.

I paused between the trees, hidden in shadow, trying to figure out what I was dealing with. The woman was definitely human, that much was clear by her scent. She was conventionally hot. Maybe I would have given her a second glance a few weeks ago, before I'd fallen head over heels for the girl with golden hair and a smile that spelled trouble.

The dark-haired woman sat on the ground, leaning back against the front door, her knees pulled up to her chest as she *wailed*.

Was this the *other woman*?

This seemed like drama I did not want to involve myself in. I was about two seconds from backing away when the flattened tire caught my eye. Great, so she was wailing like a banshee *and* stuck.

Ugh.

Fine, I'd change the tire, but that was it. Maybe it would earn me some good karma that I could cash in later when I tried to convince Ria to move back in with us and never leave.

Maybe we could banish Noah to the cottage until he got his shit sorted? He could sleep among the wood shavings and think about what he'd done.

Right. Crying lady first. I cleared my throat loudly and walked into the clearing surrounding the shitbox cabin, landing my feet a little heavier than usual so I wouldn't scare the crap out of her. The crying was already hell on my sensitive ears. I wouldn't be able to cope if she started screaming as well.

"Hey. Are you alright?" I called out lamely.

"Who are you?" she sniffed, shrinking into the doorway a little further.

"My name is Eli. I'm Darren's... neighbor."

"Oh," she replied, relaxing a little. "I'm Paisley. Darren's girlfriend. Or I thought I was." She sniffed dramatically and I gave her a tight smile. Awkward. As. Fuck.

"Er, do you have a spare?" I asked, gesturing at her flat tire.

"Oh yes. In the trunk. Would you help me? That would be so amazing!" she gushed, standing up and brushing the dirt off her jeans.

"Yeah, no worries," I muttered. Fortunately, despite her entirely unsuitable clothes for the weather, she was more prepared for vehicle troubles with a spare, wrench, and jack all stored safely in the trunk.

I began removing the hubcap as Paisley hovered a foot away, still sniffling. "I went to his office to surprise him and they told me he'd gone on vacation. Out of state! I couldn't believe he'd leave without telling me, so I came up here to see for myself."

Ugh, I didn't want to hear any of this. I hummed absently, concentrating on the task at hand, removing the nuts and sliding the jack under the car.

"Are you and Darren close?" Paisley continued. I grunted a negative, biting down on the stream of insults relating to Darren that popped into my head.

"Oh, he's so great," Paisley said breathily. Lord, this woman was a talker. "So charismatic, you know? Unfortunately, that means I have a lot of competition for his attention," she laughed sadly.

Er, no. That was definitely not how it was supposed to work. It shouldn't matter if he had the charisma of a celebrity, or of an old lump of clay. If he was seeing someone, they should have his full attention.

Darren was just an asshole.

I tuned Paisley out as she continued to list Darren's mediocre achievements like he was out there curing cancer and building schools with his bare hands in his free time.

"All done," I muttered as I lowered the vehicle and pulled the jack free, moving to the back of the car to return it to the trunk.

"Oh you're amazing, thank you," Paisley responded absently, staring at the phone in her hand. "Guess I'm going back home. Maybe I should go straight to the airport, show him how dedicated I am," she added with a forced laugh.

I grunted again, Noah-style, slamming the trunk shut. I bet this was how he communicated with the humans he had to help when he was on duty.

"How could he go all the way to New York without at least telling me first?" Paisley sniffed, looking as though she was working her way up to a wail again.

"New York?" I repeated, a chill of fear snaking through my system, freezing my lungs.

"His ex lives there, and he keeps saying they have unfinished business, even though I *know* he wants to be with me," Paisley replied, shaking her head. "She probably just has some of his stuff or something."

Denial was a hell of a drug.

Fuck. Fuck. Fuck.

"Gotta go, good luck getting back into town," I muttered, turning around and jogging towards the trees, leaving Paisley yelling something behind me, but I didn't have time for her.

I had to get back to my brothers, and *we* had to get to New York. Ria may be with her brothers, but no one could protect her like we could.

No one could *love* her like we could, but first we had to make sure she was safe.

Watch out, New York. Two obsessed and one reluctant bear shifters were coming your way.

Author's Note

Thank you so much for taking the time to read Gilded Mess! I hope you enjoyed it. These characters have been so much fun to write — unapologetically messy, so much fun, and all still figuring their shit out in various ways that society mostly expects us to have done by their age. I've loved immersing myself in their story, which is why the wait for Golden Chaos isn't long — it will be out next month.

A big thank you as always to my reader group for their support and enthusiasm about this idea, Michelle for taking the plunge into beta reading, TS for being my sprint buddy and voice of reason, my husband for all of his emotional support, and a particularly big thank you to my alpha reader, Lucy. She's always amazing, but this book literally wouldn't have happened if she hadn't sent me the Goldilocks meme that inspired the whole thing. I joked about writing a bratty Goldilocks with three bear shifter brothers. We laughed, talked about something else, then a few days later I sent her a sample because I just couldn't get the idea out of my head. Lucy, you're the best!

Colette x

For book discussion threads and the latest news, join the Reader Group on Facebook, or subscribe to my newsletter at coletterhodes.com.

Read on for a little preview of Golden Chaos...

SETH

PROLOGUE

"Pack your shit, we're going to New York."

"What?" I asked in confusion as Eli stormed in the front door, chest heaving with exertion, stomping mud over the floors I'd *just* mopped. His shoulder-length hair had escaped the man bun he was usually so diligent about keeping it in, and was almost black from the rain that was falling hard outside.

Mom snorted from her spot on the sofa, drinking the cup of tea she'd demanded I make for her. "You will not traipse around the country after that girl."

There was no question in her tone. No room for argument. She had spoken and expected her words to be adhered to.

Noah sat at the table looking between me and Eli. He and I hadn't looked so much like twins since we were kids, but with Ria gone, I'd lost the motivation to keep my beard neat and trim my hair. Another week of hair growth and only Noah's bulkier size would differentiate us.

Noah opened his mouth to speak before slamming it shut again. He wasn't as subtle as he thought he was. He thought he was all unreadable grumpiness, but I saw the flash of hopefulness and the intense weariness in his eyes that he was trying to hide. Plus the guilt. There was always guilt.

"Remember, we talked about taking things slowly?" I asked carefully. Eli's eyes were wild, glowing with the need to shift as he roughly scraped his hair back into a bun. He was difficult to reason with when he got like this.

"Two weeks of nothing isn't *slow*, we're just not doing *anything*," Eli snapped, and I couldn't disagree with him. The idea had been to figure out the situation with Mom and potentially beat some sense into Noah before we tried to pursue something with Ria, but it was difficult to do either of those things when Eli and I were avoiding them both.

"You are not pursuing anything with that *carrier*. Noah, don't forget that job I asked you to do. You can't run off until that's done," Mom ordered, a vein in her forehead throbbing. All three of us ignored her.

"Darren's gone after her. We have to go to New York. Now! Fuck, he's probably there already," Eli insisted, storming past us and jogging up the stairs.

I threw aside the kitchen towel I'd been using to dry the dishes and moved towards the stairs, fighting back my initial panic response to shift and rip the threat apart.

"Why didn't you lead with that?" Noah barked, surprising both myself and our mother by immediately standing up and striding towards his room like he was going to pack.

"Noah," Mom snapped, setting her cup down and standing, eyes blazing. "What are you doing? You said you were going to find those papers for me."

"That can wait. I'm going to kill Darren, like I should have done the first time," Noah muttered. "Hurry the fuck up, Seth!" he added, glaring at me over his shoulder like I was the one who had somehow convinced Ria to leave the first time round.

"You're coming with us?" I asked, mystified. I had no idea how or why he'd rushed Ria away in secret, but why go to all the trouble if he felt strongly enough to want to follow her to New York at the first sign of trouble?

Noah was an unsolvable riddle sometimes.

If he hurt her, I didn't know what I'd do. What my *bear* would do.

He paused with his back to me, looking back over his shoulder at the floor. "Yes."

"Why?"

"Yes, why?" Mom snapped, with a lot more hostility in her voice. "None of you ever think of me."

"Because it's the right thing to do," Noah replied swallowing thickly, ignoring Mom.

"Nope, I'm going to need a better answer. You didn't care about doing the right thing when she left," I replied coolly.

"That's exactly what I cared about," Noah snarled, turning to face me, eyes glowing as his bear surfaced. "She was leaving anyway. You were both too attached. It would have destroyed you."

"That wasn't your decision to make, Noah," I gritted out, torn between frustration and anger. He just didn't *get* it. "Our pain is not your responsibility, and you only caused more with the way you treated her. Don't come if you're only going to make things worse. Eli and I can handle Darren."

Mom huffed indignantly, sitting back down as I made my escape upstairs. Obviously, I wasn't worth trying to convince, so she wasn't going to bother. I was sure Noah would get another earful before we left, though. God knows what papers she wanted him to dig out for her.

"Are we really doing this?" I asked Eli as I stepped into the room we were sharing. He'd already thrown two duffel bags on the bed and half-filled his own.

He glanced up at me incredulously. "What, you'd just leave Ria alone, knowing Darren is following her around like a fucking creep?"

"Obviously not," I replied drolly, pulling a stack of t-shirts out of the drawer Eli was letting me use now that Mom had made herself comfortable in my room. "Taking care of Darren is a given. That's not all you want to go to New York for," I added pointedly.

I was trying not to think too hard about the logistics. None of us had even been on a plane before, and the concept of being so high in the air was a little terrifying.

Bears couldn't fly.

Don't think about it.

"I can't do this going slow shit, Seth," Eli said solemnly, pausing his packing and looking up at me, eyes pained. "I miss her like a fucking lost limb, you know? We don't know how she's doing, or even exactly where she is. I can't live like this."

I nodded silently, my throat feeling strangely tight. The fire — and our subsequent years raising ourselves in the woods, struggling to get by — hadn't robbed Eli of his capacity to *feel*. I used my art to exorcise the emotions directly out of my body, while Noah pretended they didn't exist entirely.

Eli let his emotions rule him — the good and the bad.

"Just don't scare her off, okay?" I asked gently. "For all we know, Ria is doing just fine without us. She's a young, beautiful woman. She's probably been out partying with her friends this entire time. She's probably happy."

Books by this author:

Empath Found series:
The Terrible Gift
The Unwanted Challenge
The Reluctant Keeper

Deadly Dragons duet:
The (Not) Cursed Dragon
The (Not) Satisfied Dragon

Cheeky Fairy Tales:
Gilded Mess (Three Bears #1)
Golden Chaos (Three Bears #2)
Scarlet Disaster (Little Red #1)
Seeing Red (Little Red #2)

State of Grace:
Run Riot
Silver Bullet

Standalones:
Fire & Gasoline
Blood Nor Money

Printed in Great Britain
by Amazon